Amy Jenkins created the BBC2 television series *This Life* and wrote and co-produced the feature film *Elephant Juice*. She has also directed three short films. Film rights in Amy's first novel *Honeymoon* have been sold to Columbia Pictures.

Critical acclaim for Amy Jenkins and *Funny Valentine*:

'Absorbing . . . Stevie is an engaging Everywoman for the twenties/thirties generation . . . there is a humanity in her take on relationships that ensures that *Funny Valentine* will be as popular as the rest of her oeuvre.'

Observer

'Terrific. Jenkins has hit a winning formula . . . She's adept at creating endearing and comic characters, and spinning them into an entertaining yarn . . . will hold you captive until the last page. A successful follow-up to Jenkins' debut best-seller *Honeymoon*, and fans will recognise the witty one-liners and fast-paced plot.'

Daily Express

'So does Jenkins bring anything new to the telling, and does she rate a special mention as one of the [Cinderella] story's many authors? Yes, and yes . . . She is the queen of witty one-liners.'

Guardian

'A humorous look at the nature of fame.'

Reading Evening Post

'Funny and fast-paced.'

Bournemouth Daily Echo

D1322585

ALSO BY AMY JENKINS

Honeymoon

AMY JENKINS

Funny Valentine

FLAME
Hodder & Stoughton

First published in Great Britain in 2002 by Hodder & Stoughton
A division of Hodder Headline
First published in paperback in 2002
A Flame paperback

1 3 5 7 9 10 8 6 4 2

A CIP catalogue record for this title is available
from the British Library

ISBN 0 340 75055 3

Typeset in Sabon by Palimpsest Book Production Limited,
Polmont, Stirlingshire
Printed and bound in Great Britain by
Mackays of Chatham Ltd, Chatham, Kent

Hodder & Stoughton
A division of Hodder Headline
338 Euston Road
London NW1 3BH

Funny Valentine

With many thanks for encouragement, inspiration and support to: Jenne Casarotto, Sheila Crowley, Alison Dominitz, Sue Fletcher, Karen Geary, Harriet Graham, Tracey Hyde, Sarah Lutyens, Maria Matthiessen, Jessica Porter and Carolyn Tristram. With love to Polly, Milly, Flora and Nat.

1

. . . it's been said that flowers are Mother Nature's way of showing us that she loves us stop and we must be loved stop whatever the cost we must be loved – actually make that at all costs – at all costs we must be loved stop in a few weeks' time it will be Valentine's Day stop perhaps the doorbell will ring stop perhaps a glorious array of fat and succulent red roses will be there to greet us stop we will gather them into our arms with a happy heart comma but only because we cannot see the trail of misery, injustice and disease these perfect blooms bring dragging behind them stop and all in the name of . . .

'LOVE!'

My voice booms out, amplified a million times across the sea of faces tilting uniformly in my direction, a field of sunflowers searching for the light. The crowd is enormous. It could fill Tiananmen Square. It stretches as far as I can see in every direction.

'LOVE!' I boom again. 'What is it *for*?'

There's movement below, the crowd rustles, there's a shaking of heads, an uncertain murmuring, and then it starts to produce, first here, then there, then everywhere, bubbling up to the surface, little red things. Small, red, fluffy objects. At first I think these objects are hats. I think the crowd are throwing their hats in the air and the hats are dancing above their heads, like lottery balls in an airstream. But then I make out that these red objects are not hats, but hearts. Small, red, fluffy hearts.

Somewhere somebody is screaming. Maybe it's me.

It might have been right then that I woke up. It might have been an hour later, two hours later. Did I dream about a horse as well? Was that before or after? But now I'm sitting up in the bed, sheets twisted around me, my heart pounding. I'm drenched in sweat. Not because of the nightmares but because it's so damn hot in here. So relentlessly, brow-beatingly, numbingly hot. I'm in a saucepan and the lid is on.

Sitting up like that, I sense someone in the room. I freeze. Stop breathing. There's someone in the room. I don't want to turn my head, I don't want to find out, but I turn my head despite myself and I see him. A scream starts –

There's a man in my bed. Asleep.

I stifle the scream. It's Rico.

Of course. Rico.

I remember now. No need for alarm. I *like* Rico.

Sort of.

I untwist myself from the sheet and pad naked across the lino floor to the bathroom. I hold my wrists under the cold tap. The water isn't cold enough, it's warm. I give up, go into the bedroom to pick up my tape-recorder and reporter's notebook. I go back and sit on the edge of the loo. It's the only place to sit that's not the bed.

Holding the tape-recorder, I rewind a few seconds and replay. My voice recites the following, sounding synthetic and tinny through the tiny microphone: 'fungicides, insecticides, nemoticides, dichloropropene . . .' I pause the tape to write these names in my notebook. Then I press play again and take notes where relevant: 'February the third, two thousand. Bought Elida another meal. She earns less than twenty p an hour and is named after a shampoo. She told me she got pregnant coming up to the Mother's Day rush last year. She had to have an abortion or she would have been sacked. The flower-pickers' centre say they get sixty new cases a week of bad rashes from the chemicals. They cause miscarriages too. Elida snuck me into a greenhouse and I saw the flowers. It's funny to think of them as unnatural things bringing unhappiness. So programmed to think of them as beautiful. Got a sense of the flowers being forced, or nature being forced, and felt really sad about it. Like seeing an animal being beaten. Also I don't like feeling so powerful with Elida. I think she thinks I'm the great white hope. I'm Father Christmas and Mother Teresa wrapped up in one.'

At this point on the tape, you can hear a moped backfiring, a man's voice shouting . . . my name, as it turns out: 'Stevie!'

I was coming down from the savannah and, turning a corner, came abruptly upon a cavalcade of vehicles sweeping up the dusty road. It was reminiscent of the kind employed by Latin American dictators: a couple of jeeps loaded up with important-looking equipment followed by a big old Mercedes with dark windows. The cars whipped by scattering all in their path, the 'cavalcade' feel provided by dusty boys on mopeds looking a little like outriders. It was one of these boys who shouted to me, then slowed, executed a wobbly U-turn and, abandoning the chase, puttered back in my direction. On closer inspection, this outrider turned out to be not a boy at all but Rico, who is Italian, very much a man, and a friend . . . sort of.

Hadn't seen him for, what? A year? When was the Cannes débâcle? Couldn't remember. My brain was fried. But this was Colombian extremis and we were glad to see each other. We did the 'My God, what are you doing here?'s and retired to the nearest bar.

Rico was in pursuit of something he calls – with his strong Italian accent – a sea-leb. Sea-lebs are pretty rare in Colombia, but great flocks of them swarm across the western world. They are undeniable pests.' I said, 'There are hundreds of species on this planet in danger of extinction and it's damn unfortunate that the sea-leb is not amongst them.' He told me I was funny – or I obviously thought I was – and that this particular celeb (a huge one, apparently) likes a bit of gritty Latin realism in her pop videos. Rico is a paparazzi photographer.

'What does this pop star think poverty is?' I said, as scathing as I could be. 'Some kind of set dressing? A condiment? A type of seasoning to be peppered liberally all over her first-world ego in order to add some *spice*?'

Rico rolled his big old eyes right up into his furrowed forehead. He'd heard it all before. 'Stevie,' he said, 'what exactly are you doing here?'

'*Trying* to be a journalist,' I told him. Well – I'm not *really* a journalist, am I? I mean, I can't seem to get my foot in the door. Okay, the *News* said they'd take a look at anything I came up with. No commission, though. The *Daily News* is a low-brow high-brow; a British broadsheet with a tabloid heart. It's against my principles, really, to write for them, but it's the only paper where I have a decent contact. According to Rico, I have too many principles. If I had fewer I would have more work and I could buy myself some nice clothes. We always have this same old argument, me and Rico. But is it possible to have too many principles? Easily. 'This is not a simple world, Stevie,' he says. 'Things are not so black and white.'

He really isn't my type, Rico. He is stocky and hard and always a little tanned. He's losing his hair young and crops it to a bristle to disguise the fact. He's got a big head – his body is one taut muscle. He's like a human bullet, Rico, an Italian paparazzi dynamo and he's polluting the world with an oily slick of celebrity trivia. He's not my type, but whenever I see him I want to fasten my lips to his big fat ones and stay that way for quite some time.

I told him how much I disapproved of him. There are flower workers out there far more deserving of his photographic attentions. He agreed with me. He said he hates the sea-lebs too. Why else would he go around the world trying to ruin their lives? Didn't I realise he's fighting for a cause, just the same as I am? In fact, he said, he thought he and I should work together one day – we'd make a good team – and then maybe I'd finally earn some money (and get some nice clothes).

I was only wearing a T-shirt and jeans, but good ones actually, *Italian* ones, thank you very much. What did he want me to wear? Black lacy corsets and satin skirts? Also, I told him, I wouldn't be seen dead earning money by violating the privacy of pop stars and suchlike, and he asked me if I was defending them now. Well, they are human beings too, are they not? Well, no, okay, they're sea-lebs – but, still, it's not right. Rico said all celebrities have waived their human rights, and this is a fact upheld by the courts of many countries, because they made a deal with the devil long ago.

Who's the devil, Rico?

Not me, he said, not me.

And that's how it went with Rico.

'Stevie?'

Is he coming in here?

I look around – nowhere to hide. Nowhere to hide my tape-recorder, even – I am naked and so is the bathroom. Untreated plaster walls, stark toilet pan, sink, shower head, and that is all. A cockroach to wipe your arse with and that's if you're lucky.

I saunter out casually and slide the tape-recorder into the first available hiding place – Rico's jeans pocket, his jeans that are hanging on the back of the door. Don't want him to think that I'm the kind of person who's up in the night talking to myself. Don't want him to think that.

He's still in the bed. He looks very brown against the white sheets in the half-light. I have a simple desire to touch the little pad of flesh just above his armpit, where it's soft but hard, hard but soft. Rico, however, is busy being Rico and that makes things more complicated.

'*Amore mio*,' he says, and tucks some hair behind my ear as I sit down on the edge of the bed, 'I get sick of the beautiful people, you know, it's too much candy. You're so real, that's what I like about you.'

He gives me a look and half-way through it I realise he's never given me this look before. I know this look. It's *the look* and, sure enough, I can feel my blood reacting. It starts to thicken, it starts to curdle.

'Rico,' I say, in tones of genuine astonishment, 'you're not going *soft* on me, are you?'

'You English,' he chuckles indulgently to himself, 'you understand nothing about love.'

'Oh, I know all about love,' I say, and raise my hands to mime two inverted commas around the offending word.

'But seriously, baby,' he says, and lights a cigarette to show he means business, to indicate an intention to ease the brain into gear, 'I've been thinking about you.'

'Goodness,' I say.

'You see,' he says, a jaded, self-conscious enthusiasm burning in plain brown eyes, 'that's why you drive me crazy.'

I look a question mark at him, but he doesn't explain.

'I want to tell you something.'

'Must you—'

'You and I. I think, maybe, one day, who knows?, we could be something.'

'I don't think that's true.'

'But seriously,' he says.

'You barely know me.'

'I know you.'

7

'Do you mean that you're "in love" with me?' I make the inverted commas again, but less viciously, I suppose.

'Maybe. It happens, you know. Between a man and a woman.'

'A man and a woman?'

He laughs at my tone of voice. '*Amore mio*—'

'Hey, I'm not *amore* your-o—'

Suddenly, he grabs me. 'I'm trying to tell you something,' he says.

I pull away, throw on the first piece of clothing I can lay my hands on (his shirt) and dive out of the window on to the balcony. There's a papaya tree right up against the building. Easy to climb down. When I get to the lower branches I swing there a little, enjoying the sensation, the stretch in my body, then let myself drop to the peaty earth. It feels better down there.

Behind the trees dawn is trying to come but it's fighting clouds; another hot, dirty day struggling to be born.

'Do you drive all your men away?'

Rico has come out on to the balcony above me in only his jeans, a cigarette on his lower lip. He perches sideways on the rail.

'Only the ones I really like.'

He doesn't say anything, and I watch the tip of his cigarette glowing and fading, glowing and fading, a fierce firefly in the branches of the tree. I lean against the trunk.

'I think I've finally grown up,' I say. 'Everything is fairly boring. Nothing personal, I just mean that when

8

you're twenty-eight – not trying to be funny but you've pretty much done everything.'

'You haven't loved,' he says.

My insides furl up like a caterpillar under attack. 'I don't believe in love,' I say. Then I say it again slowly, for his benefit: 'I – don't – believe – in – love.'

Or perhaps it's for my own.

'Be serious.'

'Oh, I believe in loving cats and dogs and children and partners – sometimes – but I don't believe in romantic love. Of course, there's the momentary rush of hormones and chemicals that encourages us to mate, but it's biology – it's no more inherently mystical than the nicotine in that cigarette you're smoking.'

He takes a contemplative drag as if testing my theory.

'You want me to be serious,' I say, 'I'll be serious. Romantic love, you see, and all that goes with it – i.e., marriage – the whole thing was invented by men to keep women in chains. The idea of monogamy was introduced by men because they needed to keep tabs on the reproductive source – women. Women were naturally polygamous – did you know? – originally, to increase the chances of successful reproduction. By the way, Rico, in your jeans pocket – the left one – yes, there – my tape-recorder. Oh, thanks. You couldn't turn it on, could you? So, anyway, men invented the couple and "commitment" so that they could keep tabs on their children – a source of wealth and power – and anyway it was easier to control society when people were corralled into easily manageable family units. Economic imperatives kept the whole thing up and running for a millennium or so until recently when women went and got themselves liberated and the western world got all liberal too, and then where was the glue? So this idea of romantic love, much derided by our ancestors, is making a big comeback. It's becoming the moral imperative, just like religion used to be. How else to keep coupled up?' Pause for breath. 'I have to protest against something that enslaves me. Don't you see?'

Rico lights another cigarette. I catch something of a smile as the match flares in the half-darkness. 'You're crazy,' he says. He chucks my tape-recorder at me, then leans over the balustrade looking down at me.

I catch the tape-recorder and check it, thinking it won't be on, but it is. I say, 'Romantic love is the ad campaign for institutionalised domesticity. People think they're getting happiness. They actually get confinement, compromise and divorce.'

'You're funny,' he says, and laughs.

'You too. I mean, what did you think we'd do? Set up home together? We wouldn't last five minutes.'

'*Allora*,' he says. 'Maybe I'm getting old.'

'Sentimental.'

We look at each other a moment.

'What does this remind you of?' he says.

'What?' I say. I don't get it.

He makes a gesture indicating me down below and him up above. '*Romeo e Giulietta*,' he says.

'Well,' I say, 'there you go – they came to a sticky end.'

'*Sticchi?*'

'It's an expression. You know, sticky – like caramel.'

'Huh?'

'Dead,' I say, 'dead, dead, dead. They ended up dead.'

'Why does love frighten you so much?'

'Rico,' I say, 'can't we just fuck?'

'*Certo*,' he says. '*Certo*.'

2

We finally get off the plane and I bowl along the airport corridors: all those muted greys and blues. The planes are nuzzling into the gates on the other side of the plate glass, their big noses dripping on to the rain-wet concrete below. This is the way to walk down airport corridors: to bowl. Fast. With a neat little air-stewardess trolley-bag trilling along behind you. Except I haven't got a neat little air-stewardess trolley-bag. But I see myself as bowling along anyway. That's how I see myself.

I have considered writing a book: *Walking Tours of Well-known Airports*. The walks could be graded. One star for the easy ones, four stars for walks the elderly or frail are not advised to undertake (domestic departure gates numbers 12–15 at London's Stansted airport, for example).

I have considered this idea. I have also rejected it for being too frivolous.

As I walk, I pass a little news kiosk and stop to pick up a copy of the *Daily News*. Turning the pages, I soon discover that my incisive, if angry and somewhat kill-joy, flower story has been spiked in favour of a Celebrity On/Off Round-up, a boxed-out presentation, with photos, of the current status of celebrity love affairs.

When I regain the corridor I really do walk fast, my cumbersome rucksack forgotten. I am fuming to myself, lost in my head, in a world of my own, an all consuming universe, filled as it is with hypocrisy, injustice and corruption.

'Hello, is that the *News of the Schmooze*?'

'It is. Dick speaking.'

'Hello, Dick. It's Stevie here.'

'Stevie, what can I do for you?'

'How about getting one of your brain cells and rubbing it against another and seeing if anything happens?'

'You're referring to the demise of your flower piece, I take it.'

'Yes. The one that got booted off in favour of a Celebrity On/Off Round-up. Never mind that the flower workers are a modern-day equivalent of the slave trade!'

'Your story was angry and somewhat kill-joy.'

'So it should be.'

'Stevie, the fact is, people like a Celebrity On/Off Round-up. News of a celebrity marriage biting the dust can really make the day go with a swing, don't you find?'

'Well, yes – it is cheering—'

'And so does it not occur to you that the Celebrity On/Off Round-up might serve a higher purpose than at first appears? The people *en masse* make a very wise judge – they know what they need.'

Dick, of course, never says anything like this in real life, but when we argue in my head he does.

I'm still walking furiously.

'The Offs are really where it's at,' Dick continues.

14

'There's a mild interest in the Ons, it's true, but only because they must by necessity precede the Offs. The Offs satisfy our deep need to know that a state of happy, coupled permanence is virtually unachievable, although society tells us it shouldn't be. And just think, maybe the day will come when we will finally have read enough Celebrity On/Off Round-ups to truly understand that it's perfectly natural to fall short of this crazy norm. And then, perhaps, we wouldn't have to dress life up so much, with those forced flowers you make such a fuss about.'

'Interesting but – OUCH!'

I bump into someone. Quite hard. Clearly some arrogant bastard who thinks he owns the world and isn't looking where he's going. Someone in a hat.

'Don't you look where you're going?' I shout.

'You were talking to yourself,' he says.

Before I can gather myself, answer this, get a proper look at him, any of these things, not only is he gone but I find myself staring at the ceiling – I've never studied an airport ceiling before: it looks like it's made of Styrofoam – and also at another man's face, a wide black face with many flat planes like a Cubist painting.

I'm on the floor. The descent was sudden and enjoyable – I feel somewhat exhilarated, in fact. I didn't so much hit the floor as arrive there, my fall being expertly achieved then broken by the owner of the many-faceted face. And I am, so to speak, in his arms.

I do turn my head a second however, to see what has become of the man I originally bumped into, the man in the hat. He is being hurried away by a group of people in expensive shoes – I see only their feet. I turn back to my oppressor.

'Hello,' I say – politely.

'What's your game?' he says.

My game? What's my game? That's a very good question. I receive a fleeting image of a man in a lemon yellow sweater swinging a golf club. But no. Golf certainly isn't my game.

So what is?

'What are you playing at?' he says.

This is just as difficult.

'I'm sorry, I really don't know what you mean,' I finally manage. 'Why are you sitting on top of me?'

This last question I ask in a pleasant way. I don't mind him sitting on top of me. I feel quite safe. Quite cosy, even. He smells nice too.

But I'm a little puzzled.

He pulls back. I can see the thought crossing his mind that perhaps I'm not playing the game he thinks I'm playing. The thought is like a cool breeze that springs up unexpectedly from the north. It ruffles his eyes.

'You just accosted someone. You don't do that.'

'I bumped into someone. Accidentally. I was thinking about something else.'

He looks at me now with enormous amusement, a great glow of geniality seeping out from under his facial armour. He gives a little giggle. 'You bumped into *someone*?'

'Yes.'

'You don't just bump into Louis Plantagenet.'

'Who?' I say.

If I'd been amusing before, now I'm downright funny. He guffaws. His face is split by a grin, cracking open from side to side. 'Who?' he echoes. '*Who?*'

'Look,' I say, 'I've been out there saving the world. Who is this guy?'

He's not at all sure I'm not taking the piss. But he can't resist educating me. '*After Eight*, *Science Fiction*, *Outrage* . . . surely you saw *After Eight?*'

'I've heard of it. A film, isn't it? I don't know if I saw it. Maybe. What was it about?'

'A guy gets kidnapped by this girl and they drive through the desert and he doesn't realise she's involved with some bad guys—'

At this point a pair of blue serge trousers arrives in my line of vision. Close up they look very bobbly. They need to be de-bobbled. I look up beyond the trousers to see an airport security guard.

'What's going on?' he says.

'We're discussing *After Eight*,' I say. 'Have you seen it? Apparently a girl kidnaps a guy.'

My oppressor stands up and sets me free in the process. I clamber into an upright position beside him.

'Michael Chambers,' he says gruffly, and flashes some kind of ID at the security guard. 'This young lady accosted my employer Louis Plantagenet. Probably a fan of some kind. She seems fairly harmless but you can't be too careful in this day and age – know what I mean?'

'No, I do not know what you mean!' I immediately say. 'I've never heard of Louis Whatshisname and I am not harmless and what, in God's name, is *this day and age?*'

'I wasn't talking to you,' says Michael Chambers, as I now know him to be called.

'Have you seen *After Eight*?' Me to security guard.

'You haven't?' Security guard to me.

'I don't think so.'

'You'd know if you'd seen it.'

'Louis Plantagenet gets kidnapped by Grace Farlow and they drive off in that red Volkswagen Beetle.'

'Oh, that! I saw that! I remember the red Volkswagen Beetle – in the desert.' I think about it some more. 'Is *that* Louis Whatshisname?' I say, and find myself glancing involuntarily or the spot where we had collided. My colour increases slightly, my pulse, fractionally. The word 'wow' forms somewhere in my left temporal lobe and wants desperately to come out. I won't let it.

'Exactly,' says Michael Chambers. 'Louis Plantagenet! Louis fucking Plantagenet!'

'There's no need for swearing,' says the security guard, reminding Michael Chambers of his presence.

'Hey, listen,' he says to the guard, 'we're all set here. I don't think we have – ahem – an ongoing situation.'

'Wrong, wrong, wrong,' I say hotly. 'This situation is going on and on and on. I'm a journalist. My job is to expose this cosy little fascist state you've got going here. What's more, I'm going to sue your smug arse. And your boss's.'

Another giggle from MC. 'Peace on earth,' he says.

'You messed up, Michael Chambers. This was a false arrest.'

'Can I buy you a coffee?' he says. 'And you can call me Mike.'

'You may not buy me a coffee – Mike. I don't approve of coffee unless it's Fair Trade.'

'All right, then,' says the weary security guard. 'I'll leave you two to it, shall I?'

The offices of the *Daily News* are mostly made of glass. Transparent office cells rise up layer upon layer, sliced open like a vivisected insect. It's still raining and the building appears to be sweating. Water on glass. It's a good look – like water on young skin.

Entering the vast reception area, I hear the distant rumble of self-importance and another noise; an indistinct buzz. Not so much a sound, perhaps, as a vibration: all that news coming down the wires. News rolling in every day, eternally breaking and dissipating – so much news, pounding uselessly like waves upon the shore.

'I'm here to see Dick Leaf.'

The receptionist looks me up and down. I am suddenly conscious of my shaggy sheepskin jacket. Her hair is pulled back with the exactitude and neatness that only air stewardesses can normally achieve. It looks like it's painted on to her head. She is wearing a head-set of the kind made fashionable by pop-stars.

'You are?'

'Stevie Dunlop.'

She can't find me on her list. 'Are you expected?'

Always unexpected. Ha. Ha.

'Look, could you just phone him and tell him I'm here?'

She dials a couple of numbers but she's dubious. 'Stevie Dunlop?' she checks. 'With?'

'With?'

'Who are you with?'

Oh. Without. Most definitely without.

'I'm freelance.'

She nods despisingly.

'Getting his voicemail,' she says. 'Message for Dick Leaf. I have a Stevie Dunlop in Reception for you.' Then, to me, 'Take a seat.'

A Stevie Dunlop.

So. There are others.

Half an hour later – a long time to wait especially for a deputy-arsehole-nobody-features-editor – I am wearing a large degrading, although not degrad*able*, plastic visitor's badge and standing in the lift. The lift, of course, is as transparent as everything else. It rises in a stately fashion and I with it until at last The Dick's shoes appear in my eyeline, then his legs, belt, shirt, collar, until finally our faces are level.

'We'll have to walk and talk,' he says, and sets off along the inner circuit of the central atrium, his well-tailored orange Paisley shirt flapping behind him. He has a blond forelock that falls repeatedly over his pale and weaselly face and is removed repeatedly by his pale and ghostly fingers, sinister and long. He also has platinum-blond eyebrows – which, for some reason, give me the creeps. 'Louis Plantagenet is in town and I'm going to have to do the interview myself. He's just a *huge* story at the moment and I can't trust him to anyone else. Do you like my shirt?'

'Huge? Huge why?'

'Louis is just in a class of his own at the moment. What can I say? He's the biggest thing since – since—'

'Since the last biggest thing? Which you've now forgotten.'

'Well, as you know, *Science Fiction* went through the roof, it just went stratospheric. There's no other word for it. I don't know if you know what the figures were but . . . anyway, phenomenal. And there's all the on/off with Grace Farlow to spice things up. Plus, he's decided to do this left-field indy film thing and it hasn't tested that well in the States, which is why they're opening it here. I think it's going to go belly-up, but you know what? It doesn't matter. It doesn't matter! Because it's Louis trying to be genuine, trying to find his roots, and everyone's going to love him for it.'

'About my flower workers—'

'Listen, Stevie.' Dick stops for a moment and turns to me for added emphasis. 'We've done flower workers.'

'Done them?'

'That's right. A couple of months ago.'

'But they don't know that. They don't know they're done. Somebody should tell them, really – otherwise they'll just keep on labouring and suffering—'

'Your piece – how shall I put this? It's gone cold.'

'Cold?'

'It's just not hot.'

'Not hot?'

'Listen, I feel for the flower workers. I do. But we can't *torture* our poor readers, you know. It's not what they pay us for.' We arrive at another set of see-through lifts and Dick presses the button to go down. 'How fab is this watch?' he says, and holds out his wrist for me to inspect.

The lift arrives bearing well-polished shoes that descend slowly past our eyes and turn out to house a distinguished-looking gentleman with a comfortably lived-in face. We nod to him as we get into the lift and I notice that Dick bridles and simpers a little more than usual in the man's presence, then suddenly hisses, 'Of course, it was my section that pretty much *broke* Louis Plantagenet,' as if this was a reasonable *sequitur* to our previous conversation. There's a winding-down noise and the lift judders to a halt between floors. We sigh collectively.

'Nobody panic,' Dick commands. 'This keeps happening.' He gives the alarm bell a jab with his finger. 'The power cuts out or something. It'll start again in a second.'

The distinguished gent and I stand there in an unalarmed silence that Dick, after a moment, feels obliged to fill.

'I feel reasonably confident, of course, that if there's any truth in the Grace Farlow rumours then I'll be the one Louis breaks it to. He's a very private guy, you know. A very private guy.'

Silence. I decide it's best to leave Dick's ridiculousness hanging in the air and hope he strangles himself with it.

'But I have a sneaking feeling,' he goes on, 'a small suspicion that Louis Plantagenet and Grace Farlow are destined for each other. Did you see them in *After Eight*? They sizzled. Believe me, absolutely sizzled. You could have fried an egg on the screen – a dozen eggs. It's going to be the love story of the century when they finally get together – or the tragedy of the century if they don't. For them, I mean.'

A scoffing noise comes from deep in my throat somewhere. I can't help it. Dick offers me a hankie.

'That was a scoffing noise,' I say, rejecting it. 'I'm scoffing. Did you know that, in terms of world population, at any given moment there are thirteen million people out there with whom we might be "romantically" compatible and three hundred and sixty thousand with whom we might easily think ourselves to be "completely in love" and, on average, we meet thirty-seven point two people a year who could potentially be a life partner – for the "happy ever after"? I don't think I'm going to worry too much about Louis Plantagenet and Grace Farlow.'

Dick's eyes are popping. Even the distinguished-looking gentleman seems interested.

'Where did you get the figures?'

'Oh,' I say, 'they did a study.'

'They?'

'Yes – *they*. The great *they*. The *they* who know things about life and get everything organised and decide things. The *they* that is everyone except *us*.'

'But—'

'Except, of course, for them *we* must be the *they* because for them we are not the *us* – anyway—'

'Stevie!'

'I'm sorry, but that made-for-each-other shit is just bollocks,' I say, and elegantly put, I think. For good measure I add, with some authority, 'Louis Plantagenet is a wanker.'

'You've met him?' Dick says. He seems a little scared by the idea.

'I bumped into him at the airport this morning. The guy makes so much money – for what? For being our hero? He's not a hero. He walks around with a bodyguard, for Christ's sake – he's a *coward*. The bodyguard assaulted me. I'm going to sue. You know what? I hate celebrities. Celebrities invade our head space, loot our bank accounts, and colonise all meaning in life. They make our non-celebrity existences seem rinky-dink, empty and insignificant, and then they want to go around infringing our civil liberties with their *own private police force*! Did you even read my flower story? Did you read about Elida? *She*'s a fucking hero. But no one wants to hear about her.'

Dick appears to be breaking a light sweat. I can see he wants to clamp his hand over my mouth and say, 'Ssssssh!' but he doesn't quite dare and it's all got something to do with the quietly distinguished gentleman in the corner.

'What is more,' I say raising my voice slightly, to agitate him further, 'these celebrities are a plague on the earth. And they must be *dealt with*. They are cancerous cells poisoning our life force – our very blood. They must be cast out, obliterated, destroyed.'

At this, the lift starts to move again, without any fuss. There's a small hiatus while Dick recovers himself with a sheepish look directed not at, but in the direction of, the distinguished gent. He then gives a little laugh and yodels, 'But it's all so boring without celebrities.' His voice catching strangely in his throat. He's gone for an I'm-not-ashamed-of-my-ironic-immersement-in-trash-culture tone, but doesn't bring it off.

The lift glides into position on the ground floor and the doors start to open. Escape seems imminent. But no – the doors close again. It's the distinguished-looking gentleman: his finger is on the door-close button. Dick and I both look at him. Trapped. Perhaps for ever. Trapped in a see-through lift with a distinguished-looking gentleman.

'You?' he says to Dick. 'You are interviewing Louis Plantagenet?'

'Yes,' Dick squeaks.

In the silence that follows, the older man turns his head so that his deliberate gaze comes to rest upon me. A moment later Dick does the same, his eyes as round and glassy as marbles.

3

I can tell the man's a bailiff from the size of his biceps. He looks like an off-duty bouncer. He's wearing a tight little blouson flight jacket that accentuates a large, jutting behind and he's standing on our doorstep in the washed-out afternoon sunlight, the kind that sometimes appears half-way through a winter's day. He looks like he's been standing there for a while. He looks like he's waiting. His mate is in a dirty white van at the kerb, reading a copy of the *Sun*.

We've had bailiffs before. When you've had them once they keep coming back, like herpes. You get a feel for them – sometimes you can tell it's them just by the way the doorbell rings.

I pause on the other side of the road. I can't go into the house. It is vital not to open the front door when there are bailiffs around. Once you've opened the front door, you are moments away from the TV being carted out. But they don't often violate a closed front door. The Englishman's home being his castle and all that.

This particular home is a big dilapidated town-house overlooking the railway lines in Paddington. You can tell it's a squat because sarongs bought in Goa are hanging up in a couple of the windows in lieu of curtains. The white stucco façade is the colour of a dead man's skin and peeling badly, the house having outgrown its grandeur long ago, with its servants' quarters and its coach-house. It was probably always too big for its boots, this house, and now it looks sadder than your common-or-garden slum.

I cross the road and mount our neighbours' doorstep, give bailiff man a little smile.

'Stevie Dunlop?' he says immediately, glancing at the document in his hand.

'Er – no. I'm the *neighbour*. I live here, not there. I'm going to this house, not that one.' I use my finger to underline my points, like I'm speaking to someone who's both hard of hearing and mental.

'Oh, really?' he says.

'Yes, really. Do you think I'd let someone like you prevent me getting into my own house?'

'I don't know, miss. People do all sorts to avoid paying their bills.'

'Oh, yeah? Well, maybe that's because they're sick of lining the pockets of the fat cats – they're sick of giving their lifeblood to the corporations who continue to make sure that ninety per cent of the world's wealth is owned by ten per cent of its people!'

'Like I said, miss, people do and say all sorts.'

'Please don't call me "miss".'

'I didn't catch your name.'

'I didn't throw it. Can I ask you something? Do you *like* hanging out on people's doorsteps arguing? Does that make you feel good about yourself? Do you sleep at night?'

'People buy something, they gotta pay for it. The law's the law.'

'People get *duped* into buying stuff.'

'People like you?'

He's really making my blood boil now. My head's about to blow off and I've been on a plane all night – no sleep. I consider hitting him.

'Do *you* like yourself?' he continues mildly. 'Do you like hanging out on doorsteps arguing? Do *you* sleep at night?'

'Listen, I'm for the oppressed. I sleep at night.'

'For the oppressed, but against me?'

'Definitely against you.'

'Who else are you against?'

'Oh . . .' I cast around wildly. I don't know where to start.

He's enjoying this. He leans back against the railings, rolling the document in his hand into a tight baton and striking the palm of his free hand with it.

'Would you say you were *for* more people than you're against? Or against more people than you're for?'

I tell him I've forgotten something at the shops and march off down the street. I take the second left and double back along the small track that runs behind the house, between the dustbin sheds and the railway line. I drag out one of the dustbins, climb up on to it and, using my plastic raincoat to dull the noise and protect me from the glass, I grab another dustbin lid and smash the skylight above our back door. I reach inside, grab the old servants' bells, which are still hanging there, and haul myself through.

Inside, the house has a heartbeat – the dull thump of bass. Someone's home. I find Phil and Jay in Phil's room. The window is blacked out and there's not one square inch of the room that isn't loaded up with some kind of computer equipment, but the feel is not high-tech, more like a grungy futuristic fantasy. Wires hang like intestines, keyboards – parted from their plastic covers – lie undignified and exposed for what they are; cardboard and little dots of tin. On the ceiling, neon tubes are twisted into indecipherable glowing graffiti. There is no furniture, just cushions and a mattress, and the only light is a red bulb dangling naked from the edge of the incongruous carved mantelpiece. The boys are sitting on the floor performing the smoking ritual – Rizlas, tobacco, lighters, small pieces of torn cardboard, ashtrays – seven cans of baked beans are stacked in a small tower as the centrepiece. Siege mentality.

'Where've you been?' they say. They often appear to speak in unison. Of course they don't, but they give the impression of it somehow.

'Hello,' I say sarcastically. 'Colombia. Flower pickers.'

'Flower pickers?' they echo. They look confused. They sound confused too, but they always sound confused. 'Bailiff's here,' they say. 'Bummer.' Or, rather, bumm*errrr*.

'How long has he been out there?' I ask.

'All day,' one of them says.

'We think it's the cable TV from last year,' says the other.

Then, 'Blood!' they both cry, pointing in horror at my foot.

I look down. Blood is, indeed, dripping out of the bottom of my jeans, running down the heel of my boot and soaking into the pig-pink candlewick bedspread that does for a rug on Phil's floor.

I sit down rather suddenly and see that I've ripped my jeans and, with them, the flesh above my knee, ragged tears in both. Inexplicably, really – because it doesn't even hurt – I start to cry.

'Bumm*errrrr*!' the boys moan distantly.

Some time later, I don't know how much, as I'm curled up on a bean-bag feeling a victim – and how being a victim makes time fly – the boys come back from their hourly patrol and announce jubilantly that Esther is on the doorstep.

The sound of Esther smartly ripping a cheque out of her cheque book (after having filled in the stub, of course) is like a short burst of machine-gun fire and can be heard quite clearly from the bedroom.

I manage to stumble down to the kitchen despite my injuries, which, to be honest, are superficial. Esther will be putting the kettle on. In fact, Esther already has the kettle on and is coaxing some delicious look-ing baklava, from the deli round the corner, out of a paper bag and on to a plate. This is as it should be.

When she sees me she gives me a wink and says, 'You needn't have climbed in, you know, the back door's never locked.' She reaches behind her and demon-strates by opening it easily with a quick twist of the handle.

'How do you know I climbed in?'

'Blood on the lintel.' She winks again. A habit of hers, which she carries off with a kind of Cockney-sparrow confidence.

Esther is long and bony – her elbows make the sharpest corners I've ever seen – without being the least bit brittle. She has a hardiness about her, a bit like a goat going up a rocky mountainside. She always wears black, always, always, and usually polo-necks. Her dark hair clings to her head and wisps forward to her chin like a perfectly fitting cloche hat, and she's not exactly pretty, but her face isn't the kind that brooks doubt; it just looks right somehow. She never wears makeup and she doesn't need it – her features are so well defined, it's like God did the makeup Himself. All in all, she's about as boyish as a girl can be while still managing to resemble Audrey Hepburn.

'Get some cups,' she says. She has a low, gravelly Portobello voice and a rasping chortle laugh. She smokes roll-ups and used to be a call-girl, or so she claims.

I have to move two bicycles to get to the kitchen sink. Once there, I gingerly extract four mugs from a mountain of washing-up that rises, as formidable as K2, from filmy grey water. Esther's been in South Africa for a week making a commercial – hence the dirty dishes.

I'm the one who found Esther – about two years ago, when I was picketing a florist for an organisation I helped set up called Fight 4 Fair Flowers. My sign said CAN'T BUY ME LOVE and I was risking frostbite holding it up in a pair of fingerless gloves. Esther, I don't know why, took a shine to my sign and then to me, and I haven't been able to shake her off since. She'd arrived at my elbow with a steaming cup of coffee, introduced herself as Esther Eliot, and given me her scarf to wear. I had to refuse the coffee as it was from a well-known chain. She didn't care. Esther can always take no for an answer.

When she came to visit 'the commune', as we call it – although the only thing that's communal about it is the tiny bathroom and the atmosphere is more factional than communal – Esther declared that she had finally found the way she wanted to live. I think she saw the commune as a way of having a family without actually having one so she put herself forward to take the empty bedroom.

I'd originally moved in with Jay, but we split up when he ran off with the Portuguese girlfriend of his own best friend. When he came back two months later I had, by general agreement of the communards, taken his room as my own and he had to settle for a large alcove on the first-floor landing with a rigged-up curtain to shield him from the stairs. Things were difficult for a while but then one of the factions moved out. Two more bedrooms became free; Jay got one and Esther the other. Phil, being a founder member, has always had the best room on the top floor – best because you don't get disturbed by other people's comings and goings.

So now it's just the four of us, each with our own small piece of territory. We're not really a commune any more. The commune was based on the general principle that property is theft. I don't think the fact that Esther has all the money and lets us steal it from her makes us a proper commune. These days, the house is best described as a tense and unsatisfactory place of residence where everybody argues and Esther pays the bills. Make that a tense and very draughty place of residence. I've never known a house with such draughts: they whip through of a winter like express trains. No central heating, of course.

At first the boys were against Esther. Before they met her. Esther has a proper career as a focus-puller and she earns serious money shooting commercials and pop videos with some of the best cameramen and women around. This financial functionality was definitely against her in the early days, unabashed earning of money being pretty much frowned upon by the communards. But, like I said, that was before they understood Esther. When they caught on to the bizarre fact that, in between jet-setting, she liked nothing better than to be mending their clothes or baking them cakes for tea, they soon came round.

She moved in an XL king-size divan bed and made it the only feature of her room, which she did up in Saatchi gallery Spartan style: she brought in a plasterer and a great deal of white paint and coaxed hard angles out of the spongy old building that we wouldn't have believed possible. When you go into Esther's part of the house you feel as if you've walked into another dimension. The bed notwithstanding, Esther declared herself a confirmed spinster and born-again virgin. She says she doesn't 'do' sex or relationships, has never liked sex much – something to do with her short stint as a call-girl – and, anyway, the traditional family having been exposed as a hot-bed of dissatisfaction and breeding ground for dysfunction, she says the way people should live now is with a fluid family of friends, who are just that – friends. The boys call her Celibate Eliot.

I don't know if it was these principles, or just plain old good-heartedness, but Esther soon became our support system. We 'borrowed' money from her to pay the gas and electric and to mend the hole in the roof and get a new fridge. But the debt was the third-world kind and kept having to be written off. I earned bread-line money writing a weekly website review for a magazine called the *Conscientious Consumer*, but it only just kept my head above water. The boys, meanwhile, were developing a biodegradable coffin, the success of which was apparently going to be huge, but the process was slow, what with all the shagging and the dope-smoking and the dreadful amount of paperwork you have to get through, these days, apparently, to be deemed eligible for the dole.

After Esther has successfully blackmailed Jay into going to the supermarket to buy washing-up liquid, amongst other things, and Phil has retired upstairs to check his e-mails, I tell her that my flower story got spiked. I feel I have to tell her. She paid for the flight to Colombia.

Esther is rolling a cigarette at the big wooden table that occupies most of the kitchen and has twenty-five ancient jam-pots in its middle. Behind the blacked-out windows a train rattles by on its way to Penzance. We only hear the trains, never see them. The house used to be an anarchist hang-out and for some reason they painted the back windows black, the ones overlooking the railway line. Maybe the orderly – these days, fairly punctual – operation of the trains had been an irritation.

'One day, I'm going to scrape that black paint off those windows,' I say. 'Either that or jump out of one.'

'Hmmm,' she says. 'What's up?'

'I got stuck in the lift with the editor of the *Daily News*. He wants me to interview Louis Plantagenet. Can you believe it?'

'Shit,' she says.

'I think it was something I said to the Dick about there being thirteen million soulmates out there for everyone and—'

'Thirteen million?'

'Oh, I don't know – I read something once. I can't remember exactly. I made it up. Anyway, it obviously took his fancy.'

'You and Louis Plantagenet?'

'It's incredible, don't you think? They'd go to any lengths to corrupt me. Any lengths.' I shake my head sagely, bitterly. 'Well, they're not dumbing this baby down. Not this baby.'

'But what did you say to him?'

I said NO, of course. NO. NO. NO. NO.

'I said I was busy.'

She looks at me. There's a lot of distance in the look. She's observing me as you might a rare bird. I wonder if something changed while she was in South Africa.

'You know what you need?' she says mildly, putting the roll up cigarette to one side and not lighting it. 'And I don't want you to take this the wrong way—'

I'm pretty sure I'm going to take it the wrong way. That would be fairly likely.

'What you need is a kick up the arse.'

Esther has never spoken to me like this before. In my mind's eye, I see myself rising up before her like an offended eagle ruffling my feathers, I look down my fearsome beak with my fearsomely beady eye, I take flight: I speak, I soar to the heights of eloquence explaining that I am eternally righteous and she with her Kleenex commercials will never be. I come in for the kill, dropping like a stone from the sky with pinpoint accuracy, I take her by the scruff of her neck and I savage her to death. I see myself doing all of this, but what I actually do is rest my elbows on the table and bury my face in my hands.

'I said, don't take it the wrong way,' she says, with more of the usual Esther cosiness in her voice, 'Obviously, I like the way you're so passionate about things, but there's a balance to be struck – don't you think?'

'For balance,' I say, 'read compromise, read sell-out.'

'Not necessarily. As an established journalist, you could bring your original take on things to all sorts of issues. You'd build up a reputation for yourself, contacts, a power base, and then you'd be much better placed to spread the word – you'd reach a much wider audience. Think about it.'

I look at her unsmoked cigarette for a while, and then I turn my head and look at a budding daffodil stem poking young and green out of a pot on the front window-sill. I wonder if it will flower in the silence. Eventually I say, 'Why aren't you smoking your cigarette?'

'I don't know. I don't know what's wrong with me. I feel a bit—'

'I can't interview Louis Plantagenet,' I burst out. 'I'm suing the guy for assault and wrongful arrest. Or I will be, as soon as I issue the writ. His bodyguard attacked me at the airport.'

'Don't be ridiculous.'

'He did. I bumped into Louis at the airport – quite by accident, not my fault at all – and his bodyguard arm-wrestled me to the ground. It was an outrage.'

'But you never look where you're going.'

'You're on his side?'

'Stevie, this Louis thing could be your big break. You've already got a story to tell – you could use the airport thing – and if you get in with the editor you have a much better chance of getting the kind of commissions you want . . . and being taken more seriously.'

'It's hardly a big break. It's one of those conveyor-belt interviews where you have to be in and out in fifteen minutes. I'm about as likely to show what I'm made of as the Colonel's secret recipe.'

Esther is suddenly looking very grey. I suspect she's not agreeing with me. This is all most unusual, and I start to feel a little like I do when I find out someone votes Conservative after I've already slept with them.

'No way am I pandering to that bullshit,' I say, to underline things a little.

I sense she's not happy with me. When she retches violently into the empty Baklava bag, I know she's not. Then she's up and, still bent over the paper bag, heading for the downstairs loo.

I follow. I find her kneeling beside the loo hugging it like it's her best friend.

And I used to be her best friend.

'Esther,' I cry, 'I'll do it! I'll interview him! Whatever you want! I promise. Look! I'm calling Dick now.'

I run for the phone and bring it back to make the call in front of her. She's sitting up, wiping her mouth and streaming eyes with pink loo paper, and there's a watery smile on her face.

It's remarkable we've *got* loo paper – she lucked out there.

'It's okay,' she says. 'That prawn cocktail I ate on the plane.'

'I will do it, though,' I say, sitting down on the edge of the bath, 'because you're right.'

Esther is always right.

4

'You have thirteen minutes.'

'Thirteen?'

'The other two are for the change-over. And this,' she hands me a sheet of paper, 'is the list of subjects we will not be taking questions on this morning. Read it carefully.'

With that, the woman with the clipboard and the designer specs – two narrow black slits – perched on the end of her nose is gone. I look down. I am standing on a luxurious carpet bearing a bold asymmetrical pattern. I follow the line of asymmetry to where two pert little leather armchairs are angled towards each other for intimate conferencing. I sit in one of them. Out in the lobby smartly suited staff bustle about in the offensive and hard-nosed manner that is the unmistakable sign of exclusivity in a hotel.

So this is where the rich have-it-alls come when they want to feel alienated and not good enough.

'So this is where the rich have-it-alls come when they want to feel alienated and not good enough?'

'Excuse me?'

'SO THIS IS WHERE THE—'

'No need to shout.'

41

He looks at me for the first time. Before when he'd looked at me he'd been in character, Louis Plantagenet looking up to greet the first journalist of the day, exuding amiability, while at the same time saving himself, offering only surface contact, ready to eke himself out, one drop of juice at a time. Now, for a split second, he looks at me as Louis, the real Louis, and I'm frightened by two things: one, his shaved head, and two, his vulnerability.

'You're scaring me,' I say.

'I'm scaring you?' he says, eyebrows raised sky high, all seamlessly jovial, all sewn up again.

'By which you presumably mean,' I say, after a moment's thought, 'that, in your opinion, I am more scary than you. And furthermore, if that is indeed the case, that I have no right to be scared by you when I am so scary myself. Correct?'

Suddenly he smiles. The smile lights up the room – to say nothing of the corners of the universe; it lights up Santiago and powers the national grid of Western Australia; it sends the satellites whirling around the earth. It grabs me. It whips me round on a rollercoaster ride before it sets me back down on the ground.

When it's over, things seem a little different. The world seems . . . well, it seems kind of warm and fuzzy, actually, it seems pretty nice. I imagine this smile could change my life. 'What are you *doing*?' I say.

'What?' he says. 'What am I doing?'

'Smiling,' I say.

He laughs. This is more manageable than the smile because it isn't *directed* at me as such. Laughing is his own thing. So we just bounce around in the sheer wholesomeness of his laugh for a while and then, as before, drift slowly back to earth.

'So,' I say, trying to gather things a little. I look down at my reporter's notebook for guidance.

None.

A blank page stares back at me – it is, it occurs to me, as blank as my mind. As I suspected, Louis is like a virus that is infiltrating my files and erasing my hard disk.

'So?' he says, and I look up. He has these big eyes, set wide so they take up a lot of his face. His angelic face that manages to be masculine too. The tips of his shaven hairs form a fine grazing on his skull, the colour of newly minted gold coins.

'Sorry,' I say, 'you seem to have erased some stuff.'

'Erased?' he says. And then, quite politely, 'You know, I haven't really followed a single thing you've said since you walked in here.'

I can sense old Slit Eyes rising silently from her chair, painstakingly placed as it is – by the door – not so close as to intrude upon our conversation, but not so far away as to prevent her hearing everything that's going on.

I panic. I hold up the tabloid newspaper I have bought on the way here. It's folded and I let the bottom half drop so that the front page is revealed. It bears a picture of Louis with his new haircut. The words CANCER SCARE roar out of the headline.

'Is it true you've got cancer?' I say.

'Jesus Christ!' It's clearly the first he's heard of it.

He's up from his sofa: he wants to get to the offending object, the newspaper. The coffee table is between us with its wide glass top. Louis brings his foot up and kicks the glass hard. It rises up and careers sideways, sending vase, flowers, coffee cups, pot and sugar bowl sliding, crashing and smashing to the floor.

I half rise and propel myself backwards and away, knocking over my own chair in the process. The unbroken sheet of glass wobbles, then settles on the diagonal, upended, resting on a corner of the frame. Slit Eyes is back among us waving her clipboard.

'We've got it under control,' she shouts. I don't know whether she's talking to me or to Louis. 'It's all under control.'

Louis now breaches the coffee table, stepping in and out of the exposed frame. He is very calm, pale and clenched, but burning underneath. I can tell by the fine layer of moisture that begins to prick up on his skin and the very slight, very held, shaking of his hands.

'Fuck them,' he says calmly. 'Fuck them.' And then, to Slit Eyes, 'You can cancel today. You can cancel tomorrow. You can cancel the rest of the week. I'm not giving those bastards one fucking word, not one fucking word. Do you hear me?'

'But, Louis—'

'I said cancel everything.'

'But you can't.'

He looks at her. 'They want me dead. Fine. I'm fucking dead,' he says.

Slit Eyes is left with no choice but to turn to me. 'You were told!' she yells.

The piece of paper – I didn't read the no-go piece of paper.

'Leave her out of this,' Louis says, so I act the fearless journalist and leave.

Back on the asymmetrical carpet I find The Dick floating towards me like a bad dream. 'Lucky you were in first. Apparently, he's thrown a wobbly. Did you get anything good?' he babbles excitedly, his breath coming fast and short. 'Looks like you're the only one who did.'

It's not until I glance down at my reporter's notebook, its pages as shiny and new as the day they were recycled, that I realise I didn't get anything at all.

Jermyn Street. London. A place of many stripes, wide stripes and thin stripes, loud stripes and pinstripes. Stripes that run obediently and vertically, up and down the legs and arms of suits and shirts, only veering from the norm when they cut diagonally across some of the more risqué ties.

The street itself is a stripe, a narrow, deep furrow with a pleasingly Dickensian pub, a churchyard and shops selling gentlemen's perfumes, which give it a sense of old London, not old London repackaged for tourists but real old London where everything was slow and dignified, unglamorous and staid. Outside Fortnum and Mason, a traffic warden is refusing to play the game and insisting that a chauffeur-driven Jaguar may not wait on the double yellow line.

Louis and my friend Mike – from the airport – are up ahead. They walk fast, Mike one carefully measured step behind Louis. Louis has his suit collar up and his fedora pulled down. He looks like a gangster in his brown pinstripe suit, but the slightly flared trousers give him away. They hang loose and relaxed on his long slim frame, a little skew-whiff, a little short of the ankles, flapping a little in the speed of his hasty advance.

I've never *followed* a person in the street before. I have been following the two of them since they left the hotel on foot. I feel a little hysterical and giggly, I have an involuntary grin playing on my lips. I imagine myself dodging into doorways as Mike looks round, but in fact this isn't necessary. I'm surprised Mike hasn't spotted me, but he hasn't. Instead, he's covering the opposite pavement. He repeatedly glances over at a thickset man in a bulgy yellow Puffa jacket who's going the same way as us.

One second, the two of them are there in front of me, the next, Louis has gone. It takes me a moment to work out that he must have dodged into a shop. Mike is still there. He swings round full-circle but doesn't register me, his eyes rolling right back round to Yellow Puffa Jacket.

Yellow Puffa Jacket just keeps on walking. Mike watches him go. I watch Mike watching him go. Eventually Puffa Jacket's gone far enough that Mike does another sweep with his eyes then goes into the shop. At which point Yellow Puffa Jacket turns right round and comes back towards the shop. When he gets to within a few yards he pulls out his phone and makes a call. He looks like he's reading the name of the shop, the street number.

This could be interesting.

I don't know what to do. I have no plan. So I walk

on over there and go into the shop. It's a free country, right? A bell rings loudly at my entry, terrifying me. I leap guiltily, then quickly busy myself examining a table of pastel-coloured ties laid out in rows like stripy candy.

'Just looking,' I mutter, at an approaching assistant. There's no sign of Louis.

'I'm sorry, madam,' the assistant says, his hands held wide as if to shoo me out the door, 'the shop will be closed for the next half an hour or so.'

The door goes again. The bell makes us both leap. It's Yellow Puffa Jacket. The jacket is so garish in this temple of sober, thoughtful testosterone, so loud and so yellow, it's an offence.

The assistant turns his full attention to Yellow Puffa Jacket and gives him the same line he gave me. I skedaddle sideways through an arch into another section of the shop. There's a door to the street here too, and I open and close it quickly so that the bell rings, giving the impression of departure. Another Puffa jacket outside on the pavement registers briefly, this one blue. The Revenge of the Puffa Jackets. I retreat quickly backwards into the dark recesses of the shop, find a wardrobe and step inside, shutting the door behind me. Your fearless reporter.

It's quite stuffy in there. A wardrobe full of suits. I plan to stay not very long: it reminds me of Gran's wardrobe when I was a child and going into it to search her coat pockets hoping for small change. It used to stink of mothballs in there, made me choke, a fusty, dead smell. The smell of old age, I'd thought. I'm busy with this sensory flashback when the door at the other end of the wardrobe slides back and Louis joins me.

Huh.

He barges through the suits, puts his back to the wall and slides down it to a squatting position where I can't see him. The suits hang so that they only reach half-way to the floor – there's more air below. I am standing. If he turns his head he might see my legs. But he doesn't. And if I stand very still there's a chance he won't see me at all. He's completely silent, possibly meditating. I go through denial, horror and extreme embarrassment to a kind of distanced – won't this be a good story to tell my grandchildren – appreciation of the situation. I would like more than anything to call Esther and tell her I am hiding in a wardrobe full of suits with Louis Plantagenet. At which point the psychic switchboard puts my call through with reversed charges. My phone rings.

Louis doesn't even jump. He does nothing.

Do I take the call? What's the protocol? In a wardrobe?

I pull out the phone. It's Esther. I squat down so Louis and I are face to face.

'Would you mind if I took this call?'

'Would you *leave*, please?'

I turn off the phone and make to obey, sliding the door back at my end of the—

'Excuse me.'

'Yes?'

I turn back, except now I've got a medium-weight pinstripe in my face and I'm forced to squat down again.

'I would appreciate it,' he says quietly, reluctantly, 'if you wouldn't write about this.'

There's something in his voice – in him . . . I begin to see why people might, generally speaking, prostrate themselves at his feet and cry, 'Yes! Yes! Whatever you say.'

'About what?' I say, raising my eyebrows innocently and buying time to remind myself that if I don't write about this I won't have anything to write about, and what will Esther say?

'About this.'

'This?'

'This!' he hisses, and both his hands shoot out as if to grasp the whole situation. 'This hiding in the closet.'

There's a silence while I consider my options and Louis puts his hands back where they came from. His bony knees are sticking up in front of his shoulders and his hands are clasped between his legs in one big fist, which he swings up and down agitatedly, his elbows propped up on his thighs. I notice how quiet it is in the wardrobe, muffled. The suits provide padding, I suppose.

I take a deep breath and explain to him that I had absolutely nothing to do with the cancer story and was just fascinated to know how he felt about it, and that I desperately need to earn some money and get my career into gear, so to speak, and in some ways my interview with him was a part of this new leaf I am turning over, this new approach and—

'Are you trying to do a deal with me?' he says.

'I suppose I am.'

'Well, do it, then.'

'You give me a thirty-minute interview and I don't tell about you hiding.'

'I'll give you until Mike comes to get me.'

'Where? In here?'

'Go – go – begin. You're wasting time.'

'Okay,' I say, pulling out my tape-recorder, my mind reeling. 'Err – why are you hiding in a wardrobe?'

'The short answer is because I don't feel like having my picture in the papers today. I shaved my head, by the way, for a cameo I did in LA yesterday.'

'What's the long answer?'

'Too long to print.'

'Off the record?' I say, feeling foolish. But worth a go, I think.

'There's no such thing as off the record.'

But I want to know.

A flaw in his logic occurs to me.

'But the hiding in the wardrobe could be said to be "off the record" – right? So, given that that's off the record, and you're trusting me on that, couldn't there be other things that are off the record? I mean, given that we've already got a sock drawer, we could put more than one pair of socks in it. Right?'

'A sock drawer?' He looks over at me and I'm not sure if he's amused or exasperated.

'Okay,' he says, after a moment. 'Off the record . . .' and here he pauses and looks at my tape-recorder until I get the message and switch it off '. . . the guy out there, not the one in the store, the one on the sidewalk, is a paparasshole called Rico Bargello.'

In the blue puffa jacket.

I don't know what my face does but Louis shoots me a look and says, 'Do you know him?'

'I've heard of him.'

'He's trying to set me up. So I have to stay in here until Mike clears the street.'

'Set you up how?'

'He sends in his stooge –'

Yellow Puffa Jacket.

'– to shove a lens in my face and try to get either me or Mike into a fight. He stays outside and shoots the fight through the window. It's good for him. He gets to create a story, make money, and make me look like a bastard – all at the same time.'

'Did he get you?

He gestures with his hands. 'I'm in here, aren't I?'

I ask him why it's off the record, why he doesn't want people to know that he gets treated like that, and he clasps his hands together again and squeezes his fists until his knuckles show white. I'm not sure he's conscious he's doing it.

'The rule is – never complain.'

'Who made up *that* rule?' I say, outraged – I don't know why, any cause in a storm, I suppose.

'Your queen,' he says. 'Never complain. Never explain. That's the royal rule. Do you think I can smoke in here?'

'You *smoke*?'

'All the time.'

'Is the all-American hero allowed to smoke?'

'Well, let's see,' he says. 'I guess if it's the all-American cowboy hero, he might be allowed to smoke. Especially,' he flashes me a half-measure smile, 'if it's his only vice.'

I get his eyes for a moment along with the smile, and when they move away again, I note that I miss them. He puts the cigarette in his mouth but doesn't light it – the suits, I suppose.

'Have you ever thought of doing a deal with Ri – with that photographer?' I eventually say.

'Katrina's always wanting me to do deals.' Slit Eyes, presumably, and not a popular suggestion, it seems.

'I mean in a way, if you think about it, someone like Rico could be on your side. He's part of what sells you. You could see him as one of your distributors – work with him.'

'Rico Bargello is not on my side.'

'Okay – but knowing his type, he's probably open to a deal. You could let him have one picture in exchange for him leaving you alone for the rest of the time you're in London.'

'A picture of what?'

'I don't know. Pick some girl to get "caught" with. So what if they think what they think? They think it anyway. Throw them some crumbs. I mean, it seems to me – you could, if only for your own peace of mind.' A look of panic crosses Louis's face. 'What?' I say.

'Are you in league with him?'

'No!' I say. 'He's not my type.'

'Okay,' he says.

'Deep breaths.'

'Okay.'

I don't say anything more for a moment, wanting to be sure he believes me.

'I'm sorry,' he says eventually.

'And has it ever occurred to you,' I go on nervously, 'that maybe you antagonise people – people like Rico. I was er, well, for example, I was wrongfully arrested, shall we say?, by your bodyguard at the airport for bumping into you by mistake.'

This surprises him. He jerks his head up to me. His eyes are incredibly alert and, again, when he turns his attention away I notice that I want it back.

'I hope he apologised,' he says.

'And you just blew out all those interviews at the hotel.'

'You know how many interviews I did for this movie in the States? One hundred and fifty in two days. Do you have any idea how brain-numbing that is? You get to the point when just answering one more question feels like lifting the hundred and sixty-pound weight at the gym – you're sucked so dry, you're sucked drier than a snake in a pit. You can't even open your mouth. You get home and someone calls and you can't even bring yourself to pick up the phone. By the way, I did the European press that first time. They don't need any more interviews. This was meant to be a small indy-type movie. I'm here for the première and I'll go to the première – they can live without their fucking interviews.'

'They pay you well for it, though.'

'They pay me well for it.' He nods, but his eyes are blank. 'You see what happens,' he says, 'when I complain?'

I blush slightly, like he's caught me out. To cover myself I pick up the tape-recorder. 'You'll be out of here in a minute,' I say.

'But I'm doing life.' He says it so low I think I've misheard him.

'Sorry?'

'Nothing. I was joking.'

'No such thing as a joke!' I say glibly.

'Excuse me?'

'Freud said it – there's no such thing as a joke.'

He laughs. He looks down to where his fists are clenched together; the unsmoked cigarette is now sticking out between his middle fingers.

'We're still off the record, I take it?'

'If you even *think*,' he says, waving a long, finely chiselled finger in my direction, 'of printing this . . .'

He doesn't finish the sentence, which is most effective. My mind is free to roam – visions of Mike coming through the kitchen skylight with kneecapping equipment dangling from his belt.

He glances up at me again and sees that I'm watching his clenched fists. He looks at them too and unclenches. I notice now that he has a similar tension in his jaw. A little tic. It's part of what defines his face. His jaw holds his determination, his resolve, his self-control, but also all of the vulnerability that requires such defensiveness.

Reading my mind, he makes a fist and rests his chin on it for a few seconds. It's a familiar gesture. I must have seen it in a movie.

'I get jaw ache sometimes,' he says, with a frown.

I hold up my tape recorder and turn it on. 'Tell me

about you and Grace Farlow,' I say over a discreet tapping on the wardrobe door.

'I'm sorry', Louise says, 'but your time is up.'

5

I get home to find the boys in the lounge. Lounging. The two of them, on cushions, in yet-to-biodegrade coffins – smoking. Illegal drugs, no doubt.

'I just met Louis Plantagenet,' I can't resist saying.

'Cool,' they say. 'What's he like?'

'He's about your age,' I say, 'and he can sit up already and stuff like that.'

'Cool!' they say.

'Where's Esther?'

They don't seem to know. At this point I remember her call – turn my phone back on and pick up her message.

'She's been taken to *hospital*!' I yell.

'Bummer,' they say. 'Bum*mmer!*'

'We've got to go there,' I say. 'Now!'

'Bum*mmer.*'

And so saying they clamber out of their coffins.

We find Esther sitting in a wheelchair in a corridor that looks like one of the hospital's intestinal tracts: exposed pipework streams above our heads. She's been released from Casualty and has been parked there while a taxi is called. We wait to share it with her on a row of smart turquoise bucket seats – strangely incongruous in the otherwise war-torn décor.

'I'm okay,' she says, 'I had some pains but it was sort of a false alarm. I just have to take it easy for a while.'

'False alarm about what?' I say.

'Oh, you know, small technical hitch, but it's all okay. Baby still on board.'

At which point there is a long silence. *Long* silence. Wondering if we heard right.

'Whoa!' say the boys. 'Hold on a minute!' And for some reason they both stand up.

'Baby?' I say. 'What baby?'

'I'm pregnant.'

'How far gone?'

'About an hour and forty minutes.'

We look at her.

'That's how long I've known about it. Apparently it's been in there for four months.'

Surprise.

It's not often in life that I am truly surprised: events – even unexpected ones – mostly come along tinged with a sense of the inevitable. Not this one. This isn't in the master-plan.

We all look at her belly. Now we know it's in there we can see a small bump. Esther puts a hand on it. 'It started to show the minute they told me I was pregnant.'

Phil stamps his foot. 'How are we defining "celibate", Eliot?' he demands.

The boys both look very off-balance, slapping their pockets – metaphorically speaking – the way you do when you've just discovered you've lost your wallet.

'How did you not know?' I say.

'What I thought was a spate of,' Esther mouths the

words in my direction, '*light periods* turned out to be,' mouths again, '*spotting*.' It's a received wisdom that we don't talk about the more prosaic facts of life – like periods – in front of the boys in case they (a) lose their innocence or (b) faint.

'So who's the lucky guy?' Phil says. 'I mean it's a mistake – right? – so it can't be a turkey-baster babe.'

Esther's eyes dart in my direction. 'Malaysia,' she says defiantly, 'on the beach.' Esther went to Malaysia a few months ago to make a Bacardi commercial with a big-name Hollywood director. 'Film sets are steeped in tradition.' She shrugs. 'What can you do? And sometimes the focus-puller has to sleep with the director. It's just one of those things – like toasting the hundredth slate with a glass of champagne.'

'Slate?'

'On the clapperboard.'

'Oh,' we all say.

'You know what crews are like!'

'No,' we all say.

'Especially on location.'

'So?' we all say . . . collectively, bearing in mind her antipathy to sex and having mutual visions, no doubt, of sand, surf and gentle breezes in the moonlight.

She just curls a lip in reply.

It suddenly occurs to me that congratulations are in order. 'Congratulations!' I say.

'For what?' she says. 'I've fucked up my life.'

'You'll make a wonderful mother!'

'Oh, yuk.'

'We'll share it with you!'

'Oh, yeah! You're gonna have my baby for me?'

It occurs to me she's still in shock. 'Well, not exactly,' I say, 'but I think you'll find that this is *our* baby.' I look at the boys, gathering them in with my glance and trying to ignore a strange melting effect at their edges, which makes them appear to be shrinking visibly before my very eyes. 'It's *our* baby,' I say again, sternly. 'Isn't it, boys?'

Esther has been told that she is at risk of miscarriage and must do a lot of resting between now and the birth, most of it in bed, which happens to be Esther's least favourite place in the world and is where we put her the minute we get her home. She's allowed to move around the house and even go out for walks and so forth, but work is out of the question.

Esther may not be so keen on the baby idea, however it's not lost on her that she'll be handing the bread-winner's baton to me – interviewer to the stars – and that this might provide the very kick up the arse I need.

'You got some good stuff?' she says.

'Yeah!'

'What's he like?'

'Fabulous.'

'Did you ask about his daily routine like we talked about? What time he gets up and so on.'

'All that stuff.'

'What *is* his routine?'

'He gets up at six,' I say, 'and goes running for an hour. Wherever he is in the world.'

'Doesn't surprise me. Was he handsome in the flesh?'

'Incredibly.'

'Fit?'

'Of course.'

'Muscles?'

'I guess. But lean.'

'Tall?'

'Taller than me.'

'Did you like him?'

'Loved him!'

'Did he like you?'

'Adored me.'

It's no good. I am forced to tell her the truth.

'Do you mean to say,' she says, 'that you have interviewed him twice and neither time did you get a single printable word?'

'That is exactly what I mean to say.'

She thinks about this for a while. 'What's he really like?'

I tell her he's probably as egotistical and paranoid and fucked-up as the rest of them, but it's hard to tell because – well, basically because he's so attractive. I don't mean the looks, although that's part of it. He's attractive like a magnet. He pulls you in. It's like he's incredibly precious somehow, but I don't mean precious in a pretentious way: I mean literally valuable, special. Yet he's got this air of humility – it's very convincing. But he seems troubled somehow, quite troubled.

'Interesting,' she says. 'You must get back in there, back in the saddle.'

'Too late, I think. Anyway, how?'

'Easy. You jog around the park at six – like he does – and you pretend to bump into him.'

'I made that up about jogging at six. I didn't ask about his daily routine.'

'You *made it up*?'

'Yes, yes,' I say, and wave my hands in a dismissive manner to indicate that we should move on swiftly and not bog ourselves down in these sorts of insignificances.

'You *made up* a detail like that?'

'What? I was humouring you. You're sick. Sick people get humoured.'

'It's just, well, that's quite elaborate. He runs at six – that's not just lying, that's—'

'It wasn't *elaborate*. All movie stars jog at six. You're pregnant. I'm meant to be the breadwinner. I didn't want you to think I wasn't winning any.'

She considers me a moment. I can see her having an idea. 'Go to the park, at six, and jog. He's bound to be there. Like you say, all movie stars jog at six.'

'But even if that's true, which park? It could be any park. He's not staying at the hotel. He rents some house in South Kensington.' I can hear the edge of a whine creeping into my voice: I know I'm on slippery ground.

'Guess the park,' she says, and picks up a magazine. 'How hard can it be?'

I can't make any kind of article out of what I've got. I've tried, but I can't. Every single thing I want to say about him I can't say without breaking our agreement. So I am walking to Kensington Gardens in what seems to me to be the middle of the night – five thirty in the morning, to be exact. I have worked out that this is the most likely park for Louis to jog in.

The world has a just-woken look, a little rumpled, a little hung-over from the night before. The light is different, raw, and the streets are empty, which makes them look like a studio set upon which adventures might take place given lights, cameras and action.

There are signs of life around, but not much life itself. Life is referred to, rather, in the overflowing rubbish bins, in a newspaper-delivery van speeding by and a few public servants here and there heroically engaged in supporting our city's infrastructure: a postman, a street cleaner, and – also deserving a mention – the traffic lights changing from green to yellow to red and back again, manfully playing to an empty hall.

I often wonder about the people whose job it is to organise the traffic, people whose lives are consumed with the science of traffic. How do they decide a particular junction needs a no-right-turn sign? Do they sit around tables debating it? Do careers rise and fall in consequence of good and bad no-right-turn signs? Do they have annual award ceremonies – 'And the award for the Best No-right-turn Sign goes to . . .'? For some reason I imagine these obscure traffic people working underground in a bunker. Unsung heroes.

In the park, there are daffodils – 'beside the lake, beneath the trees, fluttering and dancing in the breeze'. I cannot look at a daffodil without that line going through my head. It's quite a curse. But they are picturesque, the daffodils. I want to pull them up and put them in a box and have them for ever – but not them, in fact, rather the feeling they bring. But it wouldn't work, of course – in a box. I look at the daffodils again and try to recapture the feeling. I'm straining for it now. Doesn't work. I give up – fuck the daffodils – and walk on.

I position myself by the Queen's Gate, far enough away to give myself a view of the whole of the gate area so that I won't miss him when he comes through – *if* he comes through. I don't exactly hide behind a tree, but I loiter near one. I put my hands in my pockets, pull them out again and wish I'd bought a newspaper to read. Occasional joggers come past and feign disinterest in my skulking activities, except one burly Yank who calls out, 'Good morning,' in a very American God's-in-His-heaven-and-all's-right-with-the-world way.

I am unbelievably self-conscious behind my tree. I wouldn't be surprised if curtains are twitching in the embassies that line the park. Perhaps police have been called. At this very moment, alarm bells are ringing at stations across the area – maybe even Special Branch is involved. I am going to be *found out* and I'm so preoccupied with all of this that it barely registers that half an hour has gone by and Louis is a no-show.

Clearly I have got the wrong park. I abandon the whole enterprise. Total collapse. I decided – and I don't know where this comes from because it's not my way, but come it does – that the only answer at this time of the morning is a large cappuccino and a large cake. I may even go to Star – Star – Star – well, anyway, a well-known coffee chain. That's what I will do. If I'm going to collapse it may as well be completely.

I don't think about Dick, I don't think about Esther and the boys, I don't think about the baby – I just know I have to get across the park to that coffee and cake and *then* I will think, then I will think about what I will do.

I like to put off thinking to another time. A time when it will be a better time to think – when I am in the right ambience, the right energy loop – yes – in that glorious future time, *then* I will think. I will think well, I will think justly. I will think productive, wise and useful thoughts. For now I will just drift. I will let my mind fill with the flotsam and jetsam that is its usual traffic, and I will walk through the park thinking of whether I should change those size-six trainers I bought for a size five and a half, whether they aren't a *tad* too big or whether it's good to have a bit of breathing space for the toes. I will think of the time – this is one of my favourites – I went a stop too far on my tube ticket and they wouldn't let me pay the extra: I had either to go back a stop (thereby using London Underground's resources further) or to pay ten pounds to be released from the station. I will re-feel the anger at this injustice pounding uselessly in my chest. It will make me walk faster. I will also, no doubt, see an illegal cyclist whizzing along the park shortcuts where he shouldn't be, and I'll think about the time Jay was working in Camden and how he'd cycle home along the canal towpath and how he kept getting pushed in – bike and all. How outraged we were! How nasty a place the world seemed. Then one day, I found myself walking along the canal towpath and I saw the signs: CYCLING STRICTLY FORBIDDEN. I'll think about how I wish I'd been there to push him in too.

I am deep in this scene. I am passing the thrusting presence of Physical Energy – naked man on rearing horse – but I hardly notice, I am so deep in with Jay and his bicycle that it barely registers when a slim figure, the hood of his sweatshirt pulled over his head against the chill, jogs quietly past minding his own business.

I hesitate. What seemed possible in theory now seems impossible. To talk to him, to interrupt him in his private life, to ask him to rescue me from my own foolishness. In the imagining of this moment I had felt somewhat righteous and justified. He was, after all, public property of a sort. It was absurd – *yes! absurd!* – that he should expect me to write anything intelligent about him after a thirteen-minute interview. In any case, we had a special bond, he and I: we'd been in a wardrobe together. He owed me.

But he has only to flit past, self-absorbed and unaware, pursuing his own life, for my intimate preview of the scene to be swept aside. He owes me nothing, of course. How dare I intrude?

He disappears between some trees and that's that. I carry on in the direction of coffee and cake. I walk all the way to the far gate with an unmistakable sense of life slipping away. It's not a nice feeling. It's a very fearful feeling – an ice cube sliding through my guts, melting slowly in my belly. Here I have an opportunity and I'm letting it slip, slip, slip away. I'm always wishing life would be more surprising, would take more unexpected twists and turns – and yet, if I'm not careful, I find myself taking the easy road.

I take a deep breath. I turn back into the park.

'Hello again.'

It's him. He jogs on the spot a little, not exactly smiling but his eyes are friendly, very alive. He is always so alive. I wonder if it's something he eats.

'Hi,' I say.

There is a fractional pause between the two of us. So small only a quantum physicist could measure it. But we know it's there. It's like a pit, a small failure. It is hard to come back from. There is something unsaid and neither of us can grasp what it is. The conversation has nowhere to go without this thing that neither of us can name. We must move on. He must move on.

'Well . . .' His on-the-spot jogging begins to turn him away from me.

'*Wait!*' I yell.

He waits.

'Listen,' I say, 'it really wasn't fair last time. It was all off the record.'

He glances at me a moment, considering this, the light in his eyes doing a searchlight swoosh into my head-space like a spotlight sweeping the night sky. I see him registering that I am keeping to the deal.

'Wasn't fair?'

'Well, I didn't really get my part of the deal, did I? I didn't get my interview.'

'And whose fault was that?'

'Mine.'

He thinks about it. 'You can jog with me,' he says finally.

You can jog with me. He is saying that I may run beside him if I wish. Good. But there's a problem. I may – but I *cannot*. I cannot run. I'm not sure exactly how far I cannot run, but I know I cannot run to the off-licence on the corner of our street – it shuts early at nine and we can never quite believe this and always have a last-minute panic – which is . . . I'm not very good at distances but I would guess under 150 yards from our front door.

Now, when I say I cannot run to the off-licence, I mean more precisely that if I set out at a run I am forced by shortness of breath and excruciating pain in my calves to stutter to a walking pace before I am half-way there, however eager I am to arrive on time. I really cannot run. And conversation – *conversation* – while doing so is out of the question.

I look down at my feet in the vain hope that I will be saved by my shoes. I know exactly what shoes I am wearing but, compulsively, I imagine a situation where I am wearing different shoes, high heels, for example, and I look down anyway, I can't stop myself, just in case . . . just in case . . .

'You've got your running shoes on,' he says encouragingly.

Running shoes! It's true that I found these shoes in the section of the shop entitled 'Running Shoes', but that just means fashion items that you may also run in if you wish – *but you don't have to. Ever.* (My italics.)

He sets off. I'm forced to set off beside him.

'I'm afraid,' I say, pretending not to be out of breath

after ten strides, 'I'm not your normal celebrity hack, used to interviewing on the run.'

'Hmmm,' he says.

'I normally write about injustices perpetrated by global corporations.'

He snorts. We jog on a little longer.

'Although – I suppose you *could* just about qualify as an injustice perpetrated by a global corporation like, say, AOL Time Warner.'

'Is this you being charming?' He turns to jog sideways and must be alarmed by the sight of me because he interrupts himself to say, 'Hey – I think you'd better sit down over there and rest a moment.'

I am probably the colour of raspberry milkshake. Things are getting serious on the cardiovascular front. The air is so cold it's painful to breathe. I sink on to the nearby bench gratefully.

'I'll just go round the block a couple of times,' he says.

I must have looked anxious because he adds, 'Don't worry, I'll be back.'

He sets off running – big strides, quite fast. As I watch him go, I realise that by 'the block' he means 'the park'. He's going to run round the park *a couple of times*. This is so inconceivable to me that my mind shies away from even contemplating it – that level of determination, strength, self-discipline . . . masochism?

I settle back into my bench and before long find myself indulging in an armchair workout. By which I mean I sit there and plan to get fit. I have never had any real desire to get fit but there's nothing I enjoy more than planning a future regime, 'planning' and 'future' being the operative words. A punishing schedule swims tantalisingly into view: daily visits to yoga classes and early-morning runs in the park, up at seven, carrot juice for breakfast. I must start slow, I decide, set manageable, attainable goals—

All of sudden I see him on the horizon and a short while later he's coming past me.

'How's it going?' I yell.

He either doesn't hear or doesn't answer because he goes right on by. I'm starting to get cold now. I get up and jog a little on the spot – just to warm myself up. It's good to get a little air into my lungs, I think, into my blood, into my brain – get a little perspective.

The perspective, when I get it, is as follows: I am in a park and there is a superstar jogging around me in large circles and he will go on to greatness and I will go on to nothingness. He will misuse his influence because he has nothing to say. I, who have so much to say, will never be heard.

He's coming round again. I stand with renewed determination like his trainer on the edge of his path, ready with my next question as he comes past. 'Are you sleeping with Grace Farlow?' I yell.

He's gone again. I can't pin him down. I can't get him in my sights, even for a second. This is his talent, of course, to be mercurial. He is everything his audience wants him to be and nothing. He is a blank screen on to which we project our desires.

He's coming back. I sit down quickly, not wishing to

be seen to be trying too hard. He slows to a walk and comes to sit beside me.

'I'm sorry,' I say, feeling ashamed. 'They want me to ask you about Grace.'

He sticks his legs out and leans back, propping his head on the back of the bench to stare up into the leafless trees. He's barely out of breath. 'Can I ask you a question?' he says.

'Of course.' I look up into the branches too, to see if there's anything I'm missing.

'Why are they so keen for me to be fucking Grace?'

Suddenly the branches aren't so interesting. Suddenly I like Louis.

'Romantic love is a tyranny,' I say darkly. 'The kingdom of coupledom is a police state.'

He sits back up, looks at me. 'I'm not even going to ask what you mean by that.' He pauses for a beat. 'What do you mean by that?'

'Think about it – we don't have many institutions, these days, that control people as effectively as the idea of happy coupledom controls people. Everyone wants in. No one wants to be out in the cold. Everyone tries to do it for life and feels bad if they can't. It means they've got us where they want us, in controllable little units, under constant surveillance, mind, body and soul.' I'm talking fast, willing him to understand.

'They? Who's they?'

'Why does everyone say, "Who's they?" You know – *they*. The paternalistic capitalist society. They want to keep people in orderly domestic units in order to control the labour force and to take money from them

71

more efficiently, and also to keep people feeling they're missing out on the dream, so then they have to keep on buying products to try to get the dream.'

'Are you serious?'

'Why not?'

'Well, it's natural, isn't it, to want a family? A natural instinct.'

'Is it? Marriage was always pretty much a business arrangement until about two hundred years ago. Romantic love only became fashionable when people started reading story books – novels – although even then most people considered romance between a husband and wife to be in very bad taste.'

He laughs.

'I promise you,' I say. 'They did.'

'But people like falling in love.'

'Of course. Passion exists – temporarily – fuelled by body chemistry, dopamine when you first meet and also norepinephrine. A nice little cocktail. The effect is similar to cocaine.'

'And we all know where that leads.'

'Exactly. The Greeks knew. They always equated passion with suffering. And in France, in the days of courtly love, passion was considered quite fatal.'

This makes him laugh more. It's a great laugh, beautifully structured. It has a hesitant first act, a won't-you-join-with-me second act, and a confident third act, rolling out purposefully, all obstacles overcome. He's good, Louis. I guess that's what they pay him for.

'The happy ending is a relatively recent invention,' I say, and look away. Crocuses are pushing through in the grass on the other side of the path. Crocuses are very pushy little flowers. 'I'm not saying,' I find myself adding dutifully, 'that people don't love their families and so forth, but that's a different kind of love: *agape* as opposed to *eros*.'

He looks at his watch, jumps up. 'Shit! I've got an eight o'clock. Someone from your paper, in fact – name of Leaf.'

THE DICK.

'I'll walk to the gate with you,' I say, bleakly.

We walk for a bit.

'But seriously,' I say, breaking the silence, 'what about an interview with me? In depth. Let me really spend some time with you – defences down – so I can write something authentic. That's the way to win them over, don't you think?'

'I don't think there's any winning.'

'Look,' I plough on, 'I can understand the mess you've got yourself into. I can see how it happens – how in the beginning you would assume that people just know that you're nice and that you mean well. I mean, you're a success – you would assume people have goodwill for you and get your jokes and so forth. And then, when you say something ultimately wanky, you assume everyone knows your tongue is in your cheek. You think people will understand why you're forced to sweep through airports with aggressive-looking bodyguards. You just assume that people will assume the best. Why shouldn't you? But then, along with the success, comes a load of people who don't want to assume the best at all. They want to assume the worst. They wilfully take things at face value. They refuse to give you the kind of breaks they give ordinary people every moment of the day and they decide Louis Plantagenet's a wanker. And in a way, if you sound like a wanker and you act like a wanker, who can blame them?'

I pause for a moment. His eyes are out on the horizon. I forge onwards.

'And, if you think about it, maybe that's what wankers are. Wankers are people who don't mean to be wankers. People like you.'

'Goodbye,' he says. Quite polite.

Don't go.

'Wait!' I shout after him. He doesn't stop. In fact, he breaks into a run.

'You can look me up . . .' I call out, at the top of my lungs: 'WWW DOT FAIR FLOWERS DOT COM FORWARD SLASH STEVIE—'

Hopeless.

Useless.

He doesn't seem to have heard.

Don't go.

So, The Dick has muscled in on it. This is not good. What now? Walk to the tube. Go on with life. It's the only thing to do – or burst in on their breakfast, guns firing, tell The Dick I'm not going to stand for this, beg Louis to give me the interview instead.

I think I'll just walk to the tube.

I can see them now: Dick simpering and Louis think-ing, well – Louis thinking about me—

Stop – right there.

The End. Game over. *Auf wiedersehen.* Goodbye.

6

'You told him he was a wanker?'

'Yup.'

'I see.'

'But nicely.'

'Nicely?'

'Yes, nicely.'

When I'd got back from the park I'd found Esther not only up and feeling better, but insisting that we walk up to our favourite juice bar on the Edgware Road.

'What about the baby?' I say.

'Perhaps it'll fall out on the way.'

The juice bar is small and mostly decorated in horrible orange-coloured pine, which gives it the feel of a sauna. There are only three minuscule tables squeezed up against the right-hand wall, and it's not a great place to talk due to the deafening roar of the blenders, but the juices can only be described as liquid heaven. I order a Fusion Fantasy and suck it down in one go.

'Tell me again how it went,' Esther says, using her straw to hoover juice drops neatly from the inside of her plastic lid and then to stir, with some satisfaction, the thick gloop of Velvet Underground still waiting for her in the cup.

I look from her brimming cup to my drained one and sigh. I tell her again.

'The wanker speech was reckless,' she says.

'The wanker speech may have been ill-advised.'

'Are you falling for him?'

'No!'

'I just think, if you're calling him a wanker, you're probably falling for him.'

'How do you work that out?'

'Like in old movies. If a woman slaps a man round the face you can be sure he turns her on.'

'I'm not falling for him.'

'Just checking.'

There's a little silence.

'Try not to fall for him,' she says, after a while.

She appears to have forgotten that I'm unlikely to be interviewing him further. I don't like to remind her.

'You know what I keep thinking?' she says after a while, darting in for a quick sip of juice. 'I keep thinking, what are babies for? I mean, what are they *for*?'

'How do you mean?' I say, my hair quietly standing on end at this evidence of her state of mind.

'Well, first, as far as I can see, people have children in order to love them, but then they spend the whole time shouting at them. I just don't get it.'

'I think it's the other way round. I think they have them to *be* loved.'

'Second,' she says, forging on, 'women who just bring up children and do nothing else – if they were bringing up girls and those girls grew up just to bring up children who were girls, well, that would be *completely* point-less. No?'

'Um,' I say.

'Do you see what I mean, though?' She gives me a passionate flash of her eyes.

'Sort of. But you're not going to give up work, are you?'

'No,' she says.

When we've finished our juice, Esther insists on paying – out of habit. I look at the coins changing hands and wonder where the next ones will be coming from. On the way out of the bar – and under cover of the noise and bustle in the street – I ask Esther if she's planning to contact the baby's father.

'No way.'

'But maybe he could give you some support.'

'God forbid.'

'Is he single?'

'I suppose.'

'I mean,' I say hesitantly, feeling like I've walked out rather too confidently for the high dive, 'I think you must have liked him quite a lot to sleep with him – really, knowing you. I mean, he's probably quite a reasonable guy.'

And/or rich?

'Listen,' Esther says, swinging around to face me and using her firmest tone, 'you know my idea of hell on earth is the nuclear family.' And with that she sets off to cross the road – four lanes of rush-hour traffic – yards from the pedestrian crossing. I go after her, risking life and limb. I tell her I've always thought the nuclear family was something to do with having a fall-out shelter at the bottom of the garden during the Cold War.

'No love,' Esther says, when we get to the other side. Esther is an only child, daughter of a couple of West London antiques dealers who were famously in love. A legend in their own liver-sausage-sandwich lunchtimes, now retired to Wiltshire and no longer in touch with their daughter. The couple's love for each other had been legendary on the Portobello Road and she had grown up in the shadow of its myth. But Esther ran away at fifteen to live wild, only returning home intermittently to pilfer and sell their most valuable and portable pieces (she was well schooled) for which they never forgave her. When asked why she rebelled so violently and why she is now so resolutely single, having had parents who set such a glowingly romantic example, Esther talks about animals and the way you sometimes can't tell if they're fucking or fighting. She says that, on the inside, her parents' embrace had seemed nothing but deadly, the two of them locked together in mortal combat disguised as amorous legend.

Suddenly I notice a Baby Gap on the other side of the street. I must have seen it a hundred times before, but this time the shop's purpose registers and I have an idea.

'Come on,' I say to Esther, and taking her arm, I drag her in. I position her by a table laid out with purple Babygros featuring sherbet-yellow rocket ships launching themselves in fiery style from sleeve, midriff and thigh. I pick up the smallest size and hold it up in front of her. 'Look,' I say.

'What?' she says.

'You made something to go in it.'

'And?'

'We're going to need all the help we can get.'

'It's no good,' Esther says. 'I don't want some *man* interfering.'

'Okay,' I say, embracing defeat. 'Okay, okay The man-woman thing – it just doesn't work, does it? It really fell apart in the second half of the twentieth century.'

Esther laughs delightedly at this sudden opening up of historical perspective right there in Baby Gap.

'Esther?' I say.

'Yes, babe?'

'I love you.'

'I know,' she says. 'The man-woman thing – let's face it – is a recipe for disaster. Men are so angry with women, women are so angry with men.' She shakes her head. 'And why wouldn't they be? *Why – wouldn't – they – be?*'

'Quite. It's like Northern Ireland. Except worse. Centuries of bloodshed. The battle of the sexes – it's been raging since time began. And the wounds are as fresh as ever. I mean, if you think about it, they only recently gave us back our bodies. They only gave us *the vote*, historically speaking, just the other day.'

'Fuck!'

'And then women's liberation came along and made it all *worse*. I mean, before, at least there was some kind of enforced consensus. Now it's just open warfare. And babies are the final frontier.'

I put the tiny purple baby suit back on the table with some distaste. *Made in a sweatshop anyway.*

My phone is ringing somewhere deep in my sheep-skin jacket.

'Your phone is ringing,' Esther says.

'Yes,' I say.

The minute I answer the phone I wish I hadn't. It's The Dick. I consider hitting divert – I could always say we'd been cut off – but I don't. I go over to the window where the reception is better and stare rabbit-like into the headlights of my encroaching doom.

'Sweetie,' he says.

Sweetie.

He's never called me that before.

'I've got some very good news.' Him.

'Really?' Me.

His voice is different, somehow. I try to put my finger on what it is . . . something . . . There's a note of . . . of . . . It comes to me with a jolt – admiration. There's a note of admiration and possibly even a tinge of . . . respect and even – dare I suggest it? – an edge of – no, there can't be – yes, there is – *fear.*

'Louis feels he's been misrepresented in the British press, that they've taken it the wrong way that he's playing such an all-American cowboy hero in his latest role, a sheriff, and the juxtaposition of that with the entirely spurious gossip about girls and cocaine hasn't been good. He feels he's been very controlling when it comes to the press and that partly this has fed the problem. He's *furious* with his PA, apparently – she seemed lovely to me, very stylish. But, anyway, he doesn't feel it's been handled well.' He stops as if the rest is somehow self-explanatory.

'Well, that's fascinating,' I say. 'Thank you for sharing.'

He ignores me. 'Your *very* brief encounter seems to have left him with a *very* good impression.'

'Must have been the blow-job.'

'Sorry, what did you say?'

'Never mind, I – er – I bumped into him in the park this morning. That may have had something to do with it.'

'Oh, wow! wow! wow!'

'What?' I shriek, frightened suddenly by his enthusiasm. 'What?'

'Oh, that's glorious! Elenka – my assistant – has just come into the office in the most exquisite coat. She's been doing the shows this week. I *love* that orange. It's a *juicy* orange. So, Louis thinks the *News* would be a very good place to place, as it were, a longer, more in-depth piece – a profile, perhaps. And I was, of course, the one who *broke* him over here and I feel – *I feel* – that, despite your endemic personal kookiness, you could genuinely be the right person for the job. I really agree with our editor – he has *such* a good instinct for this sort of thing.'

'Okay,' I say, a slight tremor creeping into my voice. 'So—'

So?

The Dick seems to be having trouble gathering himself, as if, now he's swum this far out, he's wondering if he'll make it back to shore.

'Louis is in town until Friday and he suggested you – er . . . He suggested you just sort of . . .' Is that a tremor in his voice? '. . . hang out with him for a few days.'

'Okay.'

'So—'

So?

'Well, he's waiting for you. You'd better get your skates on.'

'Dick—' I say, but there's a deadness on the line and I realise he's gone.

In the back of the car, I snap on my tape-recorder and hold it urgently to my mouth: 'Eleven forty-one a.m. Great Titchfield Street, W1. Waiting for Louis. Drizzle. People walking towards their offices holding sandwiches. The back of the driver's head. He has a spot on his neck. Tan leather seats with a pinprick motif on the central panel. Shame about the pinprick motif. *Faux*-mahogany dashboard and fittings. Driver now picking spot on back of neck—'

'Real mahogany,' says driver.

'The driver is Mike,' I continue into the machine. 'He is also Louis's bodyguard and general Man Friday. Mike, tell me about Louis. Is he – is he a *genuine guy*?'

'Hey, leave me out of this. I'm not saying a word.'

'Gagged by a draconian confidentiality contract, no doubt.'

'Turn that off or I'll take it away from you.'

'Aha – bodyguard slightly to right of Ghengis Khan, who has already performed false arrest on your fearless reporter's person, now threatens to remove reporter's tool of trade. That'll provide a good bit of background for the article ... I'll make it a side-bar. You can have a whole side-bar to yourself, Mike, entitled "The Bodyguard". Think of that.'

Mike turns in his seat, he looks at the tape-recorder, he looks at me. 'I will say this,' he finally says gruffly, his eyes filling a little, 'Louis is a *good person*. He's real, you know, a real guy.'

'Not a fake guy, then?'

'Not a fake guy. I'd lay down my life for him.'

'You'd *die* for him? Do you think that's appropriate? Do you think that's sane?'

'Hey, I'm not saying another word.'

'Why do you think he agreed to take me around with him?'

'I will say this, it's not to get in your panties – if that's what you think.'

'It's not what I think.'

'Louis isn't like that. Whatever they say in the press. He respects women.'

'Respects women?'

'Uh-huh. I will say this, I think it's down to the fact that he lost his mother.'

'Did you meet her?'

'No, ma'am. She died before Louis was two years old. In a car accident.'

'And his dad?'

'I told you, I'm not saying another word.'

'But then you do.'

Mike opens the car door. 'Do you want a soda?'

'A soda?'

'Diet Coke, something like that?'

'*Diet Coke?* Jesus. No, thanks.'

Mike looks suitably chastened and tells me he only said 'diet' because the ladies, they usually drink the diet and not because I needed to diet or anything – in fact, I might benefit by gaining a few pounds—

'Mike,' I'm forced to interrupt, 'it's got nothing to do with dieting and everything to do with global corporations. I try not to drink the stuff.'

He goes to get his soda. A few moments pass in which I contemplate the dry-cleaning shop across the road and think about how toxic dry-cleaning chemicals are and wonder how the dry-cleaning workers survive in there. Although, come to think of it, perhaps the hand isn't played out yet. Perhaps they won't survive. Perhaps, in years to come, the streets will be littered with the corpses of dry-cleaning workers and we will rue those smart wool trousers that were Dry Clean Only. We will rue them terribly.

Louis gets into the car beside me. He's run from his meeting. He's terrified of being recognised. He wears a baseball cap pulled down over his eyes. If anything makes him look like a film star it's the baseball cap. It should have I MIGHT BE A CELEBRITY embroidered on the front.

'Where's Mike?' he says immediately, all intensity. I'm starting to realise that he lives his life on red alert, code blue and the rest.

'Mike left,' I say. 'I don't know, it was weird – it was like he finally cracked. He read this thing in the paper. Don't be alarmed. It was scurrilous. It was about how you thought an alien from outer space was working under cover in your retinue, how this alien was spying on you. I think he thought it was him – that *he* was the alien. I told him, "You mustn't believe everything you read in the papers."'

Mike gets back into the car with two cans of 7-Up. Passes one back to Louis. Louis takes his and just looks at me.

'Who on earth decides to call a drink Seven-Up?' I say. 'Where does *that* come from?'

We've been driving all over London. Louis believes in going *to* people rather than having them come to him. He's had a meeting here, a meeting there. But the traffic's been too slow and the rain too heavy to allow for a really frenetic pace. And I've been pointing out sights as we drive around: Big Ben, Downing Street, Nelson's Column.

I'm an assiduous tour guide, giving them no peace, telling them what they should look at and wishing I had a microphone like they do on the tour buses. Worse, I'm not even Croatian so I'm getting choked up with pride about my national monuments, showing them off to the infidel for all the world as if I'd built them myself. I think the sentimentality has something to do with the picture books I read when I was a child: 'They're changing the guard at Buckingham Palace. Said Alice'.

Sentimentality is something you inherit. It is foisted upon you by your parents and dogs you all your life, if you're not careful. My father is terribly sentimental about London, even though he left it and me as often as he could. *Because* he left it and me, I shouldn't wonder.

Louis has seen it all before, but Mike gets a little exercised about Buckingham Palace. 'Bucking-*ham* Palace!' he announces appreciatively.

'Actually,' I say, 'it's Bucking'*m* – you swallow the "ham". Which reminds me, are we going to have lunch? I've been up since five thirty.'

'One more meeting,' Louis says.

'You're joking?'

'Why would I be joking?'

'How am I meant to do my job if I'm sitting waiting for you in the car all day?'

'The deal was you'd go around with me.' He shrugs. 'You're going around with me.'

'You said you wanted me to write about how you're an ordinary guy, really. You said I could help you get that across to your public. You said you didn't want to come across as a wanker. Making me wait around for you all day is being a wanker.'

Mike gives a huge excited snort from the front of the car. We've stopped at the lights so he swivels round and looks with amazement from me to Louis, from Louis to me.

'What?' I say to Mike. He just shakes his head and snorts some more. 'What?' I say again. It occurs to me that the way I'm speaking to Louis is shocking to Mike.

'All right,' Louis says, quietly. 'What do you suggest?'

'Something ordinary,' I say.

'Like?'

'You think of something – it's your ordinariness.'

No comment.

'How about sightseeing, for example?'

'Sightseeing? Can't do that.'

'Can't do that! Why not?'

'Why do you think?'

'Oh, please. You're so paranoid.'

'It's not about being paranoid. It's about being public property. I can't just hang out in some museum. Everyone wants a piece of me.'

'They don't *want a piece of you*. I mean, yes, people are interested in you, but they're not that interested. They're all busy starring in their own lives, you know. They've got bills to pay, battles to fight, jobs to do. I mean, it's good of you to provide a bit of light entertainment on the old Sky Première every once in a while. But that's about it, you know. The world does not revolve around you.'

We're driving along the Marylebone Road. I clock Madame Tussaud's up ahead. Madame Tussaud's! Perfect.

'There we go,' I say, 'Madame Tussaud's.'

'No way.'

'Why not?'

'I'm in there.'

This brings me up short. But Louis is looking interested in something else. 'The Planetarium,' he says. 'Pull over.'

When we get out of the car I say, 'I appreciate your open-mindedness'.

'Don't. I'm going to show you why I can't go sightseeing.'

Cap on. Shades on. In we go.

7

The Planetarium – what marvels it holds, what infinite mysteries of time and space, the universe, that great uncharted territory, about which we, who know so much, know so very little. What a place.

The toilet in the Planetarium, however, is much like toilets all over the world. By which I mean toilets in the first world: it is not, of course, a stinking pit in the ground. In fact, the toilet in the Planetarium is tiled in white and there are four cubicles with black three-quarter-length doors.

I mention the toilet because this is where I am when the main body of the drama unfolds. I catch only the tail end of it when, coming out into the main hall, a marauding horde, a multitude, a host of – not golden daffodils – grimy schoolgirls rampages past me, screaming as if with one voice, in hot pursuit.

I'd last seen Louis at the Rocks In Space exhibition – disco themed. A party of schoolgirls had been at a lecture in a side room. Guessing the rest, I run for the side exit. Out in the street I belt along the pavement, turn the corner and there's the limo. Louis must be inside because there are girls swarming over the car like ants on a dead beetle. Movement seems impossible, so I'm surprised when the limo jerks threateningly forward. It's not enough to dislodge the girls, but it gives them a fright and they clamber down. Then the limo pulls away with a screech of tyres. I wave, but I don't expect Louis and Mike to pick me up. It's my own funeral.

The limo speeds past.

Stops at the lights.

I watch a moment, then the kerbside door opens – an invitation. I run for it.

'Lunch?' says Louis brightly, as I get in.

Mike is buying us sandwiches in an organic-food hypermarket. Louis won't go anywhere public. We wait in the car.

'It was just very unfortunate,' I keep saying, 'that there happened to be a party of schoolgirls in there.'

When Mike comes back he ducks his head into the car to tell Louis he's heard a suspicious noise. 'Looks like we've got a stickler,' he says.

'You're kidding?' I say, when I get his drift, absolutely amazed. I can't believe it. I get out of the car.

Sure enough, Mike opens the boot and up pops a schoolgirl like a jack-in-the-box. She's even got plaits.

'Hi,' I say, with much admiration.

Now here's a story.

'What's your name?'

'Harriet,' she says, quite sensibly and then suddenly her mouth seems to be involuntarily wrenched open into a great O, quite disturbing to behold – larynx and all. A piercing scream emanates from her lungs.

She's seen Louis, who has just got out of the car.

'Step out of the vehicle,' says Mike to Harriet, who is

still standing in the boot. Formidable Mike. But drowned out in this instance by the scream. 'Miss,' he says again, 'step out of the vehicle.'

For a brief second Harriet screams herself out of scream. She gulps, her eyes are on stalks – I try another question but, too late, the scream starts up again. It comes from deep down. Her eyes are latched on to Louis, her mouth craning open, as she screams this scream that is beyond her control.

'I think she's having sex with you,' I say to Louis, through the noise.

'Step out of the vehicle, miss,' says Mike. Louder.

'She'll faint in a minute,' says Louis. 'Then we'll have to deal with that.' But he's watching her. We're all watching her. It's fascinating. A crowd is gathering.

'Miss,' says Mike, louder still, 'step out of the vehicle.'

'Oh, vehicle, vehicle,' I say, 'can't you just call it a car? Harriet! HARRIET!' and I give one of her plaits a hard pull.

She pauses for breath.

'Harriet, I am Stevie, this is Mike and this, as you know, is Louis. Would you like to come for a ride with us, Harriet? Share a sandwich?'

Louis and Mike both expel breath in an irritated manner. Harriet's popping eyes swivel briefly to me then return home immediately to Louis. She doesn't scream again but her mouth hangs open as she tries to compute what I've just said.

'We'll give you a lift back to the Planetarium,' I throw in, for good measure.

*   *   *

I sit between the two of them in the back of the car. Louis is furious, but I've got my tape-recorder out and Harriet is on the other side of me so there's not a lot he can say or do. Harriet has quietened down – in fact, glancing at her pale face, I suspect she's finding the reality of close proximity to her idol a little frightening.

I reach over to the front seat, grab the sandwiches to offer them around and break the ice. 'Blue cheese with chicory and walnut?' I say to Harriet, reading one of the labels. She looks at me like I'm offering her gangrene with liquorice and cockroach. I check the other sandwiches. 'Hummus with roasted red peppers?' I say doubtfully.

'No thanks,' she says, and purses her mouth in a suspicious little *moue*.

'We're just giving you a lift back to your friends,' I find myself saying defensively. An awkward silence falls, and we ride along like that for a while.

'But this is great,' I announce eventually. 'Louis Meets Fan.' He and Harriet look at each other warily. 'Wouldn't you like to ask Louis some questions?' I say to Harriet.

Harriet proffers her guide to the Planetarium rather hesitantly in Louis's direction and asks him to sign it. Louis sighs rather exaggeratedly, presumably for my benefit. Harriet is on to it immediately. 'Don't bother, then,' she snaps, and snatches the guide back. 'I was only asking to be polite.'

The ice obviously needs breaking. 'I'm a journalist,' I say to Harriet, 'so how about I ask you some questions. Is that okay?'

'What's in it for me?' she says, and starts rummaging around in her schoolbag.

'You get to enlighten the masses about yourself and your motivations,' I say, 'and you get to chat with the man of your dreams.' I indicate Louis.

She gives a huge snort, the meaning of which is unclear and finds what she's looking for in her bag. Her mobile phone. 'I've got to text my mates about this,' she mutters, and bends her head over the phone where we lose her to an arpeggio of rapid electronic pings.

Louis takes the opportunity to mutter some threats and imprecations angrily into my ear. Harriet, not as engrossed as she appears, suddenly whips round to him and says, 'It's all right – I don't want to marry you, you know.'

'Why not?' I say. 'I thought that was the whole point.' She's back to her texting. 'Harriet,' I say, 'Louis thinks you want a piece of him. Would you say that was true?'

No response.

'Harriet,' I persevere, 'what is it that makes you run after Louis screaming and stow away in his car?'

This gets her attention for a moment. 'Don't take it personal,' she says to Louis. 'It's just a thing we do.'

'But why?' I persist.

Her eyes dart nervously, like it's a trick question. 'Well, he's famous, isn't he?'

'That's what you like about him?'

'Yeah.'

'What about his acting?'

'What about it?' she looks perplexed.

'And you wouldn't want to marry him?'

'Look, don't take it personal,' she says again to Louis, 'but now I see you you're a bit old.' A thought occurs to her. 'You're not a paedophile or anything, are you? Getting me in the car like this.'

'Who got in whose car?' shouts Louis, losing it.

We're now pulling up outside the Planetarium where a large school coach is parked at the kerb. I find myself hoping it's Harriet's.

'Oh dear,' I say. 'I think Louis thought you loved him.'

'Give me your autograph, then.'

It's a concession. She's mollifying him. She hands over the Planetarium guide again. Louis signs furiously. 'My friend's got your picture on her wall, you know, and it's a got a slimy patch on the mouth where she's French-kissed it with lip gloss on.'

He looks up at her. She starts to laugh hilariously. Louis starts to laugh too and then the two of them are sparking off each other and they can't stop. I find myself laughing as well. Laughing at the laughing. Mike grins from the front seat.

Still snickering, Harriet takes her autographed guide and opens the car door.

''Bye, Harriet,' I say.

'Wait a minute,' Louis says.

Harriet pauses with the door half open, the occasional left-over giggle escaping her lips.

I can see Louis doesn't know what to say, but he wants to say something. 'What do you want to be when you grow—' He doesn't finish the sentence, interrupted by the school coach starting its engines.

''Bye,' Harriet says, remorseless, and slams the door hard in our faces.

Louis watches her go. She runs. She doesn't look back.

'How old do you think she is?' he says.

'She told me. She's nine.'

He thinks about this as we pull away from the kerb and merge haltingly with the stagnant traffic. I glance at my reporter's notebook. 'She also told me what she wants to be when she grows up.'

'What does she want to be?'

'Famous.'

8

It's four o'clock and Louis and I are on our way to have tea with my grandmother in Westbourne Grove.

Question: Why am I taking Louis Plantagenet to meet my grandmother? Answer: Because everyone should meet my grandmother.

She buzzes us in. I can already smell that unmistakable smell. The smell of Gran: two parts Coco by Chanel, one part aniseed, three parts dust. Gran lives on the top floor of a rambling town-house, which was converted into flats long ago. I've been coming in and out of this house for twenty-five years, but today the presence of Louis gives it a new edge. I see it through his eyes, like I'm in a museum with a commentary playing in my ear: 'To your left, a dilapidated latticework radiator cover. Note the thickly ingrained dust and the peeling grey paint, the unopened overdue gas bills belonging to long-departed tenants. Note also the chill in the air, feel how it goes straight to the bone. However warm it is outside, entering this house is always like walking into a sepulchre. Note the beige threadbare carpet and the tarnished brass stair rods *circa* 1955. Listen for the lap-lap of the river of traffic on the wet streets outside and the throaty rattle of the black cabs, the noise magnified rather than diminished by entrance

97

into this cavernous, unhinged house. To your right you will see a light switch, a white circular one, the kind that is designed to pop out again once you have pressed it in and it has honoured you with sixty seconds of light. Press it now.'

Needless to say, the bulb has gone. Louis and I stomp up the stairs in the gloom. Three flights. Louis hasn't said a word since we arrived. No doubt he is struggling to overcome the auditory, sensory, olfactory *ennui* that descends upon entry into this building.

I glance back at him and have one of those moments that are becoming familiar to me. 'One of those moments' is when I catch myself thinking: I am walking up the stairs with/sitting in a car with/walking into the Planetarium with . . . *LOUIS PLANTAGENET*! A reality check that is most unreal. And most unreal of all is that I'm not really the kind of person who ought to be susceptible to these Louis Plantagenet moments. But the truly weird thing is: *I have them anyway.*

And they give me a high, these moments, they give me a buzz, like I'm standing on top of a very tall building looking down on my life. Not just any old building, a skyscraper, all chrome and glass, and it's a sunny day and, all at once, my life is full of meaning and worthy of an MTV mini-biog full of swooping crane shots and fast-slamming tracking shots, because where before my life might have seemed disjointed and messy and incoherent and not leading in any particular direction, it has now revealed itself to be a triumph of rightness, leading all the time to this moment of cathartic affirmation. *I must be okay because I am with Louis Plantagenet.*

'I'm beginning to get it,' I say to Louis. 'People take you like a drug.'

'Some people,' he says.

Standing outside Gran's front door we can hear her budgerigar chattering away in the kitchen. I'm obliged to knock. She hasn't left the door open for us. My first irritation.

Finally, after much trilling on the part of both my grandmother and the budgerigar, Gran intermittently calling out, 'Just coming,' in such a languid and desultory manner that it's clearly a lie, I rummage around in my bag, find my key and let us in myself. Gran is standing in the hallway stuffing what's left of her hair – white wisps, pale and spun like candy floss – into a knitted pink cloche hat.

'Oh, darling,' she says, 'you do barge in, you know. I'm just putting my hat on.'

'Gran, this is Louis Plantagenet.'

'Oh, my goodness,' she says, when she sees him. She holds out a hand and flushes slightly in the presence of his good looks, her hair wisping out wildly from underneath her hat.

'Pleased to meet you,' Louis says. He takes her hand, the most beautiful hand you could ever imagine, lily white, mottled blue – like a Gorgonzola – and cool as marble to the touch. Louis kisses the hand. Stroke of genius. Gran smiles and I can't tell what she's making of him.

'And you're American! But wasn't your mother clever to give you a French first name – Louis. The Plantagenets, our glorious kings, were all French, you know. Couldn't speak a word of English, most of them. Stevie, have you taken Louis to the National Portrait Gallery and shown him his ancestors?'

'It's not his real name, Gran,' I say. 'Louis is an actor.'

'Is he?' she says. 'But how lucky that you're just in time for tea.'

Tea. Such a short little word, a sweet little word. Yet the teapot, to Gran, is a monument to ritual as monolithic and stony-clad as Stonehenge itself. The ceremony must be performed every day in exactly the right way: the pot warmed, the cups in their right saucers, the water brought to a rolling boil, the milk – but what am I saying? No milk is allowed. To take milk is sacrilege with this fine Hukwa tea. My grandmother's china is old and fine and worn paper thin, much of it cracked and held together with small iron rivets, visible scars with the stitches left in. Sugar is provided in tiny cubes in a special vessel with an ill-fitting lid. Gran doesn't take sugar in tea herself, but she allows others to do so. It is a tolerated vice.

Louis looks huge in Gran's small kitchen although he folds his long legs up as small as they can go under the rickety iron table and his eyes dart about the place, absorbing the could-almost-be-Matisse-but-are-actually-by-a-friend paintings on the walls, the rustic ceramics, colourful and plainly broken, displayed on the shelves, the wicker shopping baskets hanging from the ceiling on hooks and the yellow budgerigar, Tommy, in his cage.

Gran performs the rites. She is lit up by Louis's

presence, her face as light and ethereal as her hair, and she makes conversation to match as she pours, passes and generally supervises the correct ingestion of the golden nectar.

'Are you trying to get on the stage, young man?'

'Er – no,' Louis says, 'the screen.'

'Oh, how marvellous. I love the cinema. I am a fan of the films of Buñuel. Have you had many good parts?'

'I guess,' Louis says.

'Perhaps I could introduce you to someone who could help you along. I once met a man who directed Garbo, can you imagine? I wonder if he's still with us.'

'Gran,' I say, 'Louis doesn't want to talk about work. He wants to get a feel for ordinary life in London. That's why I brought him to tea.'

I realise the ludicrousness of this last remark the minute it's out of my mouth.

'There is nothing ordinary about me,' Gran says.

'I didn't mean—'

'But it's such a shame,' she interrupts, eyes fastened upon Louis, 'about his hair.'

'Gran!' I say. 'He shaved his head for a part.'

I look at Louis and find him grinning happily, in my direction, and it occurs to me that this is a very intimate thing, this letting him see me with my gran. I often don't think about things before I do them – I just rush in. And now I'm not sure if it's right. I must be flushing slightly because, seeing this, Gran says to Louis: 'I do hope the two of you aren't thinking of getting married.'

This is so disastrous that I go beyond panic and into a kind of coma. I am overcome by the desire to yawn, which I do, and my eyes start to water. The world is becoming fuzzy and incomplete.

'I have always told Stevie she must *never* get married. Romance and domesticity do not make happy bedfellows. Men are a terrible nuisance. They go about littering the place and forgetting their keys. They lay down the law and don't tell you until you've broken it. And then you're for the gallows, by God.'

'Louis and I only met yesterday, Gran,' I murmur sleepily, keeping my voice studiously even, 'so, no, we're not actually thinking of marriage,' my eye *studiously* avoiding his, 'yet.'

'I married once,' she goes on. 'It didn't last.' She trails off into a vague silence.

'Go on,' Louis says.

'He was a bounder. Terribly handsome, of course, although pockmarked. He had this *appalling* skin from having had acne as a child. But a marvellous voice, especially on the telephone. I often think I married him for that. The minute the war came along he found a woman with money and they rushed off to exotic climes. She was called Edwina. Can you imagine a more awful name?'

Louis is flummoxed. To him a name is clearly a name. And nothing more. I can't rescue him, though, I can barely keep my eyes open. 'I think a marriage needs to be built on very firm practical foundations,' Louis says.

Gran is disappointed. 'You Americans are so literal.'

Silence. All I want to do is curl up in a ball and sleep like a hamster. A silence lingers. I don't mind. I am happy to doze.

While Rome burns.

'I couldn't wait to see the back of my husband,' Gran eventually muses into the silence. 'I simply *longed* for him to go.' And then, as an afterthought: 'You two might be lovers, though. Stevie never seems to have any lovers.'

It's enough. 'Gran!' I say. 'Stop.'

'I can't understand it,' she says. 'I brought her up to be a very eligible young woman – independent, self-sufficient, ambitious and well versed in the realities of life.'

'And that,' I say, 'is why I don't introduce my *many* boyfriends to you.'

'You brought Stevie up?' Louis says to Gran.

'I did. My daughter, Stevie's mother, took one look at Stevie and ran off to Buenos Aires. As for Stevie's father, he was travelling the world at the time. Stevie's father is rather like my ex husband, a ne'er-do-well, although his skin is better. Thankfully. He lives in Willesden.'

'Thankfully his skin is better or thankfully he lives in Willesden?'

'Don't be silly, darling. You know how I feel about Willesden. Now, then, will you stay for sherry? I've got two or three friends coming round.'

'The cronies,' I say to Louis, 'to be avoided like the plague.'

'And then we can play The Game.'

'Gran!' I say.

'Why not?'

I cringe all the way home in the car. Asking Louis Plantagenet to play The Game is like asking Bill Gates to play Monopoly. Appalling. (Although apparently not as appalling as my grandfather's acne.) The Mad Monk, the Faded Heiress and the Monocle, all competing to—

'That was *fantastic*!' Louis cries, interrupting my anxieties as the big leather lined limo sweeps us back to his house. 'I love the English. You guys are so eccentric.'

'That wasn't the English,' I say, horrified. 'That was a bunch of nutters.' The homosexual priest with the pursed lips, the blousy faded heiress with membership of the Chelsea Arts Club, the ginger-moustached country gent who apparently wore a monocle for several weeks in 1963 and never lived it down.

The cronies, ensconced in fading armchairs in my grandmother's draughty sitting room, had been very encouraging of Louis's thespian ambitions. None of them had the slightest clue who he was. At the sight of him, the Mad Monk – luckily not wearing his cassock – had emitted a high-pitched giggle, the Faded Heiress had thrown her chin to the sky and all but whinnied, and as for The Monocle, he perched on the edge of his seat and, when he wasn't taking thirsty laps of his sherry, peered at Louis like a whiskery red fox.

When it came to The Game, Gran insisted on Louis being on her side. This was followed by the writing of titles of books, plays and films on scraps of paper, which were folded into small twists and handed to the opposing team who then had to act them out.

When it came to Louis's turn he got *The Wasteland*. He walked into the middle of the room and threw up one hand in a gesture of such desolation and despair, his eyes searching a horizon so barren, that I guessed the answer in under a second. Gran was furious and complained in a wail that it spoiled the game if people guessed too quickly. I pointed out that I was playing to win. She turned to Louis and told him I was a ruthless girl, in an audible stage whisper.

In the car, Louis is still high on it all: 'You don't know how lucky you are, having a grandmother like that. She's so . . . so . . . *genuine*.'

'Yes,' I say patiently, 'a genuine nut.'

I should have known this was going to happen. I should have seen it coming. If I'm not careful Gran will hijack Louis. She'll make him her best friend and before he knows it he'll be having dinner with her and her cronies every night. I won't even be invited. And Gran will talk Louis into visits to the theatre, weekend jaunts to a charming little guest-house just outside Bath, tea in Regent's Park. No expense spared – except by Gran who will spare all the expenses she possibly can. Louis will pay. And gladly. He'll be in love.

I watch Louis lighting a cigarette. 'Do you mind?' he says, making a small deferential gesture with the cigarette just before he does. I shake my head. 'Tell me about your mother,' he says.

'Gran is my mother, I suppose.'

'But your real mother.'

'What makes a mother "real"?'

'Giving birth, maybe.'

'That's the easy part.'

'But it's an incredible thought – isn't it? – the person who gave you life. What happened to her?

'She died in Buenos Aires. Meningitis. When I was ten.'

He takes a big old drag and then says quietly, examining the tip of his cigarette, 'You never met her?'

'Unless you count birth.'

He looks out of the window. 'Your mother was on the planet for ten years and you never met her?'

'She left. She didn't want to know me. What was I meant to do?'

He turns back to me. 'Your ma had no contact with your gran?'

'None.'

'Why not?'

'Well, I guess one genuine nut would produce another.'

'And another . . .' He smiles. He means me.

9

We pull up outside Louis's house. It's a big double-fronted thing in The Boltons, set back from the street behind a wall with a formidable iron gate and a video entryphone. Beyond the gate, clean wide steps run up to a glossy black door bearing brass door furniture polished to within an inch of its life. To the right of the house is a set of garages. In between house and street two delicate cherry trees extend neatly budding branches towards the sky.

It's eight thirty and dark and the small cluster of fans that were grouped on the pavement when I met Louis this morning has dwindled to one: a middle-aged woman standing under the streetlight looking jaundiced and defeated, hunched against the cold in a beige mac. It's raining slightly and the raindrops show up only where the streetlight falls, making it seem as though it rains on the woman alone; her own private shower.

'Oh, shit,' Louis says. 'It's the mad fan. She's always here, whenever I'm in London. Just stands outside the house all day long.'

'But she's old enough to be your mum,' I say, peering curiously out at her.

'I know. Spooky.'

'How fascinating. Let's invite her in.'

He shakes his head.

'Why not? You liked Harriet in the end. Haven't you ever asked her what she's doing?'

'I don't think I want to know.'

I tell him I'm going to talk to the woman and get out of the car to do just that. Next thing I know Louis is behind me and he grabs my arm with some force.

'Stevie,' he says, 'I don't want you to talk to her. These people can be dangerous.'

'Dangerous? That little woman? Deluded, maybe. Not dangerous. And you're letting her stand outside in the rain!'

He shakes his head again, as if to warn me not to push things any further. 'You don't know everything.'

'Right. I don't know everything. I don't know much. So I investigate stuff, talk to people. It's called being ordinary.'

'Don't use that against me.'

'What is it that you're so scared of, anyway?'

'You don't understand what it's like to be in my position.'

'But I—'

'Stevie, I would appreciate it if you would not get me involved with that woman.'

'Louis, I will not get *you* involved with that woman.'

He's spotted the loophole. 'You will not speak to her!' he suddenly barks at me holding up a dictatorial finger, his face close to mine.

'You will not order me around,' I snap back.

'Then this interview is over.'

'Then fuck you.'
'Fuck you too.'

As Louis goes into the house a suggestion of warmth and light is cast into the street for a moment by the open door then immediately withdrawn. Mike drives off, leaving me standing in the wet. I become aware of the rain spotting on my face, which it must have been doing all along, but I only feel it now. I glance at the fan. Her eyes meet mine, her little face quivering inquisitively like a rat's.

I look away quickly then up and down the street as if considering what to do next. Waiting for a taxi, I decide, is the explanation for lingering. I glance at the fan again. She's still staring at me, exactly the same look, a look that reminds me of a dog wanting his dinner. It manages to be accusing and subservient at the same time. If I could see her ears they'd surely be quivering.

I sidle along the pavement until I am under the streetlight too. Still 'waiting for my cab'. I glance up at the house but all the windows are very firmly blinded. I deduce that I am quite safe from observation.

The fan is watching me.

'Raining again,' I remark.

I don't think she's particularly noticed the rain, but now she does, nodding eagerly for my benefit with her ratty intensity.

'You must be wet,' I say. 'Why don't we walk up the road and I'll buy you a cup of coffee?'

This flummoxes her. I suppose she doesn't want to leave the house, but on the other hand, this kind of attention is unprecedented and I imagine a cup of coffee with someone who is connected to Louis is riches beyond her wildest dreams.

'You were in the car with him?' she says.

'Yup.'

'Are you his beau?'

'No, I'm not his beau.'

'He's not a philanderer, you know,' she says.

'Please, come for a coffee.'

I'm shivering a little now, and I don't know if it's the cold or the journalistic excitement. Ratty glances at the house.

'He's not coming out again tonight,' I say. 'And I'd love to talk to you about all of this.'

There's a horrible all-night place on the Fulham Road, which I once ended up in at five in the morning and swore I'd never go to again – but tonight I have no choice. It's that or a dreaded coffee chain. The place has booths with soft red-vinyl benches. The fan and I slide into one of these and I'm thankful at least that they're private. I order hot chocolate and the fan orders Irish coffee greedily and with an air of knowing exactly what she likes.

When we've dealt with the drinks, I look at her a little nervously, not knowing how to start.

'You were in the car with him?' she says suddenly. 'Why were you in the car with him?'

I'm not sure whether to tell her the truth. If I tell her I'm a journalist it might scare her, she might run off. I try to think of something to tell her. My mind goes blank.

'I'm a journalist,' I say.

She looks shocked. Her eyes start out of their sockets. 'He hates journalists,' she hisses, but shows no sign of running off.

'Please tell me,' I say, because my curiosity is becoming so urgent I'd like to crack her head open and extract all the relevant information myself – like pick-your-own strawberries, 'how you came to be such a fan of Louis.'

'I'm in contact with his mother.' She leaves the explanation there as if the rest is self-evident, and the Irish coffee arrives. She takes a decisive glug. She has a row of neat vertical wrinkle lines on her upper lip. Her shoulder-length flat brown hair must be dyed. I decide she's older than she looks.

'His mother's dead,' I say. 'He was brought up by his father.'

'Yes.'

'You talk to the dead?'

'I'm a medium.'

'I see,' I say. I don't really and I feel a bit queasy but, of course, there's absolutely no point in arguing with her. I decide the only way to get anything out of her is to enter her world. 'How do you talk to the dead?'

'I'm an Internet medium,' she says proudly. 'I do it all on the Internet.'

'Wow,' I say. 'That's a clever way to get clients.' And I mean it. She's clearly taken advantage of an emerging market, although she doesn't look like she'd know an i-Mac from a crystal ball. 'How did you – er – first "contact" Louis's mum?'

'I saw *After Eight* – the film. I didn't really mean to because I'm not a great one for the pictures. But I went to visit my son in prison – I went all the way there, to Barlinnie and then I never saw him. It was a three hour wait for the next train home. There was an old cinema on the high street, a flea-pit, really. I went to the film to keep warm and kill time.'

'But what about your son? Was it the wrong prison?'

I see her mouth tensing, the lips pressing together and the wrinkles deepening. 'No,' she says, 'they said he was there but he wouldn't see me. They said he said he hadn't got a mum but I know they were lying. He must have been somewhere else.'

'And have you found him now?' I say, thinking it was understandable that the poor guy didn't want to have anything to do with his nutty mum.

'That was four years ago. I've not seen my son since. They're keeping him from me. But I know he's not dead.'

I look at her and something rather creepy dawns on me. 'Presumably,' I say, 'you'd be able to talk to him if he was dead.'

'Yes,' she says. 'But when I got home that night, from Prestwick, Rose was waiting for me.'

'Rose is Louis's mother?'

'Yes. That's the name she uses.'

'She was there in person?'

'Well, I don't see her physically. I know because of the smell. There's a strong smell of roses when she comes through.'

'What does she say?'

'She wants to be with Louis. She misses him. She'd like to communicate with him directly, but she's scared of ruining his life. She has regrets about things that happened between them. She has fears about his fame. She's scared for him.'

'Have you told Louis any of this?'

'I tried once when I first saw him but he won't listen to me. But one day he will. So I wait.' She drains her coffee. When it's finished she leans across the table to make a point, stabbing her finger into the lino table top to underline it. 'She thinks he should let go,' she says.

'Let go?'

The mad fan just shrugs.

'Let go of fame, do you mean?' I say.

She shrugs again, as if Rose's opinions are as much a mystery to her as they are to me. 'Will you tell Louis he's got to talk to me one day—' It's only half a question.

'I don't think I'll see him again.'

'Stupid girl.'

'Sorry?'

'You heard me,' she says. I look at her, not knowing what to make of her, not knowing what she means. 'He's here for two more days, two whole days,' she adds, and she clearly relishes those days, rolls them around in her mouth like two large, hot radishes.

'He's here until the première,' I say.

At the mention of the première she quivers slightly. 'Are you going?' Her eyes search mine anxiously.

'I'm meant to,' I say.

'I see all Louis's films now,' she says. 'I don't miss one. But I couldn't ever go to anything like the première.'

I look at her. 'It's mad,' I say, 'isn't it? It's the real fans who should go. Not people like me.'

'I'd better get back.' She gets up and winds her scarf around her long sinewy neck with some precision.

'I hope we can chat some more another day,' I say.

She doesn't answer. The froth on her upper lip has dried into a foamy brown tidemark. She walks stiffly away from me, opens the door only a crack and slips through, to be instantly received into the bustle of the street outside, her beige mac melting her immediately into the ordinary. Just another passer-by.

I feel uneasy. I stand in the street and look from left to right and from right to left. What is this? This is not good. My mind is skimming on the surface of things, skating like a water-boatman on a murky pond. I take in the scene as images only, the traffic, the cars' rear lights blurring into red streaks, the cinema on the corner and the movement of people around it, the all-night supermarket across the road.

Your fearless reporter. No one goes around telling her what to do. Oh, no.

Asking.

Huh?

Not telling you what to do. *Asking.* To begin with, Louis *asked* you not to speak to the fan. And he had what he felt were good reasons.

I force myself to recollect events: I argued with Louis, I did exactly what he asked me not to do, and I told him to fuck off. It comes to me – standing there uneasily in the street – that what I've done is blown it again.

I look over at the Pan Bookshop. It looks nice. It looks warm and enticing, full of browsers. People, that is, not Internet search systems. People standing in scarves and coats with their heads dipped to the open page. What a nice thing to be doing late on a rainy evening, browsing in a bookshop.

I head over there and I'm just leafing through the first thing that comes to hand when I feel a tug on my sleeve. It's Jay.

'My God,' I say.

Jay is the most eccentric male dresser I know, but he's outdone himself today. He's wearing Oxfam clothing of clashing eras coupled with his signature accessory, an ever-present long stripy scarf, so long it sometimes trails on the ground behind him. Jay has a kindly face, skin the colour of uncooked pastry, and short dusty dreadlocks. He has big round greeny-grey eyes that sometimes seem a little unfocused although, interestingly, he's razor sharp when it comes to techie stuff. If that sounds unattractive, he isn't unattractive: he just leans a little towards heroin chic.

'Gearing up for Tuesday?' he says.

Tuesday is a big day. Tuesday is Valentine's Day. Fight 4 Fair Flowers is due to picket offender florists all over London. Jay designed our website at Fight 4 Fair Flowers. He's been a sporadic ally ever since.

'Of course,' I say, and shove the book I was looking at – a book that boasts of a 'heart-stopping' collection of love poems on its fancy red velvet jacket – guiltily back on to its fancy red-velvet display stand.

Jay looks suspicious.

'What are you doing here?' I say.

'Hmph,' he says. He's not one for answering direct questions, Jay. 'What are *you* doing here?' he says.

'Louis Plantagenet has a rented house just round the corner. I spent the day with him.'

'And what do your principles think of that?' he says mildly, getting his rolling papers out of one pocket, his baccy out of the other and starting the act of creation. This action is so habitual, I'm not sure he's even conscious of it.

'You know why I'm doing it,' I hiss. 'I'm doing it for the money – because of Esther. It's a small compromise for the greater good.' Jay likes to come over as entirely innocuous, like 'Peace, man!' but actually he's the biggest stirrer I know.

'I see,' he says, sceptical. 'What's he like, then, this film star?'

'Nightmare,' I murmur conspiratorially.

'Really?' His great greeny-grey eyes light up a little.

'Yeah – blows out fifty interviews just like that.' I wave a hand to demonstrate. 'Poof!'

'No way.'

'Totally paranoid. Thinks everybody's out to get him. Won't speak to his fans.'

'Of course.'

'Probably deeply screwed up.'

'Of course.'

'Pretends to be nice and then, when push comes to shove, orders me around like I'm his servant.' We both shake our heads in contemplation of this predictable catalogue of sins. I find I'm feeling slightly better, can't think why.

'Don't you fucking hate people?' Jay says.

'Fucking hate them. This world is so fucked-up.'

'Tell me about it.'

'At least in Colombia they're up front about their corruption. Since I got back to this so-called haven of civilisation we live in, I've been assaulted at the airport, found bailiffs on my doorstep, I was thrown out of an interview yesterday and I've put up with half a ton of celebrity bullshit today – my God.' I shake my head some more.

Jay suggests a stiff drink. I say okay.

10

We go to a Mexican bar across the road and Jay looks disappointed when I order a glass of white wine.

'But this is Mexico,' he says. Jay is a free-thinker who lives by some very strict rules when it comes to alcohol. He has strongly held beliefs about what should be drunk where.

There's a waitress walking around the bar with long platinum blonde hair and a belt slung across her chest bearing shot glasses. She has tequila bottles hanging from each hip. People are buying shots off her and she slams them on the table and yodels loudly as they drink them down. Jay and I decide she is a tacky and embarrassing sales ploy.

An hour later, she's our best friend. I'm not sure how many shots we've had except that I think it's too many. I know this because the shot girl has gone away and Jay is talking about Us. The dreaded Us.

'You pushed me away,' he is saying.

'Excuse me,' I say. 'You took drugs with, slept with, bought tickets with, boarded a plane to Portugal with, and generally shagged yourself stupid with your best friend's girlfriend. How exactly does that add up to me pushing you away?'

'I was reacting to you. You were so cold.'

'Cold how?'

'I'm trying to tell you something. Don't make it like a court case. It's a feeling thing.'

'Give me broad brushstrokes.'

'You weren't enthusiastic.'

'Okay,' I say. 'You really want to have this out? Let's have this out. I *wasn't* that enthusiastic. I mean, what do you have to offer? Apart from a whole bunch of problems. I've got problems enough of my own. I'm not trying to be mean, but relationships, at bottom apart from being a general fucking nightmare, are about two people meeting each other's socio-economic needs. That's the real glue that holds the thing together. Needs not love. What needs of mine did you meet?'

'You have needs?'

'Of course I have needs.'

'You don't act like you do. I always wanted to look after you, but there was never anything to look after. You've got it all sewn up.'

'Are you trying to tell me,' I say, icy with outrage, 'that our split-up was *my fault*?'

'There was an element—'

'Listen, give up. Give fucking up. You blew getting the moral high ground. For ever. You ran off with your best friend's girlfriend. I've got the moral high ground, always will have, and there's nothing you can do about it. Not a thing.'

He stares into his empty shot glass for a while, then says, 'So you really weren't that enthusiastic?' The alcohol must be metabolising, he's less pugnacious now, more gloomy.

'You know they say your friends are just the people who got there first,' I say, not unkindly, I hope. 'Well, the same is true of lovers. You sleep with whoever's in front of you. It's true. You see it all the time. Why do you think so many men have affairs with their secretaries?'

'I thought we were in love.'

'There's no such thing. Remember?'

'I know. But that's what we thought. Wasn't it? Then?'

'I liked you. I fancied you. It wears off. That's the reality.'

'Thanks very much.'

Oddly, Jay and I originally met at a wedding. Oddly because we didn't – and don't – go to weddings very often. It was in our dancing days, a very romantic wedding, beside a tower on a grassy cliff somewhere outside Hove – two college friends of mine, the marriage long since defunct, of course. I was late and missed the vows and the food, but Jay invited me into his lair underneath the white-linen-covered tables and gave me a pill. There was music all night and we went skinny-dipping in the morning before driving back to Brighton where I was in my last year of a degree in politics. Jay had managed to elude further education and spent his days selling vitamin pills in a health-food shop and his nights selling other kinds of pills on the party scene where he was a DJ. He seemed as good a bloke as any.

We liked the same things, believed in the same things, and he was easy to be around. I didn't have to think too much. We fell into a gentle life together; it was simpler to be with each other than without each other. In a strange way we didn't even notice each other very much.

He moved into the sea-front flat I shared with girl-friends, a white stucco cathedral, too grand, these days, to be anything other than a boarding-house. The ceilings were so high we got a carpenter friend to build a platform in the living room, thereby creating a whole extra floor that we liked to call the mezzanine.

For most of the year Brighton's seaside trappings were nothing but a cruel taunt. We spent our days in lashing wind and rain under the desolate caw of the gulls. But in the summer, for a few precious weeks, the place would come into its own and we'd make fires on the beach and party all night. There are no words for the astonishment I'd feel to see the sun rising when, surely, we'd only just begun.

When I finished college, Jay didn't want to go to London, but I was ambitious. I was also sick of the seagulls. Jay, for all his drug-dealing and DJing and afternoons in Yum Yum Health Food, never seemed to have any money. He always owed his dealer or was paying off a new pair of decks. I managed to buy a car with some money I'd saved, and since I was now in the driving seat, we went to London.

At first we lived in a flat in an extremely run-down housing-association off the Euston Road. That was when the partying got a little consuming. In Brighton it had seemed spiritual – doing drugs in the open air always feels less toxic. In London it got ugly. A friend of ours was arrested for dealing ecstasy.

He wouldn't grass so he got five years. It was a real blow.

The sex drifted out of our lives – and the drugs drifted out of mine. I was trying to do scraps of journalism and earning money proof-reading for a firm of management consultants. I started getting up in the mornings – and then I didn't see Jay at all. Getting up meant going to bed at a reasonable hour and Jay was coming in at five a.m. and drinking litres of red wine, just to come down.

I thought moving was the answer and we found the commune through some road-protester friends. At first, it was a new leaf and Jay and Phil started the biodegradable coffin idea and I got regular work on a freebie alternative magazine. But things didn't really change and I began to wonder if they ever would.

Enter Portuguese temptress to let me off the hook.

'Don't you yearn to be overtaken by love's mysterious power?' Jay says, biting into a jalapeño pepper and rudely running a zebra crossing over my nostalgic thought path. I think he's quite drunk.

'No,' I say. 'But I do think about us getting back together. Despite everything.' Maybe I'm drunk too.

'You're kidding?'

'No. I think about it. I mean, I think about a lot of things. I do think about it, though. Sometimes. You do too. I know you do.'

Jay looks terrified. 'That's not why I brought Us up,' he says, 'not because I want to get back together. I brought it up because I want to know where I went wrong.'

'Oh,' I say.

'I mean, not that I don't think about it. I think about us getting back together too. I *think* about it.'

'Because, you see,' I say, 'given that love and passion are really a bad idea when it comes to relationships, maybe we *should* get back together. I mean, we get on okay. We know each other's foibles. We could have an open relationship. I mean, of course – I'm talking hypothetically – assuming we've exhausted all other options.'

'Of course – all other options.' He looks sheepish.

'What's up?' I say.

'Nothing.'

'It's like when we were going to nightclubs, isn't it?' I say. 'Everyone straining at the velvet ropes, desperate to gain admission to the Club of Love.'

'Stevie—'

'Louis, on the other hand,' I say, interrupting him, 'is automatically on the guest list.'

Of course. That's what the fame is for. This not-very-original thought strikes me with what, in my drunkenness, seems like a profound clarity. Fame is Louis's VIP pass to the Club of Love.

'Millions adore him,' I say to Jay. 'Imagine what that's like.'

'But it's not based on anything real.'

'He works hard, you know. He probably does in a week what you do in a year. For example, he gets up at six every morning and runs a long, long way.'

'So fucking what? What does running round a park achieve?'

'I don't know, but people like Louis, at least they do achieve. A year goes by and they've made two more films, got married, divorced, a whole new body, an Oscar – and what have we done? Painted the back bedroom. Maybe.'

'My, my.'

'What?'

'He's hooked you.'

'Oh, please.'

'In one day.'

'He has not.'

Jay says, 'George Orwell thought a dictator would pipe brainwashing messages into our homes and control our every move. I mean, he got it right, man! They don't have to force it down the fucking pipes, though. It gets invited in. We fucking pay for it, man. It's called Hollywood and the star system and it's making the world into one big consumerist USA.'

I stare at Jay. I'm really quite drunk now. 'I think,' I say, 'you may be right.'

'And you,' he says, 'your interview is going to help him further his evil aims!'

'It's just an article in a newspaper,' I say.

'And McDonald's is just a hamburger joint. We've got to stop him.' He bangs the table, getting wild-eyed now. He waves the tequila girl over and gets us another couple of shots.

'I'm not sure Louis is stoppable,' I say.

'They said that about Esso.'

We fling back our shots.

'Let's throw eggs,' Jay says, jumping up.

I stand up too. 'Eggs!' I cry. 'But what's an egg going to do?'

'Used properly,' Jay says and hiccups loudly, 'the egg can be as powerful as the atom bomb. Come on.'

We go to the late-night supermarket and buy some eggs. Jay insists on free range. I'm having doubts about the dignity of the enterprise but I tell myself my article is scuppered anyway. And then, in a moment of drunken revelation, I wonder if it is, in fact, made. I wonder if maybe I am the story: journalist throws eggs at subject. I think of it like modern art: a performance work.

The sight of the house and the mad fan back at her post stops me in my tracks. Of course I don't want to throw eggs at Louis. I want to *apologise* to him. He gave me his time and I gave him nothing but grief. 'We can't possibly do this,' I say, and I take hold of Jay's scarf and pull him backwards out of sight of the mad fan.

'No chickening out now.'

'We're not doing it,' I say.

'What came first the chickening or the eggs?'

'Ha ha. Gimme the eggs.'

'No.'

'We can't do this. He's not that bad. And, anyway, it would be the end of my career.'

'Since when did you have a career? Careers are corporatist.'

'Gimme the eggs!'

He won't. Very annoying. I have to wrestle them from him, which I manage to do by sheer force of determination and without breakages due to a very sturdy carton and Jay's advanced state of inebriation. I hide the eggs in the breast pocket of my voluminous sheepskin jacket where he can't get at them.

'Go home,' I hiss.

'Why? What are you going to do?'

'Nothing. Just go home. Look, we can't throw the eggs. We just can't. Trust me. I need you to leave me alone to think.'

I try to shoo him up the street. It doesn't work. He won't be shooed.

''Bye,' I say, and I cross the road and walk off in the direction of the house but on the far pavement.

'Where are you going?' he calls.

'Away from you.'

I turn the corner at the tip of the gardens. I wait about three minutes before creeping back. Jay's gone. Hiding, perhaps – but then I see his dark form at the other end of the street, weaving a little. He turns up towards the Fulham Road and disappears.

I straighten up, take a deep breath and approach Louis's house. When the mad fan sees me I give her a cursory nod of the kind that is meant to convey the idea that, although I have every right on this earth to be ringing Louis's doorbell at ten at night, I am, in fact, just picking up something left behind – a pair of gloves, perhaps – and that if I had more time I would like nothing better than to stop and talk to her but, you know, I'm just in and out for those gloves and, in any case, I'm fully aware that I don't have to explain myself – we're all adults here. So I give the mad fan this nod that speaks a thousand words and I ring Louis's doorbell.

Street entryphone would be a more accurate description. I'm a long way from the house's actual door.

'Hello.' A woman. Very curt. Slit eyes, his PR, I suspect.

'Stevie Dunlop to see Louis,' I manage to say, with no conviction whatsoever.

There's a silence and then: 'I'm sorry. He's not available.' Click.

I ring again.

'Tell him I want to apologise,' I say quickly, when she picks up.

'I'm sorry,' she says again, and this time she sounds quite sad, 'he's not available.' Click.

For a moment I find myself believing her. Perhaps because she sounded sad. I imagine Louis floating face down in the bath like a drowned water-lily. Not available.

I go down the side of the house and find a small green door set into the heavily fortified wall. I try the door and it swings open obligingly at my slightest touch. A shame, really, I'd have enjoyed climbing in.

There's only one lit window at the back of the house – at the top. Perfect. I imagine Louis tucked up in bed in his pyjamas. Tartan pyjamas. It's ten o'clock but he's got scripts to read, plus he has to be up at six for his run.

Now I just need a discreet pebble to throw up at the window. I look around. The garden is Japanese style; there's nothing but pebbles. The trouble is, they are all the size of small boulders. I'm after a gentle tapping effect. These pebbles would smash right through like Exocet missiles.

Then I remember the eggs.

I'm just reaching into my breast pocket when an arm encircles me and pulls me back against a warm body. I can hear the eggs crushing between arm and ribcage. The burly embrace is unmistakable. Mike.

'I love you too,' I say.

'One of these days you're going to go too far,' he says, and lets me go.

I swing round to face him, encouraged by his remark since it implies that I haven't yet, and catch him fiddling with something under his left armpit. It takes a moment to register but when it does—

'What the fuck—' I say. 'Is that a gun?' He's putting it away in a holster.

He cracks that smile of his. 'Yeah – it's a gun.' And he gives me a so-what? arch of one eyebrow.

'Is it allowed?'

'Allowed? Like the way you're allowed to prowl around Mr P's garden in the moonlight?'

'I just wanted to talk to him. We had a misunderstanding.'

Mike appears to consider this. 'Most people have a pretty clear understanding of "fuck you".'

'He told you I said that?'

Mike doesn't answer.

'Or do you have listening devices to go with the gun?'

'Time to go, baby,' he says.

'Just ask him if he'll talk to me. Just for one minute.'

'No way.'

'Please?'

'No way.'

'Please, please?'

'Time to go.'

'Just ask him!'

'Hey. Read my lips. Time to—'

'Mike, it's okay.'

We both turn. Louis is at the back door, the light behind him. In his dressing-gown. Jeans underneath. He stands back in a gesture of invitation into the warmth and brightness within. I go towards him. Mike doesn't follow.

'Thanks, Mike,' Louis says, and closes the door behind me.

11

'Where've you been?' Louis says.

Without waiting for an answer, he turns, runs, jumps and slides away from me down the entire length of the glossy parquet hallway in his socks, his worn flannel dressing-gown flying out behind him like Batman's cape. 'I'm in the kitchen,' he calls, disappearing down the stairs into the basement.

I follow him. When I get down there, everything is open plan: a pristine kitchen with frosted-glass panelled cupboards lit an eerie pharmaceutical green from within, the cups and glasses inside standing in neat and obedient rows. Everything else is gleaming stainless steel. It looks like nothing gets cooked in this kitchen – ever. Louis is staring into the fridge.

'Have you eaten?' he says, coming back out of the fridge with a bottle of beer in his hand and regarding me a moment. 'Where have you been?'

'Well, I walked up the road and had a coffee with—'

He's looking at me, his gaze absolutely level, absolutely inscrutable. He appears not to blink. I want to stare him out but I can't do it. His gaze is so steady it scares me. I wonder if it's an acting thing. The look is so intent, so true in a way, so . . . earnest is the word that comes to me, and it doesn't waver. You can't help thinking there's some kind of integrity behind that gaze, some kind of purity.

And I've got to lie.

'That's what they hire you for,' I say suddenly, 'isn't it? That look in your eye.'

'Huh?' he says.

'That look you're giving me now – that's your thing, isn't it? It's – I don't know – it's hard to come by, a look like that.' I flush slightly. I'm aware that we need to make friends again. Now is the time to make friends. But I am a traitor. 'I bumped into one of my flatmates. In the bookshop. We work together on Fight 4 Fair Flowers. We needed to talk tactics for a protest we're planning. We ended up having a few . . .'

He laughs at me.

'. . . drinks,' I end, shame faced.

'I thought you might come back. I wanted to tell you I'm going to take tomorrow as total vacation. My first for a while.' He offers me the beer.

'No, thanks,' I say. 'Just water.' Water would be wise. He gets me a glass of water then goes to put the beer back in the fridge. 'Are you teetotal?' I say.

'No. I make exceptions.'

'Make an exception.'

He looks unsure.

'For the sake of ordinariness,' I add. My blood-alcohol level feels a little intense in the presence of his sobriety.

He shrugs but takes a beer for himself from the fridge and I note, with a slightly sinking heart, that its brightly lit interior – large enough to house several of London's homeless – is stark, staringly empty. Eating,

I suppose, is as unfashionable as ever. I need some food to counterbalance the alcohol, to ground me a little, a life-raft to hang on to in a turbulent ocean.

Louis flips the top of his beer, sips it like that. Then he relaxes visibly, smiles, glugs down a little more and leans back against the worktop. 'To being ordinary!' he says, and holds up the bottle in a toast.

'Right,' I say, and do the same with my glass of water. 'To the man voted Hollywood's number-one heart-throb who can never be ordinary.' God, I really am drunk.

'Ahem.' He coughs. 'The *World*'s number-one heart-throb.'

'Oh, excuse me. I'm sure they're throbbing over you in Somalia.'

'You are excused.'

We look at each other.

'So what are you saying?' he says, after a while. 'I'm too handsome?'

'Let's face it, you're never going to be ordinary.'

Louis's face falls. I mean, really, it falls. I get the feeling I've said something terrible. This is ridiculous. My heart starts pounding. I don't want to hurt him. 'Hey,' I say, 'you could settle for being an *ordinary star*.'

'Oh, yeah?' he says, like it's an effort to carry on.

'I mean,' I say, 'aren't you getting the worst of both worlds here? Given that you *are* a star, you may as well be acting like one. You may as well be surrounding yourself with babes and falling nose first into piles of cocaine. That would be quite ordinary for a star. I mean,' I say, throwing a hand out into space, 'where are the dancing girls?'

'I've sent them all away.'

'When did you last get laid?' I say.

'Hmph,' he says, and gives me a small smile, lights a cigarette to cover himself.

'Do you mind me asking?'

'You know what?' he says. 'I have a problem in this area. I don't like having sex with strangers. I think it's kind of weird, kind of embarrassing.' He shrugs.

I stare at him. 'But surely,' I say, 'you must get a lot of offers. And presumably it doesn't have to be a stranger. You could get to know her first.'

'I could,' he says, and gives the cigarette a good old smoke while he's working out how to explain things to me. 'But, you know, most everyone I sleep with – they sell their story. And the really nice girls – how shall I put it? – the girls who know what they're about, they don't usually want to get involved with me. It's too much, this celeb business. Unless they're celebs too.'

'Well, there must be a good few of those around.'

'Some – but you don't want to get involved on the set. Been there, fucked that up. And when the shoot's over – it's hard to describe, but it's like that whole vibe falls apart. It was only a job, after all – and it's kind of hard to see people again. In fact, it's kind of hard to meet people generally, in the right kind of way, when your life's like mine. You won't believe it but I know a star – someone you'll have heard of – he was a virgin until he was twenty-five. And that's a fact.'

'Who?' I can't help saying.

He opens his mouth like he's about to spill the beans.

'I'm not telling you the guy's name!' he says and closes it again.

'What about Grace Farlow?'

'What about her?'

'You've kept her dangling, haven't you? All that on off on off. Poor old Grace Farlow.'

He gives one of his fantastic laughs. 'Poor old Grace Farlow,' he repeats, and rolls the words around his mouth as if they were to be savoured before being swallowed. 'Poor old Grace Farlow.' Then he shuts one eye and stares down the neck of his beer bottle and laughs again.

Finally it sinks in. 'You really don't do all that stuff they say in the papers, do you?' I say.

'No.'

'But what about friends?' I say. 'Where are the pop stars and the film directors, the models and the stylists?'

'Dunno,' he says, with a grin, then looks around as if they might be hiding in the wings. It occurs to me that he doesn't really have any friends. 'Mike's in the chauffeur's apartment. Katrina, my PR, just left for the evening.' His eyes come back to me. 'You're it.'

'You know what,' I say, 'I think you need to get out more.'

He gives me one of his more serious looks. 'What are you suggesting?'

'I'm suggesting we go out.'

'You're the boss,' he says.

'But we should eat first,' I add, thinking of my blood-alcohol levels.

'There's no food,' Louis says.

'Do you like scrambled eggs?'

The bar we go to is called Air. It's in a hotel and a bit of a celeb hang-out – the recommendation of a pop-star acquaintance of Louis.

When Louis had suggested calling this particular pop star, I'd been encouraged to think that he did indeed have friends in high places – but then the phone call itself was mighty odd. Louis called his people to have them call the other guy's people and only after the middle-men had tangled for a while did the two pro-tagonists finally speak. From my end the conversation sounded a bit like Nixon and Chairman Mao – long distance.

Anyway, next thing, we're pulling up outside the hotel in a taxi. I've persuaded Louis to leave Mike tucked up in bed. We've been told the management will get us in the back way if there are paps out front, but when we pull up there's no sign of anything untoward and we are whisked in through the front door, Louis with his collar turned up and his fedora pulled down, giving the game away as usual.

In the lobby I bump into a girl I was at school with and haven't seen for many years. I've heard about her, though – she 'made good' in the magazine business. She was one of those girls that everyone wanted to be friends with, but she never took much notice of me.

Well, she does now.

'Hello, Stevie,' eyes so busy darting from Louis to

me that she even forgets to forget my name, 'you look so *well*.'

So well connected.

'Hello, Julie,' I say politely.

At which point Louis gives me a little shoulder-squeeze that is perfectly calculated to convey a respectful intimacy between us that extends way beyond a shoulder-squeeze but doesn't extend to standing in chilly lobbies talking to unknown tail-wagging females. He tells me he'll go find our table and see me inside.

Julie gets every nuance of this little performance. I can actually see myself going up in her estimation. It's a physical thing, like watching mercury rise.

'Don't get excited,' I say. 'I'm still an absolute nobody, I assure you.'

When I get inside, the club is loud and dark and dominated by the bar. And what a bar. High church, its bottles racked to the roof in mirrored shelves, the multi-coloured liquids glowing with different lights. Each bottle, this seems to suggest, has its own particular promise – passport to any place you might want to go.

Around the bar are large, circular booths in soft blue velvet. In one I notice a posse of Brit actors who play gangsters. They have a couple of comic-book platinum blondes hanging on their words. I'm surprised. I always think real life is going to be more surprising than the cliché.

Louis has a booth to himself. It must have been arranged. I slide in beside him and we order drinks. I think I'm sober enough to manage a margarita. I'm not sober at all, but at least I'm not mixing my drinks. As we sit there, people look at us with the look you get in this kind of place, the look that says, 'Are you someone?' Usually, of course, people look away from me with disappointment. Here, they still look away, but they look away with the eagerness to be unimpressed of those who are semi-famous themselves.

With another drink inside us, Louis and I feel able to dance. The small dance floor is quite crowded and that helps. Louis does joke dancing, striking funny poses, making me laugh. He keeps his hat on. After a while we enter the zone – we dance through exhaustion and through boredom, through bad songs into good ones and back again, and just when I'm thinking we could dance all night, Louis suggests we get some water so we go back to our booth.

We've only been back a minute when the club manager materialises at Louis's left elbow, a lugubrious man with a strangely shaped chin. I think he might have deformed it with a lifetime's service to licking arse. He tells us that Rico Bargello is in the club but that he is *sans* camera and a personal friend and, therefore, will not be troubling Louis in any way.

No shit?

'I don't trust that bastard,' Louis says to me.

'What – the man with the chin?'

'No, Rico Bargello.'

'I think you're safe,' I say, and wonder how best to manage this turn of events. No doubt Rico will hound me to death once he knows I'm with Louis.

I get up.

'Where are you going?' Louis says.

'To the loo.'

I go the long way round, down the length of the bar. And, sure enough, there's Rico on a stool, his back to the room. I stand directly behind him and speak into his ear. I explain the situation as briefly as I can. I tell him he doesn't know me.

On the way back I take the long way round to expend some time before making my way to our table. For a moment I lose my bearings and I can't place Louis. Then I see her standing over him. There's something about this 'standing over him' that strikes me and I hesitate in my forward movement – something about the way they are together, her standing when there is all that room on the bench to sit, the way his head is turned up to hers, the way she is playing with something in her hand, dangling it, a mobile phone, perhaps, and the way she is looking at the phone and not at him. There is something about all of this that imprints itself. I know if I shut my eyes the picture will still be there, like a negative image on the inside of my lids. I know I will remember this moment for a while.

The woman standing over Louis is Grace Farlow. She is quite shockingly beautiful. It seems incredible that any one person could luck out so absolutely in the genetic good-fortune stakes. They tell us these people don't really look the way they do in the magazines – they tell us it's all done with computer enhancement. Not Grace.

Her even chestnut hair swings smoothly away from her face as she lifts her head, exposing an almond-shaped eye and smooth tan-coloured lips that stretch and swell right across the lower half of her face. Her body is a long lean greyhound body. An understated diamond lying on her breastbone sends an icy ray in my direction. As I get closer I see that the thing in her hand is indeed a small silvery mobile phone. Her fingers are like the rest of her, long and strong and beautifully defined. She has the habit that some tall people have of drooping her head. In her entirety she reminds me of an orchid that hasn't quite flowered to its fullest point.

When I get to the table I hesitate before sitting down. It seems to me that everything has changed. For one thing, I've turned into a munchkin.

'Oh, Stevie,' Louis says, when he sees me, 'this is Grace.'

'Hello,' I say.

Grace takes her time transferring her gaze from the phone in her hand to my face. And once it's there she takes her time in sizing me up – that *is* what it feels like, a sizing up. 'Hi,' she says. 'Louis was just telling me about you.'

'Sit down,' Louis says, and seems to mean both of us.

'I'm with Jo,' Grace says, 'Jo Hunter. We bumped into each other on the flight.' She turns and waves across the bar, inviting someone unseen in a far-off booth to come and join us. I have a feeling Jo Hunter is a big Hollywood director. I'm not totally sure.

I sit down. Louis takes the opportunity to turn to me. 'Grace just arrived from the States,' he says. 'Big surprise.'

'Yes,' I say.

We're just making room for Jo – who turns out to be a woman – when Rico stops by the booth.

Great.

'Well, well, well,' he says, and his eyes graze mine defiantly but don't settle. 'Look who's here.'

'Fuck off,' Louis says. Grace's head shoots up. 'He's a paparasshole,' Louis adds, by way of explanation.

Rico gives Grace a very blatant look, a very Rico look. 'How long have *you* been in town?' he says.

'Don't answer him,' Louis says.

I can tell Grace is responding to Rico despite herself. She reaches over and takes one of Louis's cigarettes – the lighting of which turns into a feast of sensual suggestion, starring that staggering pair of lips. 'Has she had them *done*?' I want to say to the possible Hollywood film director.

'Is this man a friend of yours?' Grace says to me, when she's safely alight.

'Nope,' I say, and I don't look at Rico.

'Just a huge fan of *yours*,' Rico says, and he gives Grace that look again. 'It's an honour to have two such great stars lighting up my humble evening.' He gives Louis a little bow. 'And you know why it's an honour? Because you two are real professionals.' With this, Rico turns to me. 'These two are *real* professionals,' he says, 'and there aren't many of them around. Not any more.'

Louis makes a nauseated noise in the back of his throat. I just watch Rico in repellent action – spellbound.

'Why don't you join us?' Grace says, but the invitation is more a throwing down of the gauntlet than anything else.

'Jesus,' Louis says.

'Why not?' Grace says. 'We already have a hack.' She looks at me. 'We may as well have a razzi too. Perhaps we'll learn something.' She drops her silvery phone on to the table and slides further along the banquette so that there is room for Rico beside her.

I don't feel good. The alcohol drains out of my system with one definitive glug and suddenly I'm sober. All that's left is a big headache and a small word – hack.

But I sit there for a while longer, listening to the small-talk, and then I ask the film-director woman if she directed the films I think she directed and she did. Out of politeness I ask her what she's been doing recently and she says not a lot, although she did recently direct a string of Bacardi commercials in Malaysia that have been winning prizes.

Huh.

Eventually Grace gets Louis to go and dance with her and the film director drifts away to the bar. When we're alone I risk a look at Rico. His eyes are on the dance floor. The crowds have cleared some space around the golden couple, but they don't need space, they seem to want to hide in each other, swaying tight together.

'Well, that's nice for Louis,' I say, 'that he met a friend.'

'Lovely jubbly,' says Rico, heavy on the Italian accent. He holds up his hands and makes a square frame with his thumbs, aiming them in the direction of Louis and Grace. 'Money, money, money,' he says.

Grace's phone suddenly lights up with an eerie blue flashing light. Rico shoots me a look, then picks it up and answers, but there's nobody there. He gives me a what-can-you-do shrug.

'Rico,' I say sternly.

'I'll take it back to her,' he says, gets up and wanders off with the phone.

I sit there, alone now, wondering what the hell I'm doing. After a while I work out I'm waiting for Louis to come back. But he doesn't. Grace comes first, her ear to the phone while she finishes a call. When she's done, she hangs up and looks at me.

'That's a cute shirt,' she says.

'Thanks.'

'Louis says he's had *the best* time hanging out with you.'

'Really?'

'Oh, he loves civilians,' she says.

'Civilians?'

'Oh, yeah,' she says, with a flash of her green eyes, and her lips stretch tight into a perfect, glistening smile. For a swift second I am reminded of a tiger. 'He *loves* civilians. He has this whole thing – this whole fantasy . . .' She tails off, converting the eye sparkles into a searing wistfulness now. 'He's *always* doing this. It's crazy. He's crazy.' She shrugs. She bravely lets the moment pass, shakes it off. Now, her face lights up again, mischievous. 'I just hope you know what you're getting into, honey.'

I want to say, 'Bravo.' The performance is just staggering. Instead I say, 'I don't know what you mean.'

'Oh,' she says, 'I think you *do*.' I notice that her eyes are bloodshot – delicately so. In Grace this manages to convey . . . not debauchery but immense sensitivity. 'You're clearly bright,' she says, 'I think you have a very bright future ahead of you,' and gives me a look from those shot jade eyes that leaves me in no doubt that I am on Death Row.

I feel like saying: 'Bright? *Bright?*' I think 'bright' is the most patronising word. 'Bright like a puppy?' I want to say. 'A puppy who remembers where he's buried his bone?'

'By the way,' Grace finishes, 'Louis wanted me to let you know you're free to go.'

'Sorry?'

'You're free to go.' She looks at her watch, a skinny diamond thing. 'He doesn't want to keep you up. He's sweet like that, Louis – always thinking of others.' She gives me another warm mischievous I'm-on-your-side-and-we're-all-girls-together-and-don't-we-understand-each-other smile. The effect is baffling. There's so much beauty, and beauty seems so inexorably linked to goodness, and yet being with Grace is like walking through country fields on a magnificent spring day and gradually realising that there's a smell on the air – manure or chemicals maybe – and your eyes are telling one story and your nose another and, well, it's only a *smell*, but somehow it's distressing, it just is, and the whole experience is undeniably thrown off key.

'Right,' I say, getting up and looking over towards the dance floor, 'but I haven't said goodbye.'

'No problem, honey,' she says, getting up too, 'I'll say it for you.'

12

I've been dreaming every night. Long involved dreams, but semi-coherent. In this one, my grandmother and I meet outside her flat on bicycles and everything is as it is except Gran is young. Her presence in the dream is strong, very pure and sweet, like a visiting angel. I love her very much. We decide to bicycle in different directions and that we will meet half-way – that is, where our paths cross. I set off. I cycle along the pavement and the flagstones are very uneven. I have to go up and down kerbs. It's hard going. When I get to our meeting point Gran isn't there. There's a bell ringing somewhere.

I wake up, the flavour of the dream still strongly with me, and in half-consciousness my heart seizes up with an inarticulate fear. I shy away from the dream, rouse myself, pull on some clothes and stumble down the stairs to make tea.

In the hall, a bundle of freshly delivered bills wedges the letter-box open. Rush-hour traffic noises funnel through and the temperature is below zero. I run screeching and shivering to the door and pull at the bills. With them comes something strangely soft and woolly – it's the work of a moment to realise that this is Jay's stripy scarf and that someone must have pushed the end of it into the letter-box as a joke. I give it a yank to pull it all the way through. It won't come. It takes me a while to work out that the scarf is attached to something at the other end. I open the front door. The something on the other end is Jay.

He's lying in a curl on the doorstep, fast asleep. On closer inspection I see he has his front-door key in his hand. I poke him a few times and say his name, but he doesn't wake so I give up. I have a morbid fear of waking people. I think it's something to do with breaking the spell. It's a little like having a morbid fear of breaking eggs – which some people do have.

I take the key out of his hand, for security's sake, then retreat with all haste to the kitchen where it is a few degrees warmer than the doorstep, but only a few degrees. I light the oven, turn it up to gas mark nine and leave the door wide open.

While I'm boiling the kettle, Esther appears wearing a padded pink polyester dressing-gown from the fifties. Inherited from a beloved aunt, I believe. It's the only thing in her entire wardrobe that isn't black. I once asked her why and she explained that this dressing-gown acted as the tension in the piece – there has to be a bum note somewhere, she said, something to hang everything else on.

She has pink fluffy slippers to match.

'My face is getting wider,' she says. 'Have you noticed? It's like my hips are opening out and so is my face. Did my papers come?'

'Huh?' I say.

'I ordered newspapers. If I'm going to spend the day resting, I must have media.'

'There's been a delivery of a sort,' I say. 'Come and look.'

I take her out into the hall and open the front door and show her Jay.

'Get up! Get up!' she yells, clearly not sharing my morbid fears. She gets hold of Jay by the lapels and by sheer force of determination manages to pull his shoulders up and spin him on his back so that his head is resting on the boot-scraper. Jay opens one eye but it's his only concession.

'Is it really possible to be so drunk that you fall asleep on your own doorstep?' I say, thinking there might conceivably be some other explanation although I don't know what.

'It's really possible,' Esther says, 'and here we have the living proof.' She gives Jay a firm kick in the thigh with her fluffy slipper. 'Get up!' she bellows at him. 'Or I'm going to pee on you.'

'What?' I say.

'I'm going to pee on him.' She seems quite business-like.

'Right,' I say.

Esther announces her intentions to Jay a second time, then begins to heave up her dressing-gown skirts and plant her feet on either side of Jay in preparation. I look up and down the street vaguely hoping, I suppose, that there might be someone to share the moment with.

Not a soul.

And, in the end, no moment either. Jay has rolled on to all fours and is crawling into the house. Once inside he struggles to his feet. He then staggers along the hall, rolling along the wall the whole way, taking the corner fast and swinging wildly into the kitchen.

Esther and I look at each other. 'It always works,' she says.

'It's a tactic you've employed before?'

'Often works, I should say,' she says. 'Often, not always.'

I don't want to think about the times it doesn't, not at this hour of the morning. I just want my tea.

In the kitchen Jay has collapsed on to the sofa, resuming the exact position he found so satisfactory on the doorstep. He's out for the count.

'How'd it go yesterday?' Esther says.

'It was all good stuff until Jay got me drunk and then things got strange – but nothing I can't rescue.' I fill the teapot and find two cups.

'Jay?' she says.

'I met him on the Fulham Road, then ended up going back to Louis's somewhat the worse for wear. We went out to a celebrity haunt.' I hear myself saying this with some amusement so I repeat the word 'haunt' with a giggle. 'He wants me to show him how to be normal. It's a good hook for the article. We went to the Air bar.'

'The Air bar is normal?'

'Well, for him – it's a start. He's not that keen to go out at all.'

'A kind of a mad recluse thing?'

'More just focused on his work. I mean, he's not what you might think. He's quite a serious bloke. He's not hanging out in the VIP rooms doing coke and fucking starlets . . .' I trail off here and Esther notices.

'What?' she says.

'We met Grace Farlow last night. She turned up in the bar.'

'And?'

'And nothing. I left.'

Esther gives me a very strange look. I feel myself going red, then white again. 'Well, this *is* a fuck-up isn't it?' Esther says mildly. 'I knew you'd fall for him.'

'I have not fallen for him!'

'Uh-huh.'

I stare at her. My blood is thrumming. 'You remember when I was obsessed with ice cream?' I say eventually. 'I worked in an ice-cream shop and I don't even like ice cream very much, but it didn't take long before I was spending my whole day wondering which flavour I'd try in my tea break because – because I had so much *exposure* to ice cream. There wasn't anything else to think about.'

'Yes,' says Esther patiently.

'Well, sometimes I think maybe I do find Louis quite attractive but that's just because – just because—'

'Everybody else does.'

'Exactly. And, if you remember, by the end of my second week at the ice-cream parlour, I was allergic to the stuff. I got eczema in my armpit.'

'But do you have *time* to go off Louis?'

'I'm not on him. That's not what I said.'

'But when is he leaving?'

'In two days.'

'Are you seeing him today?'

'I think so.'

'And he just spent the night with Grace.'

'Huh?'

'He spent last night with Grace.'

'What makes you so sure?'

'Oh, come on.'

'Oh-come-on what?'

'Just, oh, come on, that's all.'

'Since when was oh-come-on a reasonable argument?'

'Since I got pregnant.'

'You don't know what Louis did last night.'

'Seriously, do you really think there'd be all that smoke and no fire at all?'

'I'm just saying *you don't know*. You don't know if he went home with her last night or not.'

'Yes, I do.'

'All I'm saying is,' I'm getting shrill now, 'you have no *evidence*. That's *all* I'm saying.'

'If that's *all* you're saying, why are you so hot under the collar?'

'I'm just annoyed because technically there is a possibility in this universe of infinite possibilities that he did not go home with Grace Farlow and you won't admit it.'

Esther says nothing and my last statement, having ended in a shout, hangs in the air sounding dumb.

'By the way,' I say, lowering my voice a fraction, but only a fraction, 'I happen to know that the director of your Bacardi commercial was a woman.'

'Okay,' she says, with the tiniest movement of one slim carefully plucked eyebrow. 'I lied. I didn't get pregnant in Malaysia. But I don't want some fucking who's-the-father inquest going on, okay?'

'Who's the father?'

She just looks at me – stubborn. There is no one on earth as stubborn as Esther when she's stubborn.

At which point there's a noise at the front door, something being delivered. I go out to have a look. Esther's newspapers have arrived and they are wedging open the letter-box again, so I pull them through. There's a tabloid and a broadsheet. The tabloid is on top. On the cover is a picture of Louis leaving the nightclub, his arm around Grace Farlow and his nose nuzzled into her neck.

I go back into the kitchen and dump the papers in Esther's lap.

'Who's the father?' I say.

She's not going to answer me so I head out the back way.

I get on my bike and cycle over to Gran's. It's there somewhere in the back of my mind that Gran is going to die. I mean, I know she's going to die, but soon? I have the sense that if I can get over there in time I will prevent this untimely death. We haven't got long, I think. What was I doing sitting around drinking tea with Esther? We haven't got long.

I swerve crazily through the traffic and get called a 'silly bitch' and a 'stupid tart' and so forth. When I get to Gran's I leave my bike in the hall and embark on the stairs. Half-way up I can hear her grinding her coffee beans. When I get closer I can hear the clink of china on china and a cooing noise that's coming from the budgerigar.

When she lets me in I say, 'I had a funny dream about you, so I felt like coming round.'

'Must you wear those terrible boots? You've got such lovely ankles.'

I smile. Any minute now she'll start on my nose. She thinks it's a shame my nose isn't straighter. I can't find anything wrong with my nose. Perhaps I'm not seeing it from the right angle. But many's the time Gran has filled an empty hour lamenting the shape of my nose.

'Give me a cup of coffee,' I say. 'It smells like Fair Trade and I've got a hangover.'

We go into the kitchen where Tommy, the budgerigar, is still under his covers. I give him light and he chirrups gratefully. Gran is in her dressing-gown, a pale mauve silky thing, and she has black embroidered Chinese slippers on her feet. Her hair is the usual silvery cloud of candy floss around her head.

'What are you doing here anyway?' she says.

'I felt like coming over.'

'Where's that nice young man?'

'Nice young man?'

'The one that's trying to get into films. He was awfully appealing.'

'Well, he's on my mind, actually.'

'Mine too. I thought he rather liked me. Don't you agree?'

'Oh, Gran.'

'What? He said something about me?'

'No. Nothing. He did like you. Of course he liked you.'

'I knew it! I'm going to invite him to a matinée.'

'Well, there's something I should tell you about him.'

'Don't interfere, darling. I know you. You're just going to throw a bucket of cold water over the whole thing. I had your father on the telephone.'

'Really?' I say.

This is rare. Gran and Dad have a relationship that's like one long Mexican stand-off. My father married when I was about seven. I'd been living with Gran and there was never any question of me moving in with the newly-weds. I didn't know my father very well in those days. He'd travelled the world playing his trombone wherever he could get work and it was a shock to everyone when he settled down. He married a Scandinavian woman called Irena – she pronounces it to rhyme with henna. Irena got Dad into shape, made him get a teaching job that obliged him to stay at home during term-time at least. Even so I didn't get to know my father properly until I was eighteen and he decided that I was a useful ally in a world of women who didn't understand him.

Gran is now adjusting her hair in the budgerigar's mirror. A favourite occupation. If I had a penny for every time I've stood here watching her watching herself . . . I remember when her hair was an autumnal red and her long wicked lips were painted to match. Gran only ever wore lipstick, no other makeup, and had bone structure that made her look forty-two at fifty-seven. Still has the bone structure, of course.

'Sounds like trouble at t' mill,' she says. 'I think you should talk to your father.'

Your father.

'Why is he always "your father"? Like I'm to blame for him or something?'

She looks at me. 'You are an extraordinary girl. And you are absolutely right – you are entirely to blame for him.' She goes back to her hair.

I sigh. I know from experience there's no point in taking this any further. 'And you were an angel in my dream,' I say.

My father lives in a shambolic red-brick thirties house on the edge of Willesden Green. The house is very ordinary and suburban on the outside, but a Pandora's box of rooms on the inside with a surprisingly large garden. At the end of the garden is a shed that my father calls his workshop, but could also be said to be the place in which he actually lives.

I head for the main house first. I've come to love Irena over the years and she can be a very good listener. I ring the front doorbell. It issues a cosy two-note chime beyond the stained-glass panelling of the doorframe. After a moment Irena opens up. She has a neat, muscly little face that wears its lines well, but today her stiff grey hair is pulled into a stern ponytail and her watery eyes look red.

'Look at this!' she says, without preamble, and shoves a piece of paper into my hands. It's a handwritten letter, thick indigo ink on good paper. My eye falls on the central paragraph first.

> My favourite moment was standing on the bridge at midnight looking over Prague. There was a slight mist on the river and you held my hand. I can't wait to see you again. When can you next get away? By the way, my love, our age difference is of no importance to me. Our souls know each other well – that much is clear.

'You open his mail?' I say.

'Of course.' Irena has lived in London for twenty-five years now and speaks like a Londoner, except when she says 'of course'. When she says 'of course' she sounds very Scandinavian and somewhat forbidding. 'I have to pay the bills. I have to write back and say, yes, Mr West will attend so-and-so recital, no, Mr West is unavailable. I have to book the flights and consult his schedule and send the invoices. Of course I open his mail.'

I hand her the letter.

'I'm leaving him,' she says, taking the letter. She walks into the kitchen ripping the thing to shreds as she goes.

'Please don't leave,' I say, and sit down in a chair. I look at her. She's dribbling the shreds of the letter on to the floor, her hands still shaking. I wonder how she can be bothered to work herself up into such a state every time this happens, to live the drama over and over again.

'You think I shouldn't leave him?' she says.

'If you left him he couldn't survive for one second. He couldn't possibly work the washing-machine. He wouldn't know how to boil an egg.'

She thinks about this for a while, as if it were news to her. 'You know,' she says, 'when I first met him he'd just bought this house – to get himself on the property ladder – even though he was almost never in the country. I think he married me to look after the house. I think he simply planned to leave me here and keep on travelling.'

The idea of my father marrying Irena so that she would look after his house is preposterous. Irena is much too much of a handful for that. Unfortunately, although it's preposterous, it's also very possible.

'I wasn't having it, of course.'

'Of course.'

'I wish I'd never met him,' she says.

'Really?'

'It would have saved me twenty years of struggle and pain.' She gets up to put the kettle on.

'I know,' I say to her back, 'he's a bastard. You chose badly, really, if you think about it,' I say. She abandons the kettle, turns around. 'I think he's just one great big narcissistic baby,' I continue.

'Hmph,' Irena says.

'What?'

'I don't think you should speak about your father like that.' I look at her. There's some colour in her cheeks. I wait for the next bit. 'After all, there's no denying he's a great man.'

'He is,' I say, with a sigh.

'Absolutely,' she says. 'A great man.'

I find the great man in his shed.

'Did you have fun in Prague?' I say, once I'm in. It's

not a large shed, but Dad has squeezed in a mildewing walnut desk and an upright piano against one wall. There are musical posters all over the walls, many of them curling in the damp.

'Prague, Prague, my little strudel,' he says, 'a city of pasty faces. I wrote this little ditty while I was there – tell me what you think.' He swivels round on his chair, reaches over awkwardly to the piano and starts to play. I'm not musical, but Dad has made sure I can recognise Mozart when I hear it.

'It's awful,' I say. 'Primitive. Beginner's stuff. Surely you can do better.'

Dad smiles ruefully and the music dwindles away under his fingers. 'Mozart's sublime overture to *Don Giovanni*. Dashed off in the small hours on the day the opera opened – in Prague. A deadline can be a marvellous thing. Speaking of which,' he swivels back hurriedly to his computer, '*Brass* commissioned this article three months ago and they need it by one o'clock today. *Brass*,' he goes on, 'in case you're wondering, is a small magazine with a circulation that has risen to, oh, several thousand, I believe, following a – ha ha – much trumpeted, if controversial, merger with *Horn Section Weekly*.'

'I won't keep you long,' I say. 'I just wanted to hear about Prague.'

'Didn't I say?' he says. 'The dumplings were delicious. I like to play my horn with one in each cheek. And you, my dear,' he suddenly looks up at me and pulls his spectacles further down his nose so that he can look at me over the top of them, 'you must stop Irena from leaving.'

'Leaving again . . .' I say lightly.

'You must tell her the truth,' he says. 'And the truth is, she mustn't be allowed to blow our lives apart like this.'

I feel like saying, 'Why not? You're a dishonest philandering bastard,' but I don't. Instead I say, 'It's okay, Dad, I've spoken to her already. I don't think she's going.'

'You marvellous girl!'

'It was easy. I just insulted you.'

His eyes go back to his screen. I remember his deadline and turn to leave. 'You so remind me of your mother,' he says, before I get to the door. He rarely mentions my mother. I turn back. 'I loved her, you know. I tried to marry her. We had several dates booked, but it turned out that getting her to the church was simply un-do-able. An impossible feat that was never to be achieved. I gave up in the end.'

'Why did you want to bother with getting married?'

'Oh, one did in those days,' he says vaguely. 'Anyway, she was the most beautiful person I ever saw who wasn't in an oil painting.'

'I know,' I say crossly. Gran has schooled me well in my mother's beauty and I don't feel like hearing about it again right now.

'She used to say she didn't photograph well.'

'I know,' I say again.

'But I think, really, she couldn't commit to the page, you know. She was like an incredibly rare butterfly and everyone just wanted to pin her to a board.'

'You did, you mean.'

'We all did. I did. You did.' He looks at me. 'She couldn't bear the sight of you. I think it made her feel so terrible because she loved you so much and she knew she wasn't going to be able to stay.'

'And you'd already buggered off!'

'She wouldn't have me around. I was allowed to visit once after the birth and then she claimed I wasn't your father. She insisted it was a man called Burton Parry who used to take her to the dogs and was killed in a road accident two weeks before you were born. I was working in Canada and when I heard that she'd left you entirely I came home and announced myself to your gran – who'd never met me before.'

'I was three by then!'

'I only heard she'd gone through a friend of a friend – by sheer coincidence. And I wasn't even sure I was your father – I was pretty sure but not one hundred per cent. When I came home we had the tests done, as you know.'

I've heard the whole story before, of course, but when Dad's in the mood I let him recite it again, partly in case I hear something new and partly because I find it endlessly fascinating – my very own Genesis, chapter and verse. He seems to enjoy it too and it's one of the only subjects he doesn't communicate about in the form of jokes.

'I couldn't take you on, of course. I had no home, no job here, no savings, nothing. And by the time Irena had come along, it was too late. You were older and Gran had become your mother and she simply wouldn't let me have you.'

'You could have insisted.'

AMY JENKINS

'I regret not insisting,' he says, sheepish, with half-closed eyes. 'But I did marry Irena and I did settle down in the same city.'

'Oh,' I say. 'Don't make out you did that for me.'

'I wanted to do better than your mother had done . . .' He trails off somewhat lamely and looks like he might be about to say something more but doesn't.

'You're not going to leave Irena for this woman in Prague, are you?

'Don't be absurd.'

'I just think, for all her talk, she might get suicidal if you left.' We both contemplate this idea and then I find myself giggling. 'Or she might remarry someone faithful and live happily ever after.'

'I bet she would,' Dad says, nodding at me with an encouraging grin. 'I bet she would,' and suddenly he's laughing rather hilariously at the idea. He swivels to the piano again and starts up 'Here Comes The Bride'.

'Okay! I'm going!' I shout at him over the din. He doesn't stop playing, his right foot banging up and down on the pedals as if he were driving a Porsche.

I turn and run.

Half an hour later I find myself walking across the Scrubs. It's starting to rain. I like London in the rain. An underground-train depot to my left, a prison to my right, a flat expanse of earth in between and nothing to break the wind. The grass hasn't been cut in a while and it brushes my knees giving my journey a cross-country feel. There's a whiff of burning petrol and a loud whining noise, like disgruntled bluebottles, overhead. Grown men in khaki jackets are flying miniature aeroplanes over by the trees. Thwarted by the rain, they're bringing their toys into land.

I turn up my collar. The wind is whistling right into my ears and down my neck. I don't like wind, but I refuse to mind the rain. I just keep going. The occasional drop splashes into my eye and sends my vision swimming and blurring; for a moment I see the world through the lens of the rain itself.

The sight of the prison makes me think about what a difference a few yards makes. A few yards that way: gaol. A few yards this way: freedom. If it was my first day out of prison, what would I do? Go swimming? Underwater, scraping my body along the bottom of the pool. Or maybe climb up high somewhere. Go to the top of Parliament Hill and look out over

London? Or get on a train and go to the seaside? Or just take a ride on a bus – on the upper deck in the front seat, vibrating all the way through the West End and back again? Or perhaps I'd just go to the airport and buy a ticket to Sri Lanka on the never-never-to-return.

They say you're meant to live every day as if it were your last, which I've always thought was daft, since no one would ever pay the gas bill if that was the case, but what if it were your first?

My phone rings.

It's Dick.

'Where *are* you?' he says.

'Wormwood Scrubs. Taking a walk.'

'Louis wants to know where you are.' He says the word 'Louis' in a kind of hushed, reverential whisper that says, How dare you be doing anything other than licking the holy man's arse?

'Does he?' I say.

'He's expecting you! Jesus, Stevie, what the hell are you doing?'

'Okay, okay,' I say. 'I was on my way over there. It's not even eleven. I didn't want to be bursting in on his post-coital breakfast.'

'That's exactly what you want to be doing. Were you there last night when they met?'

'Yes.'

'Fab-u-lous.' He says the word as if he's folding beaten eggs into cream. 'Tell me more.'

'Don't worry. I got lots of good stuff.'

'So . . .' He suddenly sounds distracted. Even in full

attention mode, The Dick habitually speaks in the absent-minded way people speak when on the phone and reading their e-mails at the same time. 'So,' he says, 'what do you think of Louis?'

I find I don't know what to say. I open my mouth to say something then close it again, like a carp.

'What did you think of him?' Dick repeats enunciating slower this time, as if speaking to the hearing-impaired.

'I think I like him,' I say finally, 'but it's hard to tell. It's a little like standing too close to a painting by Lichtenstein – all I can see are the dots. I have no idea of the whole. Do you know what I mean?'

'No.'

'Well, you know, there's a glow.'

'Glow?'

'Glare then. You know, the glare. Of him.'

'Jesus, Stevie.' He gives up. 'Have you written the piece yet?'

'No! I haven't even been to the première yet, seen the movie – anything. I'm not ready to write the piece.'

'Oh for goodness' sake, you should have written the piece before you even met him. I tell all my journalists to write first, ask questions later.'

'Are you mad?'

'NOOOO!' he shrieks.

'Sorry?'

'Oh, not you. We're doing "what's hot and what's not" and Elenka's waving some boxing gloves at me for "hot". All wrong. Anyway, call Louis.'

He hangs up. I drop the phone into my pocket and

keep walking. The rain has let up a little. Most of the aeronauts have gone but two are under the trees eating sandwiches, sitting on green collapsible fishermen's stools. There's a bench to my left and I decide to go and sit down too and generally get my bearings. It'll afford me a nice view of the prison and I don't mind taking a few moments to indulge the lugubrious mournfulness that is London in the rain.

I don't think you can grow up in London without developing a partiality for gloom. Dark grey is one of my favourite colours. I like the greasiness of rain on concrete. I like it when the night is closing in, even if I have just had lunch. I am comforted by the sound of windscreen wipers and have a fondness for traffic jams, especially when I'm walking alongside one, free to admire the quiet stagnation, the glow of the red tail-lights blurring in the drizzle. And even London's seventies tower blocks have been lent a certain glamour by all those pop stars waxing lyrical about heroin addiction. And they are best seen in the rain.

Suddenly I can't bear to be on the bench a moment longer and I set off again, heading for Ladbroke Grove. I pass two doggy women in wellington boots. They nod a greeting in my direction while their dogs chase at thirty miles an hour through the grass. In the mud-ridden car park, I find a large sleek Mercedes with darkened windows. It looks like it's lying in wait, a resting panther, its eyes lazily half closed. It's not a familiar car, not the one I rode in yesterday, so I wonder for whom it waits. Not the doggy women, surely. Then the near side door opens—

'Stevie,' Mike says, 'a little bird told me you'd be here.'

Mike is driving, so I sit up front beside him. The car hums exquisitely. The leather seat is smooth, cool and slidy. There is climate control. We glide through streets where grim housing and lesser mortals are rendered picturesque by discreetly tinted window glass. The car is designed to make its occupants feel superior. It works. For a moment I feel safe and special and chosen.

Mike isn't saying much. I break the silence with 'I saw Louis made the front pages this morning.'

No comment from Mike, but he takes his eyes off the road a second and gives me a little twinkle.

'Did she stay for breakfast?' I say.

He just shakes his head.

'That old confidentiality clause, I guess.'

'It's not a joke,' he says.

'What isn't? Grace or the confidentiality clause?'

'Confidentiality. It's not a joke.'

'Tell me one thing, why didn't they go out the back? At the Air bar.' No answer. 'Or did they go out the back and Rico caught up with them anyway?'

Mike sighs. 'They didn't go out the back,' he says.

'Why not?'

He shakes his head again. 'You're gonna have to ask Louis.'

We pull up outside the house and the mad fan is there. I give her a discreet wave as we go in. At least she's not suffering rain torture any more. In fact, the sky is clearing fast and there are dabs of sunshine here and there.

'Are you worried about the mad fan?' I say to Mike.

'I've got my eye on her. We've run some checks. She's most likely harmless. What can you do? It's a free country.'

'You seem sad,' I say, 'that it's a free country.'

He laughs a surprisingly high-pitched laugh with great gusto. 'You make me laugh,' he says, wiping his eyes.

When we get inside we're told Louis is on a conference call, so Mike and I go down to wait in the kitchen.

'Has it ever occurred to you,' I say when we get down there, 'that you *should* be talking to the mad fan?'

'Have you been talking to her?' The smile falls off his face. His brow becomes furrowed like a freshly ploughed field.

'Think about it, if you and Louis had invited her in for tea right at the beginning, or even just given her the time of day, maybe she wouldn't have developed this obsession.'

'Rule number one is never, *never* engage with these people.'

'Maybe she thinks she's protecting Louis. Just like you.'

Mike comes over very serious. 'Has she threatened Louis?' he barks.

'No!' I yelp.

This exchange, which has become quite heated, subsides like a wave that's broken. Eventually I say, 'Your gun is illegal, right?'

'Not your business.'

'Well, it must be – illegal, I mean. How did you smuggle it into the country?'

'I did not smuggle it! Man, you ask so many questions.'

'So where do you get it, then?'

'The hire shop.'

'The hire shop. Guns for hire? I'm guessing that's in the East End somewhere, right? Thugs and bouncers anonymous.'

Mike chuckles. He's warming to me again. 'You wanna see it?' he says, and he reaches under his armpit and pulls it out. As guns go, it's quite a nice gun. It's titanium in colour and neatly snub-nosed. He puts it into my hand. 'Try it,' he says.

'Is it loaded?'

'Of course. But the safety's on. You ever fired a gun?'

'No,' I say, 'but I was archery champion at school.'

'You know about aiming, then,' he says.

I stretch out my arm and aim at a hanging saucepan. I make myself solid, feet apart, arm straight out, like the cops on TV. I have to admit it feels good. It feels powerful. I always wanted to be one of Charlie's Angels.

'It's like the gun becomes part of your arm, isn't it?' I say, pretending to squeeze the trigger.

'That's it,' Mike says. 'That's all you need to know.'

'But seriously,' I say, suddenly getting freaked and giving it back to him, 'you can't really think you need a gun. I mean, celebrities don't get shot in England.' I open my mouth to go on, but then I remember a TV personality who was recently shot dead not a million miles from this very street. I close my mouth again.

'I'm just doing my job,' Mike says.

'You and Louis,' I say, with slightly less conviction, 'two words, paranoid fuckers.'

'And a very good morning to you too,' says Louis, coming in and catching this. He's wearing his running clothes. He hauls himself up to a sitting position on the counter top with one simple movement and cracks open a banana from the fruit bowl.

I want to ask about the photo, how Rico caught him, but I decide it would be giving the Grace thing too much attention. Instead I say, 'You said you were going to take today as a day off, right?'

'I can do it. I know I can,' he says, and punches the air.

'You've already failed.'

He's crestfallen. 'How come?'

'You've been running.'

'I have to run.'

'You've taken a conference call.'

'I had to.'

'Look, either you're committed to this or you're not. How many other things are there going to be that you *have* to do? Calls that you have to take? Meetings that you can't miss?'

'Nothing, I swear.' He looks chastised. 'My day off starts now.'

'What do you want to do with it?'

'I don't know.'

'What do you do to relax?'

'I don't know.' I suspect he doesn't really like relaxing. 'What do you do to relax?' he says.

'My personal favourite? TV. Daytime TV . . .' I feel

myself brightening at the very thought: sitting on the sofa watching people sitting on sofas. My mind wanders to the plush living room I spied upstairs, the deep sofas and plasma screen TV, but then I catch sight of Louis swinging his legs restlessly up on the counter and I can see it isn't going to wash. 'Okay, I'm just going to brainstorm. Shout stop if you hear anything that takes your fancy. Er, shopping, movies, football, sightseeing, fun-fair – er, Alton Towers, it's a theme park, Legoland, ice-skating, bowling, swimming – er, day spa, art gallery, zoo, parks – er, countryside,' I'm running out of steam, 'flying small aeroplanes around Wormwood Scrubs in the rain.'

'Flying small aeroplanes?' His eyes light up.

'But you're not in them!' I say quickly. 'They're miniature.'

'Well, let's hire a bigger one! And let's fly it around this worm place. Great fucking idea.'

'No, no, no,' I say. 'The worm place isn't big enough.'

'We'll go to a bigger place, then! KATRINA!' This last is yelled up the stairs and after a moment Slit Eyes' sharp little heels can be heard clipping along the parquet above. Louis can't wait, though: he runs up the stairs taking them three at a time and talks to her in the hall.

He's gone a long time so Mike and I make tea. When he comes back it's to shout down the stairs: 'North, south, east or west?'

'West,' I shout back, and he's gone again. 'When in doubt go west,' I say to Mike.

'Huh?'

'Well, yes, I mean, where is the food better? Eastern

Europe or western Europe? Where did I grow up? East London or West London? See what I mean?'

'Huh.' He's not convinced. 'Where's the Big Apple?'

'I just said it to get rid of him,' I say.

Louis bounds down the stairs – must be five at a time – to announce that it's all arranged. He's changed into real clothes. 'All arranged' turns out to mean that he and I are flying to Somerset in some kind of light aircraft and we need to be at the City airport in half an hour's time.

Whenever I take off in an aeroplane my heart leaps and I wonder why I've been wasting time on the ground. I watch the earth banking and falling away, sliding past the window, houses, cars and trees becoming smaller and smaller. Eventually London fades behind us and we are over the countryside where white horses are cut into the chalk and hills take the form of lozenge-shaped barrows with lonely stone crosses set into them, like taps at one end of the bath. Stonehenge is like a mouthful of crooked teeth on Salisbury Plain. The Roman roads are long and straight and the downs go up and down. Small villages nestle picture-postcard like into the green and brown patchwork folds, overseen by the occasional stately home squatting large on its lawn, a toad on a lily-pad. On the ground, these houses would be well hidden behind walls and trees; from the air they lie open and exposed to all.

I love being able to see where roads lead, lines of desire, paths carved out by man's need to get from here to there, from there to here, a little path curving through a wood to the forester's cabin. The occasional rider trotting along the edge of a field, the occasional man walking his dog. These things rise up and fall away, rise up and fall away.

I glance at Louis wondering if he's feeling what I feel. But he lives like this, I think to myself, in the bigger picture, on the grand scale.

We land in a small airfield near Yeovil called Henstridge, and the moment we're out of the plane Louis rubs his hands together eagerly. 'Lunch!' he declares. 'In a genuine English pub!'

'We'd better get a move on,' I say. 'They won't serve a whisker after two o'clock.'

He gives me a sceptical look that says, 'Do you really think anyone would refuse to serve *me* lunch?'

'You don't know English pubs,' I say. 'You really don't.'

When we get to the gates of the airfield a hire car is waiting. But of course.

'You drive,' Louis says. 'I'm not too sure about this left-hand business.'

The man who delivered the hire car recommends a pub out towards a place called Sparkford and we head that way. But we soon lose ourselves in the country lanes so we just drive. At first it's all hedges tightly enclosing us on one-lane roads but then we come to an open valley and the country falls away dramatically to our right. On the horizon, the strange lozenge-shaped hills sit bleakly against the sky, speaking of a land ancient and pagan and immovable.

We stop the car and get out. Looking over the terrain there are places where the sun is shining and places where it isn't and places where it's neither one nor the other, where the sun diffuses in powdery plumes, where particles are strung in light from heaven to earth and back again. Down on the ground, if there's a cattle trough or the occasional small lake or pond, the water reflects hard and dark like iron.

'Whoever lit this,' Louis says, 'hire him immediately.'

'It's strange to think it's always here,' I say, 'when we're caught up in the hamster wheel. This is always here.'

'Thanks for bringing me,' he says.

14

The pub we find is called the Black Dog and they serve food until two thirty. No one takes a blind bit of notice of Louis. A couple of gloomy locals sit at the bar staring into pints and that's about it. But there's a nice fire in the grate and low beams for Louis to bang his head on.

Louis seems quite excited. 'It's so English,' he keeps saying, with relish.

'Yes,' I say, less enthusiastic.

We order at the bar. Fish pie and halves of Guinness. 'Oh,' I say at the last minute, 'and cheese and onion crisps.' Can't go into a pub and not have cheese and onion crisps.

We go and sit in the alcove by the fire. The pub's benches look like old pews from a church. There are some dog-eared games stacked on the window-ledge, dominoes and tiddly-winks and a pair of watermarked prints on the wall, hanging skew-whiff in their frames behind Louis's head. One says 'Courtship' and shows a squire gamely helping his lady over a stile. The other says 'Marriage' and shows the same squire striding off just as gamely and leaving the lady to struggle over the fence in her long skirts all by herself.

'So,' Louis says. His eyes are dancing. He's loving all

this. My hand is resting on the table and he picks it up almost absent-mindedly, then puts it down again. 'So,' he says.

'So,' I say, pull out my reporter's notebook and slap it down on the table, 'this might be a good time to—' and I don't have the heart to finish my sentence.

Louis looks down at the notebook. His eyes stop dancing.

I feel like I've taken out a ten-ton hammer and whacked it down on his head. 'I'm sorry,' I say.

'Ah,' he says, 'the interview,' and lights a cigarette.

I open my mouth to tell him that the interview is what we're here for, isn't it?, but the truth is I'm only saying it because I'm not at all sure that it *is* what we're here for. So I don't say it and then I open my mouth again to say that, in any event, we do have to do the interview at some point and that now is as good a time as any – except the truth is, now is a terrible time, so I don't say that either.

In the end I just say I'm sorry again.

'Don't be sorry,' he says, picking up his professionalism by the scruff of its neck and dragging its exhausted carcass on to the table to join my officious notebook. 'What do you want to talk about?'

I open my notebook feeling like the executioner. 'Tell me about the new film,' I say lamely.

'What about it? I play a sheriff.'

'How was it working with Candace Kelly?' This question comes to me as something Dick mentioned and sounds, in my altered state, vaguely professional and like something I should be asking.

'Oh, me and Candace,' he says, 'we had a hell of a time.'

'You hate her?'

He laughs. 'You can't ask stuff like that,' he says.

'Why not?'

'You just can't. I thought you were trying to be professional.' He glances at the notebook.

'Why can't I ask?'

'Because you can't. Next you'll want to know if we do tongues when we screen kiss.'

'Absolutely, that's exactly what I want to know. Do you do tongues when you screen kiss?'

'I'm not telling you.'

'Well, Christ, you've got to tell me something. Something interesting.'

'Ask me something interesting. In my experience the quality of the interview depends entirely on the quality of the interviewer.'

'Okay. Who was your first love?'

'Mary Jane Cuthbertson. In her Girl Scout uniform.'

'Ah,' I say. 'A fetish?'

'Not a fetish. We were ten.'

'You were a Boy Scout?'

'No,' he says. 'I didn't really have time for that sort of thing.'

'Of course. You were too busy scaling Everest or some such.'

'Why do you say that?'

'I was just remembering that you find it difficult to be ordinary. And being a Boy Scout is quite ordinary,' I say, feeling distinctly uncomfortable.

'I didn't have time to be a Boy Scout,' he says, 'because I built a house with my father when I was twelve years old.'

'I don't believe you.'

'I did. When Dad broke his back he got an insurance payment from the factory of a few thousand dollars so he bought a shack, which was all we could afford, and I rebuilt it every day after school. I put it back together until it was a liveable place – only three rooms but liveable.'

'How did you know what to do? All the carpentry and stuff?'

'I got books from the library. I studied. I asked people. Step by step I got it done.'

'Oh, God.' I put my head in my hands for a second. 'I'm sorry. It's hard being privileged. You just never have the moral high ground.'

'It's a fair trade,' he says. 'You get the olive oil.'

The fish pies come. I look down at my little oval oven dish with its wavy mashed potato lid. 'Where'd you get your name?'

'My dad called me Louis. It's my real name. He always said he was descended from royalty. There was some story that his ancestors who first came to America had royal blood. Danish, I think. I'm not sure. But fallen on hard times. Very hard times.'

'Did you believe that?'

'I don't see why I shouldn't.'

'Is that what drove you on? Did you think you were a prince?'

'No, but I always think that if someone else can have

or be something then it stands to reason that I can too. It's just a way of looking at the world, a logical equation, if you like. To believe that things are possible.'

'Were you terribly unhappy with all that responsibility on your shoulders, having to build a house and everything?'

'Not really. I remember just doing the next thing, getting the bus to school and my tin lunchbox that had Batman on it and the strong taste of the rye bread my dad made sandwiches with. He always used rye bread – he thought it was good for you. If I felt bad, it was about our situation. He was too crippled to work.'

'When did he die?'

'When I was twenty-three.' His expression tells me I'm not to tread any further down this road. After a moment he goes on, 'It was bad – nearly as bad as when Mary Jane Cuthbertson broke my heart for real.' He flashes a grin at me, a blinding light designed to throw me off course.

'The Girl Scout!'

'I loved her,' he says, 'but she dumped me. Twice.'

'Twice?'

'Yes, the first time was when we were thirteen and dating like kids but she left me for a boy called Johnny Logan who was a champion on the skateboard. I did everything I could to get her back, including serenading her at night from underneath her bedroom window on the guitar. I got her in the end. She left the second time seven years later when I got my break in *After Eight*. We shot in LA and the desert. She hated LA, she didn't want to be involved with movie people, and she didn't want me to be. But I wouldn't give it up. So that was that.'

We eat our pies for a while and contemplate the departure of Mary Jane Cuthbertson.

After lunch, we leave the car and set off walking, through the village and up to the ancient hill fort behind. There are no buildings left, of course, only a broad grassy rampart running around the circumference of the hill. You can see the countryside in every direction for miles, almost to the coast, it seems, where land and sky merge in layers of silver and grey haze. We are above the trees up here, the wintery branches like coral on the sea bed. In a nearby field a herd of cows walk in strict formation to the gate. Milking time I suppose. The neighbouring farmhouse is built of warm yellowy Ham stone and has a real orchard, stone-walled, with sheep grazing beneath the carefully staggered fruit trees.

'I want an orchard,' I say, pointing it out to Louis. 'There'd be blossom in the spring and apples in the autumn. Whenever things were bad I'd just go sit in it.'

He nods, his eyes on the orchard. And then it occurs to me that he could have it. 'You could have an orchard,' I say. 'You could have one right now if you wanted to.'

'You see how lucky I am,' he says, with a little smile, and we walk on.

At a place where the rampart is high, there's a fallen tree, dead now, forming a kind of natural bridge, an arc, and beside it a perfectly spherical deep grassy hollow.

'What do you think that was for?' I say, pointing to the hollow.

'Don't know,' he says.

'A pond? A grain store?'

'The bathroom?'

He clambers down into it. I follow and suddenly there is peace – no wind. Someone has had a fire here. There are some ashes and burnt ends of wood. Louis lights a cigarette then begins idly gathering the wood into a wigwam shape.

'Let's make a fire,' he says. He goes off and comes back quickly with more wood, building it neatly into the wigwam. Then he makes a lighting pad with some tissues from my pocket. He'd be good in a shipwreck.

There's something oddly exciting about the fire starting up, when the flames begin to lick up between the twigs. We sit close and stare into it like the oracle, warming our hands. Louis, consumed with it now, runs to get more wood. The fire makes a good noise, crackling and hissing. I discover that when I look at it and then at the sky, the sky is bluer. When I look at it and then at the grass, the grass is greener.

Louis and I sit at the edge where it's steep. We lean back and rest our heads on the hill behind.

'I like that you still care about Mary Jane Cuthbertson,' I say.

'You can tell?'

'Yes,' I say. 'It's amazing. I'm amazed.'

'Why? Because of your anti-romance thing?'

'No. I don't think it's that. I think I'm amazed you have feelings. I think it's because you're a film star. It's like we mortals made you, gods, and – as gods – we give you all this power and privilege but you're not allowed to have any feelings because having feelings makes you mortal. But then again, at some level, we don't really want you to be gods – how dare you be gods? We want you to suffer too. But then, if we bring you down, where are our gods?'

Louis doesn't say anything. After another while I say, 'Am I going to write about this in the interview?'

'About what?'

'This,' I say, 'the fire, Mary Jane Cuthbertson.'

'You're asking me?'

'I guess so.'

'What happened to your journalistic integrity?'

'I don't know,' I say, and I pull my reporter's notebook out of my pocket and look at it. What did happen to my journalistic integrity?

I open the notebook. On the last used page I've written CANDACE KELLY in capital letters. Suddenly Louis's hand arrives flat across my page. I look up startled. Louis is looking at me intently. 'Do you want the truth?' he says.

I don't know what to say. Obviously I want the truth but I want the interview too and somewhere inside me I have a feeling the two things are in danger of cancelling each other out – no, it's more violent than that: of obliterating each other.

'I liked it,' he says, 'when we were in that closet in Jermyn Street. I'm finding it hard to go back to the lies.' He closes his eyes.

'Do you lie a lot?' I say.

'Well, I don't know whether you'd call it lying . . . You tell it a certain way – you have to.' He opens his eyes. 'I lie the whole time,' he says, with a sigh. 'It's mostly all lies.'

I close my notebook and meet his gaze.

'If I tell the truth, will you tell the truth too?' he says.

'Okay,' I say, wanting to add that I'm not at all sure what the truth might be when it comes to me, but it's not the time to complicate matters.

He speaks slowly and clearly, enunciating each word. 'Working with Candace Kelly was a fucking night-mare. My whole life,' he adds slowly, 'is a fucking nightmare.'

'A nightmare?' I manage to say.

'*Science Fiction*,' he says, 'was the biggest film of all time. It was fucking phenomenal. It made me. For life. Financially, I don't ever have to work again. It got rave write-ups – so did I. They said I had the world at my feet. People told me over and over how lucky I was. And I *was* lucky, but I didn't *feel* lucky. *Science Fiction* was the most hellish experience of my life bar none. It was more painful than Mary Jane Cuthbertson leaving me. It was – it was—' For a moment he's lost for words.

'I've got this thing. There's something about my face – people make up a lot of things about it, about me. I've got this – this quality that I'm not even in control of. It's not about my acting, it's not about me, it's about what people put on to me. And the weird thing is, I'm left out of it somehow, you know? It's their show, not mine. They want a piece of me – and then it's like *that*'s not even enough. It's not just the girls who sell their stories you know, it's friends, staff, managers – or they sue me, just for the hell of it, see if they can make a buck. I get death threats, hate mail. I got this picture once – faked up – of me hanging from a tree. Lynched. People *hate* me. They love me *and* they hate me. It's a weird way to live, man.' He shakes his head. 'I spend at least half of my day wondering how to get the hell out.'

I don't know what to say.

'And then there's the fact that I don't enjoy it. I don't know that I've ever enjoyed it. It was the thing I most wanted to do in all the world – act in movies. It still is, but I've never enjoyed it. I don't think I'm very good. On *Science Fiction*, John – the director – he tortured me. He's a tyrant, a crazy man, and he knew I didn't really rate myself and he used it – man, he used it. I just couldn't get past how much I hated him – I just couldn't get past it. I couldn't even get away. We were shooting in Sydney. It took sixteen fucking hours to get home. The shoot dragged on and on. John was a madman. I mean, the real thing. Obsessive – beyond. The atmosphere on the set was a disaster. People started abandoning ship – morale was low as it can go. And then, two weeks from the end, someone died—'

He stops. I think he might be about to cry, which is a little awkward. A cow arrives at the edge of the hollow and looks down at us and – oh, I don't know – he's a manly film star and he's not meant to cry. To make it worse I can sense his pain.

I look at the cow. When I look back at Louis again, his eyes are down and he's biting his lip. I reach out and take his hand briefly like he took mine in the pub.

'I'm sorry,' he says.

'I think we should have an agreement not to apologise to each other any more,' I say.

He laughs a little and then gets up to distract himself – put some more twigs on the fire.

'Who died?' I say, when he's got his back to me safely. He just shakes his head. 'Someone in the film?' I persist. We have an agreement to tell the truth, after all. 'Or is that when your dad died?'

He looks at me across the fire. 'I guess,' he says.

'How do you mean?'

Now he looks over his shoulder as if someone might be listening.

'The cow is listening,' I say.

'You know what really, really gets me about all this? I can't ever go back. Like I've lost a leg or my eyesight and it's never coming back. Never.' He looks down into the fire. 'I've destroyed my life. I've become this "thing". Nobody sees me as an actor any more, I'm Louis Plantagenet. And I can't ever get away from him. I destroy things. The film I'm promoting this week – it's a small film, it was a good script. But it can't bear the weight of me. I've blown it out of the water.'

'But surely,' I say, 'if you step out of the whole circus, go and live on a farm in Wyoming or something—'

'And then what? I can't act on a farm in Wyoming.'

I look at him.

'I'm an actor,' he says.

'Yeah,' I say. 'It's strange how that part gets forgotten.' After a while I say, 'Will you promise me one thing?'

'What?'

'You won't do *Science Fiction II*.'

He laughs. 'I definitely won't do that.'

'And while we're at it—'

'At what?'

'The truth. What about you and Grace?'

'What about us?'

'The photo in the paper this morning.'

'Oh, we did a deal with that guy Rico. We gave him a shot. Grace thought it was great joke.' A thought occurs to him. 'In fact, I followed the advice you gave me – in the closet in Jermyn Street, remember? It's over with me and Grace, you know.'

I don't say anything.

'Look at that,' he says.

I turn to look where he's pointing and at first I don't see anything and then, suddenly, it jumps out at me as if it has just that moment appeared: a daytime moon, full but faint, becoming brighter and more defined as I look at it. A silvery ethereal presence; one moment the moon, the next a big old planet hanging in the sky.

I scramble up the edge of our grassy hollow, under the fallen tree and out on to the rampart to get the full view. If I turn my head the other way I can see the sun too, low now, clearly outlined, a creamy egg yolk in the grey haze of the sky.

'Incredible,' Louis says, joining me and swinging around full circle.

'I think this place has a special power, a kind of magic. The earth's power is very close to the surface here. There are ley lines. And Stonehenge not that far. They say King Arthur camped here, on this hill. Another Camelot.'

'No shit? How do you know so much?'

'I read the sign at the bottom of the path.'

'I never would have thought little England could be so . . .' He trails off.

'Where's your favourite place?' I say.

'The beach, I think, at Anasett Point. Have you ever seen snow on the beach? It's incredible. And in the summer, the stars at night. The earth's power is close there too.'

We stand side by side for a moment contemplating this other place.

'Where is Anasett Point?' I say.

'Small-small town – east coast. I've got a house there, on the ocean. No one knows about it. It's my hideaway. My dog lives there. He's called Boris Karloff.'

'Boris for short?'

'No. The whole thing. Boris Karloff. My dad named him. He had a thing about Boris Karloff, the actor. He thought it was a great name. And, I'm Mr Karloff sometimes. I use it as my cover name to check into hotels and so forth. That's a state secret by the way. Very few people know that.'

'What kind of dog is Boris Karloff?'

'He's just a mongrel – dirty white with brown heart-shaped patches.'

'Do you love him?'

'Of course. Sometimes I think people aren't much good and I prefer dogs.'

'It makes sense.'

'How do you mean?'

'Well, think about it, he doesn't know you're famous.'

Louis grins. 'I'd like you to meet Boris Karloff,' he says.

I don't know what to say to this. I'd like to meet him too. Then I find myself saying, 'Me?' as if checking Louis has got the right person.

'Why not you?' He reaches out and takes my hand and swings it lightly, casually. We both stare intently out at the horizon and the moon above. 'Why anyone? It happens.'

We're both still looking at that moon. When we turn away it will be imprinted on our retinas and then we'll be able to see it in our own eyes. And I know with absolute certainty that if I turn my head towards him now he will kiss me.

15

'Put your shades on,' Louis says, bent almost double to look out of one of the plane's minuscule windows across the dark airport Tarmac.

'Shades?'

In answer he slaps a big black pair of Ray-Bans across his face.

'Excuse me,' I say. 'It's February. It's England. It's er . . . night-time. I don't have sunglasses with me.'

But he's not looking at me or listening to me, even. The pilot lends me his.

'Walk behind me,' Louis barks. I fall out of the plane, tripping on the steps. It's dark, the sunglasses obscure what light there is and immediately fog up in the drizzle. 'Walk ten paces behind me,' Louis barks again.

Charming.

But as we approach the terminal building, I see the hounds straining at their leashes, worrying at the mesh airport fencing. They set up a hue and cry as Louis comes past. 'Louis! Louis! Louis! Over here, Louis! Just one!' When they see they're not getting what they want, they change course, the entire pack of them. With much jostling and collapsing of ladders and umbrellas, they set off towards the terminal building at a jolting, equipment-encumbered run.

I take my sunglasses off. This is ridiculous.

By the time I get into the tiny airport building I've lost Louis, but I can see television vans through the plate-glass doors, their roof-top satellite dishes angled to the stars. The rabid mob is being held back by one frail, elderly security guard. I look round crazily and suddenly Rico is in front of me.

'Stevie!' he says.

'What's happening? Has something terrible happened?' My heart is pounding wildly, the whole thing is scaring me. I'm imagining – I don't know what, some terrible event. It's so terrible I can't even imagine it. Something has changed the world while we were away, while we weren't looking. We should have been looking. I feel the ground slipping away from under my feet.

I grab hold of Rico. 'Tell me what's happened!' I rasp.

'It's been reported that Grace Farlow is pregnant.'

I take this in. I must have gone white because Rico says, 'What's going on with you and Louis anyway?'

White with rage.

'For fuck's sake,' I say, and I shove him hard. His camera bangs against his chest. 'I thought something terrible had happened!' I shout, the release of tension making me yell.

Instinctively Rico raises the camera, his finger on the trigger.

'Don't take my fucking picture,' I say. 'I'm with you. I'm the fucking press.'

'Well, you've got yourself a story now,' he says.

'Some fucking story,' I say, and carried on a wave of

rage I storm out of the plate-glass exit doors to where the press pack is baying. 'You fools!' I cry, but before I can fully get their attention and before I can go on, Mike is beside me, yelling, 'This way!' and grabbing my arm.

'*Miss! Miss! Miss!*' they scream. 'Who are you? Miss! Over here!'

'For Christ's sake,' I scream back. 'I'm a journalist!'

There are groans from the pack, they practically hiss at me. I want to straddle the barrier, to get to their side, to be with them. But Mike has my arm in an iron grip and is dragging me towards the waiting car.

When we get to the car it's just me and Mike in the back seat.

'Where's Louis?'

Mike nods to the road ahead. Travelling in front of us is a black limo. I can just make out two heads, Louis and Katrina no doubt, in urgent confab in the back seat. On the streets everything is dark and wet but, again, the car gives the feeling of it all being nothing to do with us.

We travel down the Commercial Road, people struggling home from the tube with bags of shopping, guys hanging out in baggy jeans yelling into mobile phones, grim parades of newsagents and kebab shops.

'How did you get Louis through?'

'We got him through – but we lost you. You were meant to be behind.'

'Yeah, I know. Ten paces. Listen,' I say, 'just drop me at the next tube station, okay?'

Mike fiddles with something at his waist and I realise he's wearing a radio-mike.

Jesus.

'Stevie wants to be dropped at the subway,' he says into it. A reply comes back. 'Louis wants to see you at home,' Mike says to me. And that appears to be the end of it.

'Over and out,' I say.

'I'm sorry?'

'Aren't you going to say "over and out"?'

He looks confused.

'Never mind,' I say. 'Look – just pull over,' this to the driver, 'I'm getting out.'

'You can't,' Mike says.

'Are you kidnapping me?'

'Louis wants to talk to you. It's important.'

'If you don't pull over now,' I say, pulling out my mobile and thinking the battery is probably flat but it's a good prop, 'I'll call the police.'

The driver ignores me.

Mike sighs, says, 'Be cool. Listen, Grace's pregnancy was leaked. By a studio she's just pulled out of a deal with. Sources close to Grace say that Louis is the father—'

'Do you think,' I say interrupting, 'that I give a flying fuck? Do you think,' and I gesture towards the window and the people out there on the Commercial Road, 'that they do? Does it matter to the world that Grace Farlow is pregnant? Really? One more single mum?'

My phone, which I've just turned on, must have some juice in it because it suddenly rings.

'Hello,' I say.

'My God,' says The Dick, 'where are you?'

'Louis seems to have me under some kind of house arrest,' I say, 'but I intend to escape at the first possible opportunity.'

'You're in there!'

'In where?'

'With them! What are they saying? Louis has the news, yes?'

'I believe so. He's in the car in front.'

'Where did Louis go today? Were you with him?'

I stay silent.

'Stevie?' Dick says.

'You're breaking up,' I say, even though he isn't.

'Fuck!' he yells. 'Stay with this, Stevie! This is your story – don't you dare leave! Stevie? Can you hear me?'

'Hey!' I yell back. 'Why is it a story that some actress is pregnant? That's not a story. That's just our sick, sick world.'

'Fuck!' he yells again, and I can hear him throwing things around and cursing to himself in the background. Then there's a short silence. Then, 'Stevie, can you hear me?' he says. His tone is different.

'Just,' I lie.

'*That*'s your story,' he says. 'Tell it the way you want to tell it. Tell us how mad it is. Write the story you want to write. But don't give up on us, babe. We need you. This is your moment. You're at the epicentre!'

'And you're breaking up,' I say.

I press the little red button and think for a minute.

He's got a point.

But I'm going home.

*   *   *

I jog down the steps into the underground station. Leaves and general debris swash about on the bleak concrete, and when I turn the corner, a powerful howling wind, channelled straight from Siberia's northern wastes, catches me and blows my scarf and jacket out horizontally behind me. I lean into it battling my way forward until I reach the next corner where the wind drops, as if the tap has been turned off, and my clothes rearrange themselves into their normal positions.

On the escalator I hear the familiar noise of a train at the platform – and I'm about to miss it. I run down the last few steps and, sure enough, I'm a moment too late. The train wipes across my vision, revealing a vast movie poster on the other side of the tracks, Louis staring out at me, his face so big I could wear his left nostril as a hat.

I stand transfixed for a moment. The impact is as powerful as if he'd suddenly arrived beside me. I look around to see if anyone else has noticed. The platform is empty. Louis and I have the place to ourselves.

'Hey,' I say.

He doesn't reply.

'Thank you for a very nice day.'

No response. He just keeps looking out at me and not exactly smiling but almost smiling, a perfectly judged expression in a perfectly judged face.

'Bye-bye,' I say.

I walk away along the platform but before long there's another identical poster. The eyes are looking into mine just as they were before. I experiment a little – it turns out that wherever I stand the eyes look into mine. That's clever, I think. But really I want to scream.

Another passenger arrives and comes to stand close by. I feel a mad urge to tell him that not very long ago I was sitting up on hill with Louis, that we built a fire. I don't suppose he'd believe me. I don't suppose he'd care.

I look up at the information board – another six minutes until the next train. Six minutes. I feel I might easily die before the six minutes is up. Six minutes is an eternity. I need to get . . .

Home. The house is empty. I can tell the minute I come through the door. The walls breathe aloneness at me. The place seems cold, like it's rearranged itself while I'm gone and become somebody else's house – or I'm seeing it through somebody else's eyes. I notice the layer of dust on top of the skirting-boards.

I check Esther's room just to be sure I'm alone. The bed is rumpled and unmade, which is unlike her, and she's not there. I go into my room and pick up a blow-up plastic beach ball and start flinging it wildly around the room shouting, 'Fuck!' at the top of my voice. The beach ball doesn't do much damage, being so light, just knocks the lampshade skew-whiff. I keep going with the ball, picking it up and throwing it, yelling until my throat is sore, 'Fuck! Fuck! Fuck!' My blood is thrumming through my veins, burning and raw. I feel slightly nauseous.

When I pause for breath, I hear a mousy tap-tap-tap at the door. I fling it open: Esther in pink dressing-gown.

'So that's what the beach ball is for,' she says, seeing it in my hands. 'I've often wondered.'

'You're meant to be out,' I say.

'I'm *meant* to be resting in bed.'

'You know what I mean.'

'I was in the bath. Is this what they taught you at that anger workshop?'

I once did an anger workshop in order to write a piece about it. 'Kind of,' I say.

'What's up?' she says. 'Louis trouble?'

'You could say. I'm calling the whole thing off.'

'What?'

'You heard me, the whole thing – the interview, the article, the première, everything.'

'Oh dear.'

'I wouldn't write about him if he was the last man alive. Wild horses couldn't drag one inky little word out of my pen!'

'Is this about Grace? I heard it on the news, that she's pregnant.'

'You heard it on the news? It's not *news*!' I yell.

'Keep your hat on,' she says, cool. 'It was Radio One.' But her eyes flash and I decide I'd better not shout again. I drop the beach ball and sink down to sit with hunched shoulders on the edge of my bed, a little ashamed.

'Okay,' I say. 'Well, for the record, this isn't about Grace. I mean it's only about Grace in the sense that I think it's wrong that an actress getting pregnant gets so much attention when there's so much real stuff going on in the world. I shouldn't be doing this Louis interview.

That's all. I'm sorry about the money. I'll get a cleaning job or something.'

Esther looks at me quizzically, then sits down on my red bean-bag. 'So,' she says, 'what happened today?'

'We went on a trip. It was nice.' I pick up the beach ball and start bouncing it against the floor.

'Stevie!' Esther says.

'Okay!' I chuck her the ball – hard. She catches it – neatly, of course. 'You were right. I've made a fool of myself.' I go to speak again, to catch the wave of confession, but it doesn't come. My mouth closes.

Esther just waits.

'I like him,' I say finally, with a groan, and I roll back on to the bed and thrash about a bit with the embarrassment of it all.

'And?'

'I don't know,' I moan. 'I'm confused. I mean, at one level it's not really about Grace – if he's with Grace he's with Grace. They're having a baby. Fair enough. It's the idea that he was lying to me. It was like a thing between us that he was telling me the truth and I believed him, I really did. But then again, he told me he lies a lot – to the press, I think he meant. And maybe I was the press. But I thought I wasn't, even though I am. And maybe it isn't his baby. It's possible, it isn't. But surely Grace would make sure there was no confusion if that was the case?'

'Oh, I don't know about that. It might suit her to create confusion.'

'At Louis's expense?'

'Maybe.' Esther shrugs.

'You know what?' I say. 'It doesn't matter – it doesn't matter because the whole thing is completely fucking hopeless from the start. Of course it is.'

'What whole thing?'

'Me and Louis. I can't believe I'm even thinking it. I refuse to spend my life walking ten paces behind. I absolutely refuse.'

'So don't.'

'But I've got that stupid fucking feeling – that idiotic delusion . . .' I wail. 'We should never have done it!'

'A snog?' she cries, agog.

'A snog. Exactly. My reaction is hormonal. That's all it is – hormonal. But horribly convincing.' I jump up and shake myself like I could shake it off. 'It's only oxytocin. It makes you want to *bond*. They did an experiment – they injected female prairie voles with oxytocin and, you know what? They bonded willy-nilly – they bonded *all over the place*.'

'How ghastly!' Esther cries, jumping up too and looking around fearfully, as if a man in a white coat might be rushing towards her at any moment bearing a syringe full of bonding juice.

'Come on,' I say, 'let's go downstairs and have a nice cup of Britain's answer to everything.'

Down in the kitchen Jay is sitting at the table. He's just come in from his weekly poker game – early, so he must have lost – smelling of whisky.

Esther begins floating around the gas cooker, posing something of a fire hazard in her pink polyester, and frying bacon. She's humming to herself.

'Well, this is all very domestic,' I say. 'Happy families. Where's Phil?'

'Where do you think?'

'I'll take him a cup of tea,' I say.

Phil's room is as dark as ever. The only light reflects bluely upon his intent features one to one with the computer screen. 'Am I interrupting something intimate?' I say.

'No, no,' Phil says reluctantly. 'Come in.'

Phil reminds me of a rat, but in a good way. He's got a small, neat body and pointy, inquisitive features. He's a scavenger by nature – most of his equipment comes from London's skips – and he's often up at night.

Phil spends much of his life in a virtual world called i-City. In i-City the participants can see each other because they are on webcams. You can create your own 'room', hang out in other people's rooms or do it one on one; i-City dwellers come from all over the world and some of them inhabit the place full time. If absent, it's only because they are, as the sign says, 'Sleeping!'

In i-City, Phil has an i-relationship with an i-girlfriend called Lux. They are i-committed to each other. Sometimes they have i-sex. We're hoping for i-babies soon.

It's one way of doing it.

'How's Lux?' I say, giving Phil his cup of tea.

'She's good.'

I check the screen. Lux is there, her long dark hair swinging on either side of her face. Lux lives in Denmark. She waves at me cheerily.

'Maybe I need an i-boyfriend,' I say. 'Maybe that's the answer.'

'Don't take the piss.'

'I'm not. I'm serious. Doesn't Lux have a friend? Someone for me?'

'I'll ask her.' He types a message on the keyboard and Lux grins and nods in the strange halting motion of pictures squeezed down a telephone line and soon there comes a small italic text reply: *What about Jay?*

'What about Jay?' I say.

'I think she thinks he's your boyfriend,' Phil says, typing away – presumably to inform her otherwise.

'She's met Jay?' I say.

'Jay visits i-City sometimes.'

'It's like the oracle,' I say, looking into Lux's dark eyes. 'You ask it things and you get replies. Ask her if she thinks Jay and I should get back together.' Which scenario is putting up its usual wallpaper in the back of my mind. It always does when things go wrong elsewhere.

Phil types in the question.

Jay needs AA, comes the succinct reply.

'What?' I say.

'She thinks Jay's an alcoholic,' Phil says.

'Come again?' I say.

'You can't tell me you haven't noticed.' He keeps his eyes down. This is territory we have never specifically broached before.

'Lux hasn't even met Jay!' I say, indignant. 'How much does she know about him? How much does she know about us?'

'She knows you found Jay on the doorstep. She knows a lot about this sort of stuff.'

'But, I mean, she's *Danish*!'

'So what?'

'Well, it's such an orderly civilised country where they actually learn foreign languages and so forth – how can she possibly understand?'

'Shut up,' says Phil, flushing up with i-loyalty.

'They *are* very clean living . . .' I mutter, chastised.

The computer gives a little ping. Another message from Lux. It says: *Jay needs help.*

'There you go,' Phil says. 'The oracle has spoken.'

'You're just smitten,' I say dismissively.

'Go away if you're going to be like that,' says Phil, and he means it. He starts typing rapidly.

'Phil,' I say, a small cold breeze of fear having sprung up somewhere around my heart, 'let me speak to her.' Phil sighs and scoots back in his chair to give me space. I bend over the keyboard.

Jay hasn't got much going on, I type. *Jay has always liked a drink. How bad can that be?*

How bad does it have to be, comes the reply, *before you do something about it?*

16

The bathroom.

I think it's my favourite place in the whole house.

This bathroom, though, was never meant to be a bathroom. It became one when a greedy landlord turned family home into boarding-house and made of every cat-swingable room a cash cow.

The room is tiny. When you open the door you hit the bath, which runs along the opposite wall and across the bottom of the window. Once in the bath you can use your toe, if you have the knack, to hook up the beaded scarf that acts as a curtain and, while lying back to preserve modesty, do some nude trainspotting. Either that or adjust your gaze a few millimetres skywards to enjoy the view of west London high-rises.

I have spent many hours in this room, in this bath. I like the feel of the thick walls close upon me and the steamy heat, the contrast of cosiness and the large flimsy window with its desolate view. I like the threadbare plum-coloured cord carpet on the floor, the old loo with the raised cistern and elaborate wrought-iron arm, the dressing-gown belt that dangles from it, serving as a flush cord. I like the murmuring grumbles and sighs from the boiler above the sink as it flares and subsides. I like the sight of my towel carefully folded on the radiator, slightly stiff from the wash, ready to encase me when I get out of the bath, like warm pitta-bread.

This room. The womb?

Yes, I think so.

And now for the complete experience: I reach out and carefully dry my hands on a towel – another towel – that I have dropped beside the bath. Then, gingerly, because I don't want to drip on it, I raise the latest edition of the *National Geographic* and start to read.

'Stevie?'

Jesus Christ.

The room is so small and echoey and full of steam and the door so close to the bath and so loose on its hinges that I can hear his voice as clearly as if he were sitting next to me.

'Stevie, I need to talk to you. Would you open the door?'

'I'm in the bath!' I call out cheerily.

Go away.

'Can I come in and talk to you? It's important.'

'I just need . . .' I cover my breasts with a bubble-bath bra '. . . okay, come in.'

Jay lets himself in very quickly knowing it's important not to admit too much cold air. Once in, he sinks to a sitting position on the floor, his back to the radiator. He doesn't look well. His skin, never rosy at the best of times, is as grey as my flannel. He keeps his eyes averted, fastened to the carpet, and looks like he doesn't know where to begin. It occurs to me, with some relief, that he's going to broach the drinking thing himself and then I won't have to.

'How's DJ land?' I say.

'Haven't had a gig for months.'

'How's the biodegradable-coffin thing?'

He doesn't answer.

'Are you all right, Jay?' I say, after a while.

He plucks at some mud on the hem of his cords. 'You know Esther's baby?' he says, looking like he might faint. 'I think it's mine.' Having made this admission, he keels over sideways, felled by his words, sliding down the radiator into a foetal curl on the floor.

I slip on to my side, my skin making a rubbery sound against the bath enamel. My heart is pounding. I've got goosebumps even though I'm far from cold.

'Jay?' I say.

He opens his eyes. He's okay.

'Could it really be yours?'

Jay shuts his eyes again, squeezing them tight, and nods a painful affirmative. My mind teeters to the brink of all that this implies – then scuttles queasily away.

'How do you know?' I say.

'I suspected. I read her diary.'

'Why isn't she saying?'

He shakes his head painfully. He doesn't know.

'Is she trying to let you off the hook?'

He squeezes out an uncertain shrug.

'Or does she want to leave you out?'

On the floor, Jay puts his head in his hands and gives a little moan.

I take the opportunity to jump out of the bath and grab my scratchy towel. 'Get up,' I say to Jay.

'I can't.'

'You have to.'

'I'm just—' he whimpers. He can't get the word out.

'Scared?' I say.

'*Esther!*' I burst into her room like a cyclone. Still in my towel.

'What?' She's lying in bed.

'You *had sex* with Jay!'

Esther is up and out of the bed in a second. 'Who the fuck do you think you are?' she thunders. When Esther is frightening, she's very frightening. She holds herself like a piece of steel, thrusting forward slightly, fists clenched. 'Barging in here like that! You can't have every fucking man on the planet, you know.'

'Why can't I?' I yell back. 'You always said you didn't want them! And now you're fucking Jay behind my fucking back!'

'Why shouldn't I?'

'He's *mine*!'

'*What?*'

'You heard me.'

Actually, I can't quite believe I heard myself. As my words sink in, I back out of Esther's room confusedly and hurry to my own, slamming the door behind me.

I stand there, my whole body ringing with the injustice of it all. I stand there for a long time, stock still, a few feet from my door. Just standing there and standing there, the whole 'thing' of it rushing through my blood, round and round, never stopping long enough in my brain for useful thought. After a while, there's a knock on the door.

Esther.

'You should have told me,' I say. 'That's all.'

'I'm sorry,' she says.

'You should have told Jay.'

'I'm sorry,' she says again. 'I was scared of what it would do to us.'

'You and Jay?'

'Yes – and all of us.'

There's a long silence. We both study the floor. Which needs hoovering.

'He's not mine,' I say.

We simultaneously look up and give each other the tiniest dot-dot morse-code smile.

More silence. More studying of floor. It still needs hoovering.

'Have you two been – er – fucking – a lot?' I manage after a while.

'Kind of every now and then, sort of by mistake, late at night.'

'When he comes to watch TV on your bed?'

'Exactly.'

I nod. And for some – to me completely inexplicable – reason, I start to cry.

'I don't know why I'm crying,' I say, the minute I can form coherent words again. 'It's not Jay.'

'I know,' Esther says.

At this point my phone starts to ring. Esther looks at my jacket, which is lying on the floor by her feet. The phone is in the pocket and its ring is getting louder and louder, more and more insistent.

'You see?' she says. 'It's him.'

'Don't you dare answer it,' I say, reading her mind.

In a trice, Esther grabs the jacket pulls the phone out and does just that. She says hello and then, almost imperceptibly, she blushes. I've never seen Esther blush before.

Shit.

Pulling my towel tight around me and leaking one small sob on the way, I make a dash for the loo and lock myself in. I put the seat down and sit down to cry until the crying has gone, which doesn't take very long. Then I sit for a while and think how familiar all this feels.

When Dad travelled the whole time, before he married Irena and when I was very small, he would use a return to the country as an excuse to call in at Gran's, laden with exotic presents. He came straight from the airport, smelling of the plane and his unthinkably glamorous adventures – bringing me dolls in national dress encased in circular tubes of clear plastic, exquisite bottles of real grown-up perfume and on one occasion, joy of joys, an entire miniature zoo.

It was all quite overwhelming. Once, when he wore a strange and smelly Afghan coat, I took fright. I ran for the loo and bolted the door then couldn't open it again. Gran had to call the Fire Brigade. I remember them shouting for me to stand back and then an axe came through the door and, behind it, huge men with kindly faces and yellow boots.

Remembering, I start to wonder if I'm acting out some bizarre unconscious desire to be rescued by men in yellow boots and the thought gets me up quickly enough. I open the door, quiet as I can, and sneak out.

Esther is still in my bedroom wandering around fingering bits and pieces of my stuff and *she's still on the phone*.

'Esther!' I hiss.

She turns round slowly but shows no sign of guilt or remorse. She also shows no sign of hanging up. 'Yes,' she says into the phone, 'I know what you mean. But I guess eventually you can do DNA testing. No?'

She listens.

She listens some more.

Christ alive.

'Of course, of course,' she croons into the phone, while waving a shushing hand in my direction to indicate that she has it all under control. 'Stevie understands,' she says. 'She absolutely understands.' And then, 'Oh, that's very kind of you. When is it? Tomorrow night? I don't think I should come in my condition, but Stevie will be there. I happen to know she's got something to give you.' Short pause. 'Well, I don't want to spoil the surprise. But – think about it – what's tomorrow?'

She laughs. They say their goodbyes. Finally she hangs up and, with some caution, looks over to meet my eye.

I frown at her suspiciously. 'What am I going to give him? What *is* tomorrow?' I say.

17

Valentine's Day dawns bright and sunny. I draw the curtains and look out, blinking, into the light.

'Valentine's Day dawns bright and sunny,' says the voice in my head – again. I guess it's going to be that kind of day, the kind of day that needs a voice-over.

A pair of cheery daffodils are nodding at me from a window-box across the street.

A happy couple.

It seems the world is one big paternity suit – so *that*'s why they invented marriage: to avoid all this. It seems people must know who belongs to whom: Grace and Louis, Esther and the baby, Jay and the baby. But can people really belong to other people? And, if they can, why does no one belong to me?

I pull down the invitation to Louis's film première from where I've pinned it to the wall and make sure I get out of the house without seeing anyone.

I go straight to Louis's house and the mad fan is there. Thank goodness. In her usual place, under the camellia so big it overflows the front garden wall. I give her the ticket to the première.

When she realises what it is, she says, 'God sent you.'

'Did he?' I say. I don't want to stay to talk, I don't

want to risk Louis seeing me, I turn to go, but the mad fan grabs my arm.

'He spoke to me once, you know,' she says.

'He did? God or Louis?' Perhaps it comes to the same thing.

'When he first came to London – a few years ago. I told him they could be together again – him and his mum. He said he'd like that. We had a conversation.'

'And he's never talked to you again?'

She shrugs. But she doesn't seem to care today, her chin is up, her eyes are alert. 'It doesn't matter any more,' she says.

'Perhaps it's time to give up,' I say hopefully. 'The première could be your swan song . . .'

'Yes!' she says, and claps her hands, her eyes shining, like an alarming little girl. 'My swan song!'

Crazy.

'I'll be off, then,' I say.

'Good luck!' she calls, to my departing back.

'You too!' I call back.

Fight 4 Fair Flowers are demonstrating all over London today, at the flower market in Nine Elms and outside one or two particularly culpable supermarkets and florists in the centre of town. I spend most of the day going from place to place. I'm writing a piece about the day's events, interviewing the punters, finding out what they think of our protest and the general commercial junket that is a modern Valentine's Day.

Come the afternoon, Knightsbridge is my last stop. There's a small posse of flower fighters on the pavement outside the florist in question. I feel obliged to hold a placard to swell the numbers. It says: BLOOMING AWFUL! It's been a long day but the spirit is strong.

Before long, a young man comes out of the florist with a large bouquet. Perfect fodder. I call over to him. 'Excuse me!'

He gives me and my placard one terrified look, says, 'I'm just the nanny!' and scampers off.

We chant again. Almost immediately a plump woman in court shoes accosts me. 'What's wrong with you?' she demands. She comes up close, peering into my face.

'With me?' I say.

'Yes,' she says. 'You! What's wrong with *you*? Trying to spoil everyone's fun. What's your problem?'

'Well,' I say, 'if "fun" is to be had at the expense of lives in the third world—'

'You PC people – you just want to ruin everything. Valentine's Day is about love!'

'Fuck off!' says someone behind me.

'But we *love* the flower workers in Colombia,' I say.

She gives me a scathing look. She's in my personal space and it's bugging me. 'You don't know anything about love,' she says. And then, with a click-click-click of her court shoes, she's gone.

'Bitch!' someone shouts after her.

I feel violated; a little shell-shocked. Normally this sort of thing wouldn't get to me, but today my skin is very thin. The gang make sympathetic noises and I can feel tears pricking the back of my eyes – oh, God. Not again. Then someone's tapping on my shoulder. I swing round, terrified the woman is back. It's Phil.

'Thank fuck I found you,' he says. 'I've been round everywhere. Your phone's off.'

'I know,' I say stupidly.

'It's Jay,' he says. 'You'd better come.'

At the hospital, Jay is away being treated by the doctors. Esther is in the waiting area.

'Is he going to be all right?' I say.

'They don't know,' she says. 'It wasn't suicide, though. I'm sure it wasn't suicide. He made a mistake.'

'Okay,' I say, 'start at the beginning.' And Phil and I sit down one on either side of her and put our arms around her.

She tells the story. Apparently, after our talk in the bathroom, Jay hadn't gone to bed as I'd thought, but had gone out again. He'd told Phil he couldn't sleep. He stayed out all night and didn't come back until lunch-time. Phil saw him again at that point. He'd told Phil he still couldn't sleep. Someone had given him a dodgy pill and it was keeping him wired. At tea-time, he took half a bottle of temazepam. Esther found him collapsed under the kitchen table.

'At tea-time?' I say, struck by the heartbreaking jux-taposition of 'tea-time' and temazepam and the thought that Jay should have been eating toast rather than little white pills.

I look at Esther. 'Did you talk to him?' I say.

'I was going to. Last night. But then he wasn't there. I was going to talk to him today.'

A nurse comes in and tells us Jay is going to be all right. She takes us down the corridor so that we can see him. Phil and I let Esther go in while we stay outside. There's a big glass panel in the wall and someone has forgotten to draw the curtain so we can see Jay's legs and the occasional Esther body part as she moves about.

'Shit,' Phil says. 'For a moment there I thought he was off to see the big DJ in the sky.'

I make sure Phil is in the loop about Jay being the father and we watch them through the glass and wonder what they're saying. As the shock recedes and relief starts to crawl along my veins, I find myself entering a gentle state of euphoria. I study Jay's white bony legs sticking out from the end of his gown and think how much I love him – in the *agape* way, of course. And Esther. I trust her completely. I know she won't make Jay do anything he doesn't want to do. I know they can work things out just fine. I can suddenly picture them with the baby – Esther handing it to Jay, Jay folding it into his arms – and I feel an unexpected shiver of joy. *Everything is going to be all right*. And then it comes to me in a flash that Jay is scared of the very thing that's going to make him the happiest of all.

I feel like telling the woman in the court shoes that I do know something about love. I feel like showing her.

I look at my watch.

Then I stick my head into Jay's room. 'Gotta go,' I say.

Esther looks at her watch too. 'You'd better,' she says.

'You're a wise woman,' I say.

I'm half-way to Leicester Square before I remember I gave my ticket to the mad fan. I call Dick but he's left the office. I speak to his assistant and she says if I've been sent a ticket my name should be on the door and I should be all right. But, if I'm honest, I'm not at all sure I RSVPd. I get her to promise she'll call and make sure my name *is* on the door, but she sounds a bit dubious about her chances at this late hour. I don't have a number for Mike or Katrina, but I scroll back through calls received and ring the number that Louis rang me from last night. An anonymous message service picks up. I can't think of an appropriate message. I hang up.

I get off the bus in the Charing Cross road and make my way to the security barriers with a pounding heart. I'm not dressed right for a start. Sure enough, my name isn't on the list. Security is tight. It's a no-hoper. I hang around for a bit, thinking maybe Dick will turn up, but then the bouncers ask me to move on.

So now I'm standing with the fans behind the crush barrier because my only hope is that Louis will see me. And that's a long shot. The crowd is ten to fifteen teenage girls deep and there are at least five between me and the barrier and this is the closest I can get. I have, however, managed to get into a position where I'm standing on the edge of a kerb, which means I'm a couple of inches higher than the people in front of me. I don't actually need to get into the première after all – I only need to do the dreaded Valentine thing.

I have a daffodil in my hand. It is now a rather wilted and battered daffodil, but it's still a daffodil. I picked it up in the park on the way.

The crash barriers carve out a wide arc across the neck of the cinema and the sleek stretch limos are pulling up twenty or so yards away. The only way Louis will see me is if he comes over to greet his fans in person. But surely he will. They've been waiting so long. I imagine myself shouting his name and him looking over in recognition.

I'm just playing out the scene in my head when the screaming starts. It has a strange effect on me, the screaming. It makes my blood rush. I use this new energy to push my way recklessly to the front. The screaming rising into the dark night like a thousand starlings taking flight above Leicester Square. At first the scream frequency is constant, but then it starts to rise and fall in correlation to Louis's movements: when he opens the car door, when he waves for the first time. When he smiles.

'Louis! Louis! Louis!' they shout, and I remember I thought I would be the one shouting his name and I laugh at myself hysterically. He hesitates by the car for a moment, not wanting to come over. He's wearing a slim cut silver grey suit and his jacket buttons are done up. I haven't seen him looking so formal before and somehow his slightness is accentuated. He has that precious look about him again, that aura of goldenness and irreplaceability – like the priceless artefact that gets the special glass box right in the middle of the museum. Something emanates from him. He shines in some way. I don't know how.

Come this way, I will him – along with the rest of the crowd, no doubt – come this way. There's a Japanese girl beside me who is cutting herself in half against the barriers and screaming so harshly I think she might be sick. She flings herself wildly towards him. And I am half with the crowd and half observing all of this with a kind of elated curiosity. I notice the Japanese girl is wearing knee-high white socks.

Louis visibly capitulates and strides over towards us. I fill up with terror, glance down at my daffodil – this is my moment. But when Louis gets nearer I realise he isn't going to notice me. He's thinking of other things. He begins to sign autographs. He's quick at it, just a twisted scribble on each page. He moves up the line until he is only a couple of people away from me. I can't attract his attention by calling out. There's no question of him hearing me. I'm trying to think what to do . . .

I pull out my reporter's notebook and write the words MR KARLOFF in big letters. Then I hold it up like a chauffeur at the airport.

I see the white of the notebook catch Louis's eye. I see his eye passing over it, the words not registering at first, then registering. He turns back, looks straight at me.

'I lost my ticket,' I say, mouthing the words exaggeratedly, acting it out, holding up empty hands etc., as I know he can't hear me. He nods, understanding. He swings round and makes a gesture towards the cinema entrance and a suited man in radio-mike runs forward.

Louis has a word in the man's ear and indicates me. He uses the man's presence as an excuse to turn away from us – the hungry crowd – flinging an arm up in respectful salute as he goes. An official approaches to give me a VIP pass and to negotiate my passage from one side of the barriers to the other. The crowd jeers derisively at the spectacle of my promotion. Feeling tatty and underdressed I cross the floodlit arena to the hallowed ground.

A wide flight of red-carpeted steps leads up to the foyer. Louis is ahead of me and there is a bank of television cameras waiting for him, each like Cyclops with one blinding eye of light. Louis must stop and make his way down the line. I wait and watch his back. His hands knead each other awkwardly behind his jacket tails. He wants to smoke, I should think. He takes sideways steps positioning himself for each crew, briefly answering one question, moving on.

I loop round and get ahead of him so that when he's finished I'll be in the right place. The daffodil is safely in my jacket pocket. I can't imagine getting it out, but perhaps I'll be able to do it when the time comes. I practise putting my hand in to grab the stalk and while I'm doing that I see the mad fan. She's standing waiting for Louis just as I am.

I'm just debating the wisdom of having given her my ticket, when I see Louis coming towards me. He pauses, flanked on all sides. We have an audience.

'I've been trying to call you,' he says.

'I brought you something,' I say.

His eyes come alive – remembering what Esther said. He gives me a quick smile. Is it encouragement? I'm not sure. My hand goes for the daffodil pocket and, as it does, I turn my head to the right. I'm not sure why. For ease of access to the breast pocket, perhaps, to facilitate the movement of the arm, as a decoy, as a gesture of defiance – like I said, I'm not sure why I do it, but when I do it I see the mad fan, although that's

not what registers first: what registers first is a narrow
flash of reflected light, like the sun on the railway lines
behind our house, glinting steel. The mad fan has a knife
in her hand.

She blunders forward and before I can even move she
has thrust the thing towards Louis's stomach. The next
second, Mike is there, knocking me sideways gathering
the mad fan into a backwards embrace. Then the two
of them are falling back against me – I'm terrified of
the weight of Mike – but the mad fan must have slashed
up at his face with the knife because Mike cries out and
throws up his arms instinctively while at the same time
flailing backwards, with his gun in one hand. Both hand
and gun hit me in the chest. I grab Mike's arm trying to
stabilise him as he goes down, but he's far too heavy for
me to hold. His arm slithers through mine leaving me
with the gun, which I keep hold of thinking, perhaps,
that it might go off if dropped, although 'thinking' isn't
really the word – there's no time to think. Only seconds
have passed since I first saw the mad fan's knife. Louis
steps forward to help Mike and the mad fan, free of
him now, makes that strange charging movement that
reminds me of a bull, and the men around Louis are
taken by surprise – they thought Mike had her – but
the mad fan has Louis all to herself and she takes him
by one shoulder as if to steady him to receive the knife,
and the men are yelling, 'No! No!' but it seems she has
all the power and they are frozen on the knife edge of
his death – so I do the only thing I can do. I raise the
gun and shoot.

I had no idea how much noise a gun going off can

make in a confined space. The noise hits me so hard that for a moment I think perhaps I've shot myself. After the brutal explosion of noise there is a momentary profound silence while all of life, having been thrown up in the air, quietly rearranges itself.

Then the mad fan falls sideways and Louis falls backwards and the mad fan hits the ground and the men are on her and take the knife from her and I have no idea where my bullet has gone. After this brief spate of movement everything becomes still for another moment. We are a *tableau vivant*, a living, breathing picture, life suspended, caught, as in a painting, where there's a sense of people breathing even though they do not move, until someone takes us off the pause button and we are running again.

People start to scream, different sorts of screams from the screams before. One of the suited men takes the gun from my hand. I am in shock so I cannot really be sure what is happening. Time is strangely elongated. There are people everywhere. I can't see whether Louis is up again. It is quite some time before I am informed that he is not.

No.

Louis is down.

18

What's happening? What's happening? What's happening? The words echo around – possibly in my head, possibly I'm saying them too. No one is taking any notice of me. There is a crowd three or four people deep around Louis. I have no hope of getting to him.

And then someone takes my hand. A warm firm grip, taking my hand like my hand was taken when I was a child. The owner of this hand is Dick.

I don't think I've ever been glad to see Dick before.

'Dick!' I say. 'What's happening?'

'Stevie, my love,' he says, 'I knew you were going to come good. I just knew it. That's why I've been nursing you all this time – like a sore throat that one day grows up to become a fully fledged case of bronchitis.'

What's happening?

'Did she stab him? Did you see? Is he okay?'

'I saw the whole thing. Follow me.' He gives an authoritative tug on my hand.

'Is Louis okay?' I say again. I must be resisting Dick's pull because the authoritative tug has become more like a wrench. 'Where are we going?'

'Stevie,' he says, looking me firmly in the eye, 'you must come with me.'

'Why?' I say, desperate. 'Did she stab him? Is he okay? What happened?'

'She didn't stab him.'

'She didn't get him?'

'No, she didn't get him.'

'Did I shoot her?'

'You didn't shoot her.'

'Is Louis okay?'

'No. Louis has been shot.'

'Who shot Louis?'

'You shot Louis.'

He watches me. I watch him watching me. He's looking for a reaction. I have none to give. His words slide around in my brain like eggs on a non-stick frying-pan. They make me feel queasy but nothing more.

'The police will be here in a moment, which is why,' he continues, 'I think you should follow me.'

With that he pulls me into the main auditorium. The people inside have heard about the fracas in the foyer – word is spreading and they are starting to stream out. We are going against the flow, but it's a good move on Dick's part. There's safety in numbers. Once we are in the vast, darkened auditorium, he pulls me towards a fire exit and we clatter through and down concrete steps smelling predictably of stale urine, then through another fire exit at the bottom and out on to a back-street on the rim of Chinatown.

A gust of hot sesame-prawn air strikes us, almost blowing us back into the cinema, but we go through the vacuum of the doorway and out into the anonymous night. Dick pulls out his phone to call for a car, but a taxi pulls up beside us with its light on like a chariot of fire. Dick parcels me in, pausing on the pavement to give urgent instructions down the phone. He closes the taxi door a moment so that I can't hear his conversation. I don't want to hear it anyway. All I am conscious of is the leathery smell inside the taxi, the throbbing of the engine, the neat grey carpet on the floor, the loud yellow disabled-access door handles and the lights of the Chinese takeaway on the other side of the road.

Someone gets into the taxi from the road side. He gives a couple of taps on the glass and we're away. I watch Dick's figure receding, so caught up in his phonecall he doesn't react to our departure and I think vaguely it must all be part of the plan, until suddenly I see Dick looking up and shouting and the sight of his horrified face makes me turn at last to have a look at my new companion – Rico.

'Don't worry,' he says, before I can open my mouth. 'I'm going to look after you. We're going to a five-star hotel.'

Huh?

'Better than five stars. Six stars. This hotel would have six stars if six stars existed. Have you stayed at the Newton before?'

I just stare at him.

'No,' he says, 'of course you haven't. You won't believe this hotel. You are going to *love* this hotel. You don't want to deal with that man from the *News*. They don't have real funds at the *News*, not for this kind of thing. I think I'll take this to the *Gazette*. The money will take your breath away – that I can promise you.

And by the way, you hit Louis in the arm. He's not in any danger. You saved his life. That's what they're saying. So, really, it couldn't be better.'

'He's okay?' I say, like an automaton, and the fear that, until this moment, couldn't speak its name sticks its head out of the cave and speaks it: *he could have been telling me that I killed Louis Plantagenet.*

But it's okay. I didn't. It's true, a few centimetres to the left and I might have killed Louis Plantagenet, but it's also true that a few millimetres to the right and I'd have missed him entirely.

I lean back in the taxi seat and my body begins to relax. It's a good feeling, like brandy seeping through the veins. Hmmm. Brandy. That would be nice.

'We'll get you some great champagne,' Rico says, as if reading my mind. 'What's your favourite champagne?'

'Rico,' I say, 'do you think of me as someone who knows a great deal about champagne?'

Rico's got no time for jokes. 'We're getting you a lawyer – he's coming to the hotel. No expense spared. You don't want to be talking to the police without a lawyer.'

Now there's a good distance between me and the cinema I'm thinking about getting out of the cab, but I also have an urgent need to talk about what's happened and Rico witnessed events. If I get out of the cab I will be alone.

'Why do I need a lawyer?' I say. 'I saved Louis's life.'

'Yes!' says Rico indulgently. 'You saved his life! And I got some great shots.'

'By the way,' I say acidly, 'I'm not selling my fucking story however many fucking stars your fucking hotel's got.'

He looks at me unmoved. Then his phone rings. He gabbles into it before slapping it shut triumphantly.

'One,' he says, and takes a deep reverential breath. I wait. 'Hundred,' he adds. Another devout pause. 'Thousand!' he finishes.

'One hundred thousand,' I repeat. 'What?'

'Pounds,' he says.

When it hits me, it hits me around the heart area, like a punch. I'm not used to this level of surprise in life. I like to think I know it all.

'They are offering to pay me,' I say, thinking he's going to laugh at me when I get the words out, that I must have got this wrong somewhere along the line, 'one hundred thousand pounds?'

'*Cara*,' he says, patting my knee, 'I told you we'd work together some day.'

'I am in a room,' I say down the phone to Esther, 'with a leather wall.' A soft pale grey leather wall, cubed, padded – like they're expecting loonies. There is a low bed set against the wall and a stern minimal sofa arrangement on the other side of the room. This is where I am pacing. Beyond the bed, a partition of glass brick divides off the bathroom. I've shut Rico in there to give me time to think and he is pacing too, on his mobile, his moving form providing a ghostly rearrangement of light up and down the glass.

Down the line, Esther sounds sleepy. She sounds

muzzy. 'How'd it go?' she murmurs. 'Did Louis get your Valentine?'

I open the mini-bar and stare into it. There are no answers in there, only small liquor bottles. I take one out, unscrew the lid and suck gently on the little glass teat.

'So to speak,' I say.

There's a suspicious silence. Esther knows me well. 'How d'you mean?' she says, and she sounds more lucid now, like she might have sat up in bed.

'Well, it wasn't your conventional Valentine . . .' I trail off.

'Did you tell him how you feel?'

'Perhaps,' I say. 'I shot him.'

She shrieks, but not because of what I've said, she shrieks because the doorbell begins ringing furiously at her end and our doorbell is the old-fashioned metal-bell kind, as loud as the hounds of hell.

'There's someone at the door,' she says.

'Don't answer,' I say. 'It'll be the press.' I give her a brief outline of what occurred at the première while she gets out of bed and goes to the window.

'Jesus,' she says, 'it is the press. They've got vans and everything.'

'Listen,' I say, 'I'm in a hotel and the *Gazette* have offered me a hundred thousand pounds for my story.'

'Stevie,' she says, 'don't scare me like that – I nearly fell out of the window. Fuck off!' This last is not directed at me, but down into the street to whoever is ringing the doorbell. 'Are you considering it?'

'I think,' I say, 'when it's a hundred thousand pounds you have to *consider* it. I mean, I was going to write about my time with Louis anyway and, well, a hundred thousand. I could buy us a house.'

'What about tax? It's not so much after tax. And we've got a house already.'

'Okay, but we could use it to look after the baby. You wouldn't have to go back to work for ages.'

'I'm gagging to go back to work this minute.'

I drop my empty brandy bottle on to the frosted-glass coffee table. 'I wasn't going to do it anyway,' I say grumpily. 'I was just *considering* it.'

'And what about Louis?' Esther says. 'Isn't that what he hates the most, people making money out of him? Isn't that what you told me? You'd be just another of those people.'

'My God,' I say, coming to my senses with an electrifying jolt and feeling a dazzling change in my perspective so sudden it gives me vertigo – like a trick camera shot that pulls back from an extreme close-up to show first the street, then the city, the continent, and finally the entire planet as seen from the stars.

'I'd better get out of here,' I say, and I hang up the phone.

19

I'm outside Gran's. I was planning to use my key but
now I'm here something makes me knock. It's nearly
ten at night, after all. So I knock. No reply. I knock
again. Eventually there's a hiss of 'Who is it?' through
the letter box.

'Me, Gran,' I say.

'Who?' she says.

New heights of eccentricity.

'Your granddaughter,' I say. And then add, 'Stevie,'
in case she's completely lost her mind. The start of
Alzheimer's? I told her to replace those aluminium saucepans.

'Oh, you!' she sighs. 'What are you doing here?'

'I've come to see you,' I say.

'Why?'

'Let me in, Gran.'

'Go away!'

'Not that game,' I say.

When I was about six, I discovered that Gran was
sneaking out of the flat at night and leaving me alone.
Fast asleep, in my dreams, I'd heard a voice calling
my name from far, far away, calling me slowly to
the surface of consciousness. I'd staggered out of my
bedroom towards the front door half asleep. The voice

was familiar, but in my somnambulant state I had no doubt that its owner was a ghost. I lifted the letter box and shouted, 'Go away!' And I meant it. I went back to bed. Gran was stuck out on the landing with her lover. She'd lost her key. They had to go to a hotel. She never let me forget it. The lover, who was married, shot himself. But that was another time.

After that, Gran always told me her secrets and I got used to being alone. Especially at night. Gran said I was old enough to look after myself. I think she always longed for me to be an adult rather than a child. Gran was a very strange mother; distant and difficult, vain and preoccupied. Funny too. She'd sometimes shout, 'Go away!' through the letter-box when I came home from school.

Now she says, 'Oh, bother.' But I can hear her throwing the bolts and the door eventually opens. I step into the hall. She looks me up and down. At which point a deafening blast of disco music sweeps through the apartment. Gran and I both jump out of our skins. The words 'Relight My Fire' reverberate into the kitchen, making the saucepans clatter against each other on their hooks, before bouncing out into the hallway and back again. Dan Hartman, if I'm not mistaken. Tommy the budgerigar looks up from his feeder stunned. And then, as quickly and as suddenly as it came, the clarion call is gone. Silence descends again. We hear the clank of dustbin lids outside and a distant train.

I look at Gran. I wonder if my hair is standing on end.

'What was *that*?' I say.

Gran looks vaguely sheepish.

'Gran!' I say.

Gran giggles, faintly. I can see I'm not going to get anything out of her so I push past her and go into the sitting room. There's a young man standing by the record player – it *is* still a record player. He is very pale and elongated and he is wearing a white shirt with a loose stripy tie like a schoolboy.

'Hello,' he says. 'Sorry about that. I'm not familiar with the controls.'

He has a long nose and soft, mousy hair. He looks like someone Gran has picked up in the queue for cheap seats at the matinée. Most of Gran's social life derives from the queue for cheap seats at the matinée. These young men tend to think she's a collector's item. They treat her like a curiosity, an entertaining one-woman show. They usually come for tea a couple of times, but then Gran starts being Gran and telling them to keep their jackets on because, well, why must she put up with their sweaty underarms?, and that's usually the end of that.

'I'm Stevie,' I say to the boy with the mousy hair. 'The granddaughter.'

'Oh,' he says, rushing forward eagerly, '*so* pleased to meet you.' He shakes my hand. 'Rupert Green. Angela was telling me about her passion for disco.'

I'm not used to Gran being called by her real name, so for quite some time I wonder who the hell Angela is. When I work it out, I say, 'I need to speak to her, actually. I'm having a crisis.' I go back down the corridor.

Gran is putting sherry glasses on to a tray and shaking

cheese straws into a bowl, humming to herself like she's in the garden of Eden pre-snake.

'Gran,' I say, 'I'm having a crisis.'

'Would you like a straw?' she says.

'No thanks. Gran, listen, who the—'

'Isn't he charming? Come along, come along,' and with that she floats past me carrying the tray of drinks.

I follow, wanting to broach things before we're back in the living room, 'Can I stay the night?' I say.

'Must you?'

'I wouldn't ask – except—'

Rupert is perched nervously on the edge of the sofa, the disco music playing mutedly around him. Gran pours him some sherry only remembering to offer me some at the last minute. When that's done she hurries over to turn the volume up a touch. 'Rupert and I have identical taste in music,' she coos.

'Gran,' I say, 'I'm having a crisis.' I turn to Rupert. 'You wouldn't give us a minute, would you?'

'Darling,' Gran says, icy, 'how dare you be so rude? To *my* guest. Rupert, sit down! And don't think of leaving me alone with this horrible girl for one second.' Then, to me, 'Where's that nice beau of yours?'

'I just shot that nice beau of mine,' I can't resist saying. 'With a gun.'

'Oh dear,' she says, mildly exasperated, as if I'd just knocked the cheese straws on to the floor. 'You're always so cross with everyone. And you know I *hate* guns.' She casts around for the right words with which to express her condemnation and her eyes come to rest on Rupert. 'Duelling, don't you think, was so much finer?'

'Oh, yes,' he says, and nods violently. I notice that a fine sweat is beginning to prick at his pale skin.

'Gran,' I say, 'this is serious. I can't go home. The world's gutter press is camped on my doorstep.'

'Darling,' she snaps, making it sound like I'm anything but her darling, 'you're being rude to my guest again. Rupert is a member of the press. He writes for *Glow* magazine.'

My eyes shoot to Rupert and he gives me a nervous, sickly smile. His ashy skin has turned a dusty olive green.

'What?' I say.

What?

'You *will* excuse us for a moment,' I say forcefully, and drag Gran out into the corridor.

'You said you met him at a matinée!'

'I said no such thing. I met him an hour ago when he rang the doorbell.'

'Jesus, Gran, you can't just invite people in who ring the doorbell. Don't you realise he's here to *spy* on us? Because of Louis.' My mind runs frantically over the things that I've said in front of him.

'Oh, don't be ridiculous. He's awfully nice.' And to my amazement she pulls away from me as if to go back into the room and continue entertaining him.

'Gran,' I hiss, 'he has to leave.'

She ignores me. I follow her back in.

'You're going to have to leave,' I say to Rupert. He gets up eagerly.

'You're not going anywhere,' Gran squeals, and he sits down again with a gulp.

'You're here on a story, aren't you?' I say.

'Well,' he gives one of his nervous nods, 'sort of. I'm just a stringer though,' he says limply. 'I'm new to all this.'

'How nice,' I say. 'Time to go. And before you do, let me make it crystal clear that Louis is not my beau and never has been. That was a joke between me and my grandmother and if you use it I will sue you.'

'I won't. I won't,' he cries eagerly.

'God, *Glow* must have been desperate,' I say.

'Now, now,' Gran says, arriving at his elbow with a sherry refill, which he gulps down gratefully. 'We can all sit down and make friends. There's no need for any unpleasantness.'

I stand my ground. I tell Gran she's behaving outrageously. I tell her it's him or me, but even before the words are out of my mouth I know it's hopeless, I know who she'll choose. I worry for a moment about him offering Gran money for my story, but then realise she won't be any use to him. Gran can only really talk about herself.

I resolve to let Rupert find this out for himself and, in the meantime, I am back on the street and it's now eleven at night and there's nowhere to go.

Except Dad's.

There's a light on in the front room so I tap on the window and after a moment the curtains twitch back and Dad's there in a cardigan, his paunch showing, with a glass of whisky in his hand. He flashes me a surprised smile. I feel my stomach expanding with the relief of it.

I should have come here first. No danger of any press here. They'd find my dad very hard to trace. We don't even have the same surname.

'Have you come to tell me your secrets?' he says, the minute he's opened the door. 'In the dead of the night?'

'Kind of,' I say, and begin the story of why I've come and it takes some time since I have to start at the beginning. He listens in a very unruffled way. Sometimes it irritates me, the way it's impossible to ruffle him, but tonight it suits me just fine.

Dad decides we must go straight to the police. He makes the phone call then drives me back into town to West End Central. He thinks we won't worry about a lawyer until we see what they say.

The police take a statement from me and won't be pressed as to whether I'll be charged or not. Louis, it seems, has made it clear I was trying to defend him, but the Crown Prosecution Service will be looking at 'all the facts of the case' before they make their decision. Louis is in the Westland hospital, but basically fine. Mike has been charged with illegal possession of a firearm and bailed. The mad fan is being held.

Back at the house, we make up the bed in the small back bedroom together and I gather from the fact that I'm not being offered the spare bedroom that Irena must be sleeping there. I wonder if she sleeps there every night.

Dad goes off to make me some camomile tea and I get, first, into a pair of pyjamas he's lent me and, second, into bed. When he comes back he hovers in the doorway a moment and I wonder at the novelty of being put to bed by my dad and how many times we might have done this if I'd grown up with him.

'Have you got something to tell me?' I say in the end – hoping he's not going to say Irena's leaving again.

'Do you remember,' he says, coming in and climbing into a horrible white rocking chair, which has been exiled to this room, 'the time I took you to that lunch party in Richmond when you were about five? There was a little boy called Simon and you played in the attic until he announced that when you were grown up he was going to marry you.'

'I remember it well,' I say, the horror of it clutching at my heart afresh. The boy had worn a plum-coloured velvet suit.

'You pushed him out of the window. He broke his ankle, you know, but you refused to say you were sorry. You absolutely refused. It was very embarrassing.' Dad grins delightedly.

'What's your point?' I say.

'I think perhaps you're in love with this man Louis.'

'And what,' I say, sitting up in bed again, 'do *you* know about love?'

'Strangely,' he says, 'for someone who doesn't believe in love you have some very romantic notions.'

'I do?'

'It's romantic to think that I cannot roam a little and love my wife all the while, that my passion must be exclusively for her.'

'You cause her pain.'

'She causes herself pain.'

'That's a hideous thing to say.'

'But true.'

We pause a moment for breath.

'I just see you making each other miserable,' I say, but I can hear in my voice that I'm on the defensive and with Dad that always means the game is lost.

'Well, look a little harder,' he says, giving the chair a big rock and shooting out of it on to his feet, 'and you might see something else. Goodnight.'

'Goodnight,' I say.

And he turns out the light as he goes even though I haven't asked him to.

When I wake up in the morning I consider leaving the country although it occurs to me that they might arrest me at the airport. As I run over yesterday's events in the light of a new day it strikes me as strange that I've slept at all. I always think it's extraordinary that humans haven't yet conquered the need to sleep, like we haven't yet conquered the weather. High-tech warfare? Still need to sleep. Shot a movie star? Need to sleep.

I wonder what I should do. I feel numb. I can hear Irena in the kitchen. I don't feel like talking to her. There's only one person I want to talk to. Only one place I want to go.

I walk straight into the hospital and no one stops me. The security presence seems benign and friendly. I approach the front desk, which is vast and curved like that of a grand hotel.

'I need to find out where someone is,' I say.

'Name?' says the guard, looking up languorously from his crossword.

'Karloff.'

He consults the computer. 'E 7,' he says, without looking up again.

I take the escalators up and have all the thoughts I usually have on the rare occasions that I'm in hospitals – like how fucking lucky I am to be 'just visiting'. I also run what I'm going to say to Louis through my head a couple of times, asking him if he still wants me to write the article. I feel the decision should be his, now that I've shot him. A thought occurs to me and I reach into my breast pocket. The daffodil is still there. Very wilted and collapsed. But still there. When I get to the seventh floor I chuck it into a passing bin.

Here I encounter a problem. The ward itself is locked and there is an entryphone and key pad on the door. I press the key with the little nurse graphic on it.

'Here to see Karloff,' I say, when it buzzes.

'Sorry, no visitors,' a voice comes back, and that seems to be that. I retire to a waiting area where there are green benches and spider plants to match. I call the number I've got in my phone for Louis and this time I get Mike.

'Are you at the hospital?' I say. 'With Louis?'

He says he is.

'Tell him I've got to talk to him, will you? Just for a couple of minutes. I'm outside the ward.'

'I don't think that's going to work,' Mike says.

'Why not?'

'Er—'

'Look, just get me in, will you?' I say. Long silence.

'Mike,' I say, 'I can't just shoot him and never see him again. We need to talk about it.' There's more silence. 'Are you still there?'

'The code is,' he suddenly says very fast and clear, 'five, two, two, five'.

That's my boy. I jump for the door and type the code in with trembling fingers. The door buzzes and I'm in. There's a main corridor, white and pristine, stretching ahead of me, and a smaller side corridor off to my right. I go straight for the side corridor, thinking I will be less conspicuous. I march along it purposefully. I know it's of the utmost importance, should any of the nurses see me, that I look like I'm meant to be here. It's not promising, though: the rooms off are all of the utility-type, not bedrooms. But then I spy a tasteful sign at the far end: VIP ROOMS, it says, with a pertinently angled arrow. I increase my pace to a jog, take the corner quite fast, and bump slap-bang into someone coming the other way.

Grace.

Startled isn't the word for it: her nostrils twitch and flare – her eyes are scared like an animal's. But, quickly, she gathers herself.

'Hello,' she says, not unfriendly but disconnected somehow. 'I'm sorry,' she says, 'that was probably my fault. I'm all over the place – not looking where I'm going. I didn't sleep last night. You can imagine.'

I feel the words are coming across a vast distance, a wide desert plain, that it's an effort for her to speak to me. The words have all the resonances they should have and yet she's put them there. She's acting.

'I fired the gun to defend Louis, you know. The mad fan was about to stab him.'

'We know,' she says, like it's no big deal.

'Is Louis okay?'

'Oh, yes, he's going to be fine.'

'I was wondering if I could speak to him.'

'He's with the doctors at the moment. And I'm going to have a coffee. Will you come and have a coffee with me?'

Which is how I end up having a one-to-one in the canteen of the Westland hospital with Grace Farlow.

20

When we're seated with our coffee she says, 'I'm actually desperate for a cigarette but I can't smoke because I'm pregnant. Ever since I got pregnant all I've wanted to do is go out on the town and dance and smoke and drink delicious cocktails. Do you know the feeling?'

I had a feeling I didn't know the feeling. Not Grace's version of the feeling, which sounded like it involved VIP lounges and cocktails I'd never heard of. But she made me think I wanted to know the feeling.

'Kind of,' I say.

'I was going to pull the plug, you know,' she says, 'but – you know what stopped me? I realised that the only reason I was pulling the plug – the *real* reason – was fear. Fear of the physical changes, fear of the birth, fear I wouldn't like the baby, fear the baby wouldn't like me. And that's terrible, isn't it? You can't not do something because of fear. And the minute I made the decision, committed to the baby, I started to see things in my life really clearly.'

She's talking fast now.

'It was incredible. I had complete clarity. It's like I saw the love. I saw where the love lies. I was talking to Brad the other day,' she pauses fractionally to make sure I register who she's talking about – *the* Brad, the great big huge massive film star Brad, 'and he had – you know – one of those bead necklaces on that spelled out his wife's name and he was fooling around and he put the letters in his mouth when he was talking to me, he was kind of sucking on them, and every time he spoke you could see her name rolling around on his tongue and I thought, *That's* what it's about. I've been looking for the wrong thing in the wrong place.'

'Really?' I say.

'You know, I think there are so many ways to live. And yet we tell ourselves we have to do it this way or that way when really it's whatever way works for you, isn't it? I'm going to make a home for my baby and it might not be a traditional home but it'll be a great home. You know, when I first got famous – really famous – I went into an eighteen-month depression. I thought I'd destroyed my life. I didn't know how to survive. But you learn. Louis will learn. You come through. I'm changing. I'm no longer afraid to reach out and pluck what I want, just pick it right off. And you know what? I deserve it. I truly deserve it. My God, it's exhilarating to know that. My therapist has been telling me to go for it and I've been resisting like crazy and now I just feel exhilarated . . . and *desperate* for a cigarette. I shouldn't be telling you this, should I?'

'Definitely not,' I say, with a reassuring smile to imply the opposite.

'I just *love* my life.' She gives me one of her stretchy smooth-lipped smiles that radiates with tainted love.

'You know I'm a journalist . . .' I say.

'On yes. We met in that bar. Louis says, by the way,

that you should go ahead and write the piece about him – what happened doesn't change anything.'

'Really?' I say, genuinely surprised this time.

'Of course. He wants to honour his side of the bargain. He doesn't blame you for anything. He's not like that. And, anyway, he's had good news.' Her eyes sparkle patronisingly as she waits for me to ask.

'Oh, yes?' Nervous now.

'Oh, yes – *Science Fiction II* got the green light. We just heard. And it's going to be even bigger than the last one. Starring guess who!'

'He doesn't want to do it,' I say.

'Says?'

'Grace,' I say, 'I really, really need to talk to Louis. Could you arrange that?'

'Of course,' she says easily. 'I'll see what I can do.' With that she picks up her mobile phone and starts scrolling through numbers to indicate end of conversation – performance over, roll credits, theatre dark.

When we've finished our drinks, she leads me back to the corridor where there is another green padded bench and another potted plant and, giving me a confidential wink, tells me to wait there.

An hour later I'm beginning to think I imagined the whole thing. The thing with Grace – the thing with Louis, even. I'm beginning to think I don't exist. I am, perhaps, a figment of my own imagination.

Or hers.

I'm a figment, that's for sure.

I've rehearsed the upcoming conversation with Louis

so many times in my head that he's started to say things he's not meant to say and, as for my own arguments, they've got so defensive and detailed, I've lost track of them myself.

I'm just about to get up and go investigate when I see Katrina the assistant coming down the corridor with her slitty specs and her clipboard.

I jump up. 'I'm waiting to see Louis,' I say. 'Grace is arranging it.'

'Stevie,' Katrina says, and I notice she has a strange look on her face, a guilty look. This is extraordinary. Guilt on Katrina is like custard on beef. Sickly and incongruous. She hugs her clipboard tight to her chest as she speaks, her beloved clipboard. 'Louis left for LA . . .' she consults her watch for accuracy, '. . . about seven minutes ago. He's going straight to the airport.' She checks her watch again, accuracy in this matter clearly being of the utmost importance, 'Yes,' she says, with a precise nod, 'he'll make the BA flight with time to spare.'

'Fucking Grace,' I say.

'Excuse me?'

I look at Katrina. Kill the messenger? Well, maybe not.

I turn on my heel and leave.

Dad has a Jaguar. Which is a surprising thing about Dad. His life seems so ramshackle and then there are these little pockets of excellence: a love of the Marx Brothers, beliefs about marriage, gentlemen's pastes that must be bought from Fortnum and Mason, that sort of thing – ways in which he defines himself that suddenly remind me that he is not just my father but a person in his own right. It's decades old now, the Jag, but it's a good one.

I put my foot down just beyond Chiswick, where the A4 becomes the M4, where two lanes become an inviting three, and you can spread your wings and shake off London at last.

The motorway is busy but fairly fast moving, and I drive like I would never normally drive. I overtake on the inside where necessary. I get hooted at – a slag in a Jag, they'll be thinking. I don't care. I have a sense that I'm doing something important. I have a heightened sense of everything around me, the road, its colour and texture, the sky, the sun breaking through the clouds.

Further out, the traffic thins a little. There are fields on either side of the road. Huge signs warning of different terminals loom and pass. A vast jet rumbles along beside the road making its cumbersome descent: nose up, feet first, like a duck coming into land.

I zip through the tunnel, inside the airport now – a mini-city unto itself – and follow the signs for short-term parking. It's complicated. I have to keep in the right lane and trust. If I miss it, I'll have to go round again. I can't afford to go round again. I lose a couple of minutes at traffic-lights. But then I'm through, taking my ticket from the machine and climbing the levels.

The car-park is really busy. I haven't bargained for this. I can't find a space. I begin to panic, knowing with absolute certainty that if a space does come free someone else will get it first. Any sense I might have in life of being in the right place at the right time has deserted me completely. It becomes personal – no room for me at the inn. I go round and round, from level to level, up and then down, down and then up. I feel dizzy.

Just as I am giving up, I find a space. I leap out of the car, flinging the door shut behind me and locking it with the remote even as I run for the lift. I stab at the lift button. It takes a century to come. When it does I'm so crazed I don't read the instructions properly. I press buttons wildly. We go up when I think we're meant to be going down. People get in. We go down again. Then up again.

'Departures?' I implore of the people around me. They are all from Bangladesh. One points at the door. I throw myself out of the lift with relief and run across a covered bridge – into the airport.

'Departures?' I call, to anyone who will listen.

'Floor below,' a passing porter says.

I can't see stairs. I run for another lift, stabbing at the button again. It comes. I get in. It goes up not down. I scream. My fellow passengers look at me in alarm. 'I'm sorry,' I say.

They all get out. More stabbing at buttons – I go down again. I'm back at Arrivals. A porter gets in with a huge empty trolley the size of a hospital bed. We go down once more. The doors open. I mount and traverse the trolley and charge to the nearest desk.

'Next flight to LA?' I say to the woman in blue. 'I need to talk to one of the passengers urgently. It's an emergency.'

I'm panting, I'm sweating, my hair is wild, but I don't

really expect her to care. To my amazement, she does. She turns to the computer with sympathetic haste.

I love her.

'The thirteen forty-five?' she says.

'Yes?'

'It just left.'

Well, I say to myself as I tramp back to the car, *you can't say I didn't try*. The gods had their say: there was no parking place.

Perhaps exhaustion has made me philosophical. But part of me has been satisfied just by coming here, just by trying. The intention is all. You don't have to win, I guess. You just have to play.

But the bit that really *gets me* – the bit that makes me want to go back and commit hara-kiri all over that shiny Heathrow airport floor – is the part when I go back to the car park and *I can't find the car*. Because I didn't memorise my level number as you are meant to and because I went up and down in the lift several times, I have no idea where it is. I go round and round the car park looking for it. And this is a big car park. Only now do I fully appreciate what a big car park this is. I'm not sure I am *ever* going to find this car. Everyone else seems to find their car so smugly, so easily. They understood the system. They took precautions. Not me.

After a while I come out on to the car park roof. A jumbo jet roars overhead, taking off into the flat white glare of the sky. There's a tinge of spring in the air and people are going places and I'm standing alone on top of this concrete car park, looking out over the purposeful airport. so full of promise and possibility, so full of potential. And while I'm doing it, I'm wondering why potential always seems to be delivering . . . somewhere else.

21

It's dark.

OUCH.

It's so dark I've stubbed my toe. How did they get the room so dark? They must have used black-outs. I strike a match. The room flickers into being around me. I watch them for a moment; spooning, innocent, their mouths open slightly, like two newborn pups in straw.

The match burns out, but I'm not done. I want to watch them some more. I strike another match. This time it wakes Esther – which I was hoping would happen the first time. She sits up.

'What are you doing?'

'Oh,' I say, 'you two seem so happy I thought I'd come and spoil it for you.'

The second match dwindles down to burn my fingers and I shake it violently plunging us back into the aforementioned darkness.

'Give me the matches,' she says. I throw them in her direction, guessing. She lights a candle beside the bed, sees the clock. 'It's two in the morning,' she says.

I go and sit on the bed on her side. Jay moans and shifts, throwing the duvet off, hot and bothered and muttering something.

He's been sober since he got out of hospital and at first he seemed relieved and there was some colour in his skin. We all thought it was the happy ending, but now he seems very low and we tend to walk around him on eggshells saying things like, 'Shall we go for a drink? Oh! I'm sorry!' while he scowls at us furiously, not because we're mentioning drink but because we're trying not to.

'How'd it go?' Esther says.

I hand her the newspaper and she opens it out. The entire front of the broadsheet review section is a picture of Louis in his cowboy hat and across it in Wild West dead-or-alive lettering it says, '*Stevie Dunlop*', and then, underneath, in even bigger letters, '*I Shot the Sheriff.*'

'Wow,' Esther says. She turns the page and inside there's a double-page spread. More shots of Louis, including one of him being stretchered out of the Odeon, Leicester Square, a shot of me at City airport in those ridiculous aviator shades, plus a small head-shot of me next to my by-line.

'Wow,' Esther says again. 'A star is born.'

'Tomorrow's chip paper,' I say.

'This is going to change your life,' Esther says, 'if you let it.'

We both stare down at my 2,500 words: 2,500 words to change my life.

Jay mutters again.

'He talks in his sleep,' Esther says.

'I know.'

'I only let him sleep here to stop him going off on midnight drinking binges. It's a temporary thing.'

'Do you two . . . ?'

'What?'

'You know.'

'Sometimes,' she says reluctantly.

'Really?'

'It's only because I'm pregnant. The midwife says pregnancy can increase the libido in some women. It's a—'

'Temporary thing?'

'Exactly.'

I look at Jay fondly. 'He's quite good in bed, isn't he?' I say. 'He's quite—'

I'm just about to mouth the word 'big' with a kind of naughty schoolgirl hilarity when Jay shoots up to a sitting position and says, 'For fuck's sake!' Then he gives us the humourless scowl that's becoming such a regular feature, jumps out of bed, grabs a pillow and stalks out of the room.

'Jay!' we both call after him, in admonishing tones, as if he were behaving with great unreason. Then we look at each other in amazement.

In the morning, we can't find Jay anywhere. Esther's newspapers have been delivered, and when Phil eventually comes down to breakfast, I show him my Louis article for real. We spread it out on the table and admire it for a while. Sweetly, Esther takes time to admire it again before asking Phil if he's seen Jay.

'Why?' Phil says. 'What have you done to him?'

'Nothing.'

'Well, he did storm off. Last night.'

'Because?'

'No reason.'

'Actually—'

'What?'

'We were discussing—'

'*What?*'

'Nicely.'

'But what?'

'You know, his . . . *bits.*'

'Bits? For fuck's sake, Esther, where did you get a word like "bits"?'

'No wonder you don't like sex,' I say, 'if you go around calling them bits.'

'That's what my mother called them.'

'Anyway, Jay's over-sensitive lately. You must have noticed.'

'He's very moody.'

'Moody?'

'Yes!'

'It's only his ex-girlfriend—'

'And the mother of his child—'

'Sitting on his bed—'

'Discussing his—'

'*Bits!*'

We all go back to reading my article.

It's cold in the kitchen and Phil puts the heater on and after a while I say, 'What's that smell?'

'What smell?'

There's a smell in the room now, sweet with an edge of fermentation. Unsettling. But undeniably familiar.

'What smell?' Esther says again.

'Jay's drinking,' I say, with sudden conviction.

'He can't be. How do you know?'

'I know that smell.'

'I promise you he's not drinking. I'd kill him if he was.'

'I know that smell. It's vodka. And it's coming through his skin.'

'Are you saying he's in the house?'

'He must be.'

I get up to check the living room again. On the way I notice the biodegradable coffin on the sideboard. It's been there so long it's become part of the furniture. With sudden conviction I lift the lid. Jay is lying inside like a vampire clutching an empty bottle of vodka to his chest.

'He can't have got drunk because of the "bits" thing?' Esther says when she and Phil have gathered round.

'No,' I say. 'Look. He's been at it for a while.' There are various other empties littered around the sides of the coffin. We all stand there and look down at him and, no doubt, we all have the same question in our heads: what next?

I take hold of the vodka bottle and poke Jay with its neck. He opens one eye and peers up at the three of us. 'Rehab?' he says.

Three months later, I'm in Dick's office. For the record: I am now officially *a successful person*. It would all be quite fun, I suppose, if I didn't feel vaguely sick the whole time. People keep telling me how lucky I am, which makes me feel even sicker because I don't think

I've ever felt worse in my whole whole life. I catch myself wondering if this is how Louis feels and then I kick myself for thinking about him at all.

Following 'I Shot the Sheriff', which was, I've been told, picked up by magazines and newspapers all over the world, I have been invited on to radio and television news programmes to discuss 'the dark side of celebrity'. I have been offered a two-book deal by a distinguished publishing house, the first book to be about 'the dark side of celebrity', the second to be about an issue of my choice. I'm not at all interested in the dark side of celebrity, but nobody seems to mind. The editor of the News has taken me to lunch at Sheekey's to offer me my own column at a substantial annual salary. The editor of the Gazette has taken me to lunch at the Ivy to offer me my own column for twice the News's price. So much money I choked on my Welsh rarebit. When I asked them what these columns should be about they both said, 'The things you talk about at dinner parties.'

'I'm sorry,' I had to say, 'I don't go to dinner parties.'

So I turned it all down, but I did manage to get myself an advance for a book about grandmothers, which I've always wanted to write. The advance is not a huge sum, but it makes a nice bulge in my Instant Saver account and the grandmother book itself doesn't have to materialise for two years so, for the time being, it can remain a twinkle in my eye. As for the journalism, I've settled for a feature-writer's contract with the News, which means I get a regular salary. Alleluia. My first story was the Louis story, of course. It wasn't a kiss-and-tell: it was a serious and thoughtful account of the time we spent together and I was paid for it as part of my regular salary. Otherwise I have a series of more weighty pieces planned and have already done an in-depth examination of the road-protest movement – I camped out for a week on a protest outside Bury St Edmunds. Next I want to go back to Colombia to do the flower workers properly.

When I ask Dick why things have changed, why he is suddenly willing to contemplate road-protest and flower-worker stories, he says, ' "Stevie Dunlop meets the road protesters" – or, more accurately, "*The girl who shot Louis Plantagenet meets the road protesters*" is a completely different kettle of fish. You see? You're the hook now. You officially have a voice. And a voice is the most important thing you can possibly have. *You* are the story.'

He really loved my Louis piece, Dick. With regard to his attitude to me, he has executed a precise U-turn. He has no shame. He has simply erased the memory of how he treated me before. For some reason, I quite admire this about him.

'So, let's talk about the flower workers,' I say, assuming that's what I'm there for.

'Flower workers?' Dick says blankly.

'I'm off to do the flower workers,' I say. 'Remember?'

'Ah,' Dick says, 'about those flower workers . . .'

I don't like his tone.

'We've got a story for you first, and then, when you've done it, you can do the flower workers to your heart's content.' He makes a gesture with his hand, a sweeping gesture which conjures up vast acres of newsprint dedicated to Colombian flower workers.

My heart sinks into my boots. There's plenty of room for it in my boots. My boots are big and roomy and they're used to having my heart come visit.

'What story?' I say suspiciously.

'Take a seat,' he says.

'I don't want to sit down.' I've noticed a lot of people lately wanting me to take a seat. In the land of the real world, in the land of reception rooms and waiting rooms and green rooms, people are always telling you to take a seat. I feel very controlled, trapped in these small rooms, made to sit in all those fucking seats.

'Just sit down,' Dick says.

'I refuse to sit,' I bark.

'Louis Plantagenet is getting married,' he barks back. 'We want you to go out there and cover the wedding.'

At this point, I'm ashamed to say, given my above feelings about seats and the way people will always have you sitting in them, I sit down.

'You're the obvious person,' Dick says, almost apologetic. Almost.

'I won't do it,' I say.

'Stevie, I'm not even going to argue this with you. You're the *only* person for this story. It's a great story. There are kids out there who'd hack off their left arm to get this story – hack it right off.' He acts this out with a vigorous sawing action, his right hand and a pen.

I stare at him.

'What *is* your problem?' he says again. 'Are you in love with Louis?' Dick meets my eye and then his lips twitch and a little colour comes into his cheeks. 'Did you sleep with him?' he says. His face is telling a whole story.

'You're jealous of me and Louis,' I finally say. 'Aren't you?'

He loves that. It breaks the moment. He throws the pen on to his desk and turns his attention to his in-tray. 'It would be a deal breaker in terms of your employment with us, I'm afraid,' he says cheerfully, 'were you to say no.' He throws me a glance to see how I'm taking the news. 'Now, tell me you're going to do it.' I look sulkily at the floor. Dick sighs. 'Just tell me you at least slept with him.'

'I didn't actually.'

'For God's sake.'

'What?'

'Tell me you're going to.'

22

When I get to LA I speak to the the *News*'s guy out there and he tells me straight off that Louis isn't in town. The word is he left yesterday and his people are saying nothing about where he's gone. The wedding, which is shrouded in misinformation and secrecy, is now thought to have been put off until the end of the month. There's some idea that Louis may have gone to the desert. Grace is in town, though, and today she's out and about, attending a swanky lunch at the Peninsular Hotel in honour of big-shot local politician Senator Donald Bragg.

The only thing I can think of to do – apart from turning around and going straight home again – is to head for the lunch. It's my only lead.

My cab drops me in the circular driveway of the Peninsular Hotel. I stand for a moment and take in the fountain and the potted plants, the valet-parking guys and the luggage porter, who is dressed like a barrel-organ monkey. It occurs to me that most people haven't got living rooms as nice as the driveway at the Peninsular Hotel – the floor tiles look like they belong in an opulent bathroom, the kind with gold taps.

I find the press pack around the corner. They are camped out on the sidewalk, up ladders with their obscenely long lenses resting on the high hotel wall. And among them – Rico.

I've never been so happy to see Rico. I practically fall into his arms. The mood I'm in, I'd be glad to see anyone – anyone.

On the cab ride over, I'd felt pretty alienated. Tired after the ten-hour plane journey, I was taking it personally that Louis had left town. Plus I've never been to LA before. I didn't know Sunset Boulevard looked like a motorway, with its unpeopled sidewalks and high-rise hotels. You can sense immediately in LA that the place has no centre. If you go to Paris or Rome, it's obvious where it's at. LA is a hidden, heartless city. You know there's an in-crowd, but you don't know where. LA, alienation is thy name.

Rico has no idea where Louis is or what I should do next. But he turns out to be booked into the same motel as me and offers to take me out to dinner, which makes the prospect of the lonely LA evening slightly less desolate. So I stand gratefully at the bottom of Rico's ladder while he stands at the top with his powerful binoculars trained on the hotel. Rico, apparently, has been obsessed with Grace ever since the Air bar in London.

After a while, he lets me climb the ladder and have a look through his camera lens. It's amazing: I can see easily through the hotel's french windows and into the function room where the guests are sitting down to their silver-service luncheon. I can't see Grace, though. Rico thinks she's sitting on the other side of the room.

Which makes the whole thing quite long and boring,

both up the ladder and down on the sidewalk. The other paps take a few shots and very sensibly pack up. Not Rico. Like I said, Rico is obsessed and when Rico has an obsession . . .

Rico talks me through the lunch – the main course looks like salmon, ah! here's the dessert, and so on and so forth. It's making me hungry so I go off and get us pizza. While Rico's eating his, he gives me another go at the top of the ladder.

The lunch is breaking up and some of the left-over guests come out into the garden where they form a group. They are still some way away, standing with their backs to me in close formation, so it takes me a moment to work out that they are posing for a photograph. At first the group is entirely made up of men in their shirtsleeves, but then Grace materialises amid them in a red dress. She's received into a central position, looking waif-like among the broad male backs. The man on Grace's right puts his arm around her and she does the same to the man on her left; a more informal shot. I tell Rico that I can see Grace. As I do, my eye is caught by Grace's hand sliding off the broad and hefty shoulder of the man beside her and wandering familiarly down his broad and hefty back. To my amazement, she then slips this same hand down into his trousers where it lingers on his left buttock for half a second.

At the mention of Grace, Rico is storming the ladder.

'My God,' I say, 'did you see that?'

'No! No!' he yells. 'I didn't see that!' He frantically rakes the now dispersing photo party with his lens.

'Grace put her hand in that guy's trousers.'

'Shit! Shit! Shit! Shit! Shit!'

'What?' I say. Having been jostled aside by Rico I am now hanging precariously off the edge of the ladder, swinging in mid-air.

'That's what I've been waiting for!' he wails. 'You can't believe how long I've been waiting for that!'

'Rico,' I say, 'waiting for what?'

'Hours! Days! Weeks!'

I get the feeling Rico won't be buying me dinner tonight after all. 'What's going on?' I say again.

'I knew it! I knew it! I knew it!' he says. He's off the ladder now and stamping his feet on the ground like an angry Rumpelstiltskin.

'Rico!' I say. I jump off the ladder and face up to him.

'In London,' he says and takes a deep breath, 'at the Air bar – you remember I had her phone?'

'Yes.'

'I pressed redial.'

'Yes.'

'You want to know who picked up?'

'Yes.'

'The offices of Senator Donald Bragg.'

Rico, to give him his due, bears his dinner responsibilities and not his grudges. That evening we go to a Japanese place where you can sit up at the bar and watch the sushi chefs slicing and dicing.

Senator Donald Bragg, it turns out, is a Republican and a family man. He is also, according to Rico, having an affair with Grace Farlow, which has been going on for at least five years. When Rico had gone back and traced the couple's movements he'd found that their schedules collided more often than could be attributable to coincidence; if the Senator had been in New York, for example, more often than not Grace would have been there too. And vice versa. A different hotel, a different *raison d'être*, but nevertheless together.

'Which means Grace was seeing the Senator before she met Louis?'

'*Certo*,' Rico says, with a definitive nod and bites into his California roll with equal conviction, causing the back end of the avocado to ooze out and plop on to his plate.

'And he's the father of the baby?'

'Of course.'

'Do you think Louis knows? Has known all along?'

'No way,' Rico says. 'No one knows.'

'Only you.'

'Only me. Only the best rat in the business.'

I must find Louis.

'You can't tell him,' Rico says, reading my mind.

'I have to,' I say. 'I can't let him find out from a newspaper.'

'If you tell him, it won't be *in* the newspaper. If you tell him, he'll tell Grace and she'll tell the Senator. They'll clamp down. They'll go to ground. I'll never get my shot.'

'I don't care about your shot.'

'You want a cover-up, *amore mio*? Because that's what you'll get. And Grace will just deny the whole thing. Think about it: you've got no real evidence for Louis. Grace has it all mapped out. She needs Louis. She needs a father for her kid. She's not going to let him off the hook.'

He has a point.

The dead fish on my plate lies uneaten and all the ramifications of the situation dart hither and thither in my mind like a shoal of very alive ones.

'Look,' Rico says, 'how about this? You go back to London, there's nothing for you here anyway, the wedding is postponed and Louis is hiding. I promise to call you when I've got my picture. It won't be long now. I can feel it's close. Then you can jump on a plane and be back here by the time the news breaks – in time to get the scoop.'

I sigh.

'In time to pick up the pieces,' Rico adds, with a sleazy smile.

I ignore him. The word 'hiding' has jogged my memory. Of course. Louis's hideaway. The beach. Anasett Point.

'You're right,' I say. 'I'll leave in the morning.' I get up.

Rico takes hold of my arm. 'Give me your word you won't tell Louis.'

I just look at him.

'The Senator is a liar and a hypocrite. You want him to get away with it?'

'So what are you saying?' I ask. 'It's in the interests of national security to keep Louis in the dark?'

'Exactly.'

'It's also in the interests of your pocket.'

'Give me your word.'
'Okay,' I say reluctantly. 'You have my word.'
'*Allora*.'

23

Pepperidge Farm cookies. Mmmm. Even the words themselves are crumbly and comforting and resonant with nostalgia. For me.

I know Pepperidge Farm cookies are nothing like the delicacy they used to be – now you can get better home-made-style cookies on any street corner – but in the days of the good old British Rich Tea biscuit, (anything but rich, as dry and plain as a ship's rusk), in the days when Dad used to turn up unexpectedly at Gran's, just back from a concert tour of the States with Pepperidge Farm cookies in his bag, they were exotic treats indeed. Especially Maple Pecan. Maple and Pecan were unfamiliarly wonderful tastes for my inexperienced palate.

I've got them mixed up with love, of course. Pepperidge Farm cookies . . . Dad . . . prodigal return . . . a gift . . . sugary pleasure . . . Easy mistake to make. But not so easy to change. Which is why I am standing in the general store in the small East-coast town of Anasett Point, admiring the Pepperidge Farm cookie display – and which is why I am filled with a warm glow. Look! There are the little goldfish ones! It's true, I no longer particularly want to eat the cookies, but I do want to look at them and buy them and own them . . . all those things.

A dog appears at my ankle and sniffs my flip-flop gingerly, with extreme caution. It's a sweet-looking dog, kindly – a mongrel, I guess, I'm not good at breeds. It has a barrel-like body, short-haired with camel brown patches, heart-shaped patches . . . I spin round. Louis is standing behind me, about ten paces away, in the white light of the chiller cabinet. He seems different – more substantial. His hair has grown.

'Boris Karloff,' Louis says. 'Come here.'

It's one of those moments when it's only possible to grasp at the present, as if for breath; everything else is beyond reach.

The dog hasn't obeyed. Louis comes towards me and bends to hook the dog's lead on to its collar. As he does he says, into my ear, 'The trouble with Boris Karloff is he doesn't know I'm famous.'

He straightens up. I smile. He smiles.

That smile.

The warm glow initially induced by the Pepperidge Farm cookies increases: it buzzes loudly around me and threatens to lift me off like a flying saucer. Louis is not angry. Not only is he not angry, he's pleased to see me.

'Fuck,' he says, incredulous. 'You're here.'

'Yeah,' I say, and then don't know how to go on, so I just stand there with a packet of Pepperidge Farm cookies dangling from my hand and – I wouldn't be surprised – my mouth hanging open slightly.

'We never said goodbye,' he says, 'did we?'

'No . . .' Again, I don't know how to go on. There's a small matter to be broached, dealt with, resolved, apologised for – I shot him.

'Well,' Louis says, and seems to remember where he is – in the general store. He makes a small well-so-much-to-say-don't-know-where-to-start gesture with a tube of wood glue he's holding and wanders over to the till. I follow and stand behind him, ready to pay for my biscuits.

'Hey, Louis,' says the store guy. He says it like he's glad to have Louis back in his store, but at the same time making a real point of keeping his dignity. I can guess how it works here. The locals have too much pride to do anything except leave Louis alone.

The guy puts the glue in a brown-paper bag and, with a nod to a neat little square of taped gauze on Louis's left arm, says, 'I heard they shot you up in London.'

'Oh, yeah,' Louis says.

'What kind of crazy would do a thing like that?'

'It's a good question,' Louis says, and he reaches over and takes my Pepperidge Farm cookies and adds them to his wood glue.

'Together?' the store guy says looking from the cookies to Louis to me in amazement. Amazement that immediately turns to suspicion. Perhaps I'm a pestering fan. 'You haven't been bothering Mr Plantagenet now, have you?' he says.

'Not since I shot him.'

Good a time as any to broach the subject, break the ice – so to speak.

The store guy thinks I'm joking. He laughs. Louis laughs. I laugh. The laughing carries us all the way through the paying part and propels Louis and me out on to the store's wooden porch. Just below in the dirt there's a rail that looks like it was once used for tying up horses. Otherwise there are flowers in baskets and bicycles littered everywhere.

'I'm really sorry,' I say quickly, seizing the change of scene as my opportunity, 'about what happened. I'm sorry I shot you. I thought I was saving your life.'

'Well, maybe you were,' he says, and he looks at me in the blazing sunlight like he's never seen me before. I'm suddenly shy under his scrutiny. 'I can't believe you came.'

Some people come out of the shop door behind us and we have to rearrange ourselves on the porch to let them pass.

'I faced up to a few things in London, learnt some stuff,' he says. 'You were an important part of that.'

'What did you learn?' I say.

But he just gives me that look again, says, 'I can't believe you're here,' again.

I'd like to get away. It seems unbearable that he should be looking at me like this, that I am being seen. I would like, as the wicked witch did, to melt into a little heap at his feet, leaving only my shoes.

'Did you see my article?' I say. 'About you?'

'Yeah,' he says lightly. 'It was cool.'

'I was sent to do a follow-up.'

Louis's face falls. That's an exaggeration. Louis never does much with his face, which is what makes him good on the screen, but now it's like the lights go out. There's a tightening around the eyes and the corners of his mouth. I know him well enough to recognise the signs.

And I want to take back what I said. I want, desperately, to retract.

So I do.

'I'm joking,' I say, and grin. 'I came to see you. I wanted to talk to you. I missed you.'

It's all true.

He reaches out and gives my shoulder a little punch. 'Let's go for a drive.'

'A lot of artists live out here,' Louis says, when we're on the road in his battered pick-up, 'because of the light.'

It's a sideways light, coastal flatlands lit by a big low sky. It makes whites very white. When we get to the beach – this turns out to be our destination, a long blousy Atlantic beach – I sit down in the sand and it has a pearly white luminescence that makes my legs, hardly tanned at all, look as brown as eggs. I pick up a tiny, tiny seashell, pale pink and perfectly formed . . .

'You know I'm marrying Grace in California at the end of the month,' he says, squatting beside me.

I nod.

'Baby and all,' he says.

I nod again.

'But it ain't mine.'

I draw an O in the sand with my shell.

'I did have a thing with Grace,' he says, 'when I first met her.' He pauses, wondering how to explain, finds a small smooth pebble in the edge of his shoe and chucks it into the sea. 'It ended and we stayed friends. I know she doesn't seem it, but Grace can be really great. She can be a bit crazy too. She got pregnant by mistake. After an awards ceremony. It was a one-night stand. Awards ceremonies can do that to you. The father is this guy – he's not in the business. She hasn't told me exactly who, but he's . . . Anyway, he's not going to do the right thing by her – even if she wanted him to. She doesn't care, though.'

He pauses again. I lean my elbows back in the sand and let my eyes rest on the unfailing horizon. I say nothing, not wanting to give myself away, not wanting to break the spell.

'Grace is thirty-four, but she feels old. Thirty-four is kind of old for a movie star, you see. She's probably got five years before . . .' He trails off.

Before the certain extinction of her career.

'Anyway, she *feels* old. She really wants the baby. She wants stability, commitment – she didn't before but she does now. And we're really good friends, you know.'

'So, it's kind of a *friendly* marriage, is it?' I say.

Louis shoots me a look to see if I'm taking the piss.

'As you know,' I add quickly, 'I think that's the best kind.'

Louis considers this while plunging his long fingers deep into the sand, grasping it in fistfuls. 'I spent such a long time wanting Grace,' he says. 'In the past.'

'Right,' I say.

'And it's a question of balance.'

'Balance?

'Grace is one of the only people on this earth who can marry me and not be Mrs Louis P.'

'But why get married at all?'

'Well, there's all those miserable journalist bastards,' he flashes me a grin, 'hounding us.' He shrugs. 'Grace wants it official.'

'And you?'

'It takes the pressure off "the world's number-one heart-throb", being married, you know.'

'That's not a good reason—'

'Stevie,' he says, interrupting me, 'I think it's going to work.'

'Okay,' I say.

'Celebs need to be with celebs.'

'Okay,' I say.

'Look what happened with us.'

'What happened with us?'

'I got shot.'

'I'm sorry,' I say. And I mean it. There's a long silence while Louis keeps grabbing the sand and I look around for my fallen crest.

'I hope I didn't mislead you in London,' he says eventually.

'You didn't.'

'I enjoyed every moment I spent with you. Well, every moment except one.'

'Thank you.'

'No hard feelings.'

'Good.'

'We should hang out for a while.'

'Hang out?'

'Yeah. Here.' He throws out an arm expansively, as if all this beauty was at his disposal, as if he was offering it to me. 'I'm not going back until the day before the wedding. After that, the madness starts. I start rehearsals for *Science Fiction II*.'

'Oh yes,' I say remembering. For some reason this is the most painful thing. 'I thought you weren't going to do that.' I forbear to mention that he promised me he wasn't going to do that.

'You know you asked me what I learnt in London?' he says. 'I made my bed. I gotta lie on it. That's what I learnt. My dad used to say, "Either you're in or you're out." He saw things very black and white. In or out.'

'So you're "in" then?'

'I've gotta be.' He flops back in the sand and shuts his eyes against the glare of the sky. 'It's the same with Grace. In or out.'

'Marry or bust?'

'We call it the merger.'

24

So Louis and I have decided that we will be friends. And why not? He has a few moments left to him of single life and I am meant, supposedly, to be covering the wedding. It seems the only thing to do – to grab life's chances while we can. We are both adults. For now, we like the differences in each other, but surely he's right. In the end they would be the very things that pulled us apart. We come from different worlds and I am realistic. I'm good at that: bite the bullet, look the gift horse in the mouth. I don't believe in romantic illusion after all – I can throw it out like so much bath water without a second's thought, baby and all.

Louis and I fall into a routine of days that slide one into the other and those can be the best days of all. We meet on the beach in the morning. I cycle from my motel on one of Louis's bikes and swim in the breakers, letting them toss me like a rag. Louis takes his morning run along the beach and hails me from the shore each morning – always behaving as if it were a surprise to see me. He never comes right into the sea, but he'll walk barefoot in the edge of the surf, rolling up his jeans and throwing a stick for Boris Karloff. Boris Karloff will swim out courageously, his paws working furiously and unseen under the water, his neck craning upwards in a desperate effort to keep his nose out of the spray. This is endlessly entertaining to us, the sight of Boris Karloff swimming.

When I've had enough swimming I stagger out of the water, fighting the suck that tries so forcefully to pull me back in. I run up the beach, my legs like jelly, and sit with Louis for a while.

And then we say, 'Breakfast?' and off we go to the café up on the highway, the café attached to the same general store that sells the Pepperidge Farm cookies.

Louis has a big strong coffee. I have tea. Every morning we say we'd better not have muffins or pancakes or waffles this morning, but every morning we have them anyway. Every morning Louis asks me to come and give him a hand with the pergola he's building in his garden to please his green-fingered housekeeper Consuela. She thinks Louis should have climbing roses. Apparently she's been on at him about the pergola for ever.

Louis's beach-house is a modern construction, but made of traditional clapboard cedar stained a dark steel grey by the sea air. Turning in from the drive, the place appears like a fortress – not a window in sight. The back of the house is curved and tall, like an enormous beer barrel. The drive disappears under the house and you leave the car underground, coming up some steps to a vast deck on the seaward side overlooking the dunes and the ocean beyond. On this side, the house diverges into more interesting shapes – more pirate ship than beer barrel. At one end the upper floor is glass-walled and glass-roofed: an open studio with a breath-taking view of the ocean.

Inside, Louis has some real art, great big canvases, abstract, dark and somewhat scary. Otherwise there's very little by way of personal signature, just long white sofas lying here and there.

But Louis and I don't spend time in the house. Not in the day and not in the evening either. In the day I sit on the edge of the dune on an old table, blasted by the sand into a pale uneven shadow of its former self. There I swing my legs and drink cranberry soda with a squirt of fresh lime squeezed right into the can. I watch Louis nailing pieces of wood together. We talk idly and sometimes the conversation runs out and that's okay too.

Then, every day, I say, 'Well, I'd better get back to the motel.' And every day I don't go. Boris Karloff comes worrying for a walk and I find myself obliged to take him on to the beach and play with him until Louis comes out in time for sunset – the next unmissable instalment. The sunset is different every day, high drama in neon pink, perhaps, or just long hazy stripes of rose strafing the sky from edge to edge.

Louis makes us walk the other way down the beach, away from the spectacle. Then, after a certain number of paces, we are allowed to turn round again and each time we turn it changes. The colours are deeper, more affecting, gaining impact from the time we spent looking away. Every time we turn we experience the magic again.

When it's over we go back and Louis brings beers on to the deck and says, as if surprising himself, maybe he'll light the barbecue. And why shouldn't he? And maybe

Consuela has left some blue fish in the fridge. And why wouldn't she? And so we barbecue some fish and sit on the deck watching the light fade and listening to the insects coming out to hail the night.

Sometimes Grace calls and Louis is gone for fifteen, twenty minutes or so. While he's gone, I resolve to see less of him tomorrow. Perhaps he does the same.

But the next day, after I've cycled back to my motel, after I've slept the sea-air sleep of the dead – the blissful, grateful dead – and woken late to hurry down to the beach for my swim, along comes Louis with Boris Karloff. And why shouldn't he? And then it's breakfast time and, well, we have to eat. People have to eat. And why shouldn't we?

And so it goes on – I don't know how many days. I'm not counting for once. I'm just being.

At some point, though, I call Dick and – God is on my side – I get his voicemail. I tell him I'm off the case. I won't be writing about Louis again and my decision is final. Then I turn off my phone. I reason that if he sacks me when I get back to London, he sacks me. I've always got my grandmother book. I've always got the little lump in my Instant Saver.

And so it goes on. It's the small details you most remember, the moments in between – who said that? Like me slipping a coin into the bubble-gum machine outside the general store, or the fisherman on the beach who thought Boris Karloff was going to eat his catch, or the white blush on the fresh blueberries bought at the roadside, or the taste of oily blue fish.

In the evenings, Louis spends hours standing over the

barbecue, spatula in hand. Either that or he leans on the rail of the deck and smokes cigarettes and listens to the sea beyond the dunes.

One night he says, 'You know, the way I look at it, there's three of us.' I look up, but he's not looking my way and he goes straight on, 'There's me, there's Grace and there's the relationship. And the relationship – the thing that exists between us – has a life of its own, a story of its own, and always has. In some ways it's beyond my control.'

Then he gets himself a fresh beer and tells me about falling for Grace.

They met on his first film. The one Mary Jane Cuthbertson left him over. Good old Mary Jane Cuthbertson. Grace was a well-established star at the time and it was an honour for Louis to be playing opposite her. It was an intimate love story, the one with the Volkswagen Beetle in the desert, but Grace and Louis managed to get through the entire movie without getting to know each other at all. Louis was intrigued, but not smitten. He was getting over Mary Jane, after all. A year later they shared a hotel one night – brought together to publicise the film.

Grace was overwrought. She cried from exhaustion and too much adrenaline and some man she wouldn't talk about. Louis comforted her. They spent the night together. When Louis woke up in the morning he couldn't believe it. He'd dreamed all his life of a woman like this. They met again and again in the following weeks, as much as their schedules would allow. They flew miles and miles to be together in short breaks from filming, taking red-eye flights with a flagrant disregard for time zones and sense. When they weren't together she called him every moment she could – what did he think she should do about this, about that? Everything seemed snatched and fleeting. What was presented as an earth-shattering problem one day would be utterly forgotten the next. She was mercurial, sometimes ecstatic, high on it all, ordering up Cristal from Room Service. Other times she'd sit up smoking all night, and crying, rehearsing arguments with her critics (hardly numerous). He can't remember ever seeing her eat a meal. He made her promise to get some help, take a break. She never did. And then, just as he realised he couldn't live without her needing him this much, that he was irrevocably in love, she dropped him. She told him in an airport where their paths briefly crossed. The reason: it doesn't feel right. That's all. Doesn't feel right.

But she kept on calling him. Let's be friends, she said. And, unlike most, she meant it. She called him every day. She still wanted to talk over her problems with him. Not her men problems, but everything else. He knew he shouldn't, for his own sake, but he couldn't say no. He knew it wasn't reasonable to love her, but love her he did. He'd always thought he could never have Grace and when this was proved briefly and unreliably false and then – sickeningly – true after all, the loss triggered an age-old pain and the only cure was Grace.

He stops there. He's leaning with his back to the rail, dangling his beer in one hand. 'But it's not like that now,' he says.

I must look sceptical because he repeats himself. 'It's not,' he says.

'I believe you.'

Then he says something about prison, which I only half catch. I go and lean on the rail beside him, ask him to say it again.

'Prisoners,' he says, 'under constant surveillance go mad. Did you know that?'

I don't say anything.

'When we were in London I was having this little idea in my head that I could escape. I was, you know, nostalgic, I guess, for being an ordinary guy. I thought maybe I could go back. It's "normal", you know, to dream about going back. Grace does it. You don't know what privacy is until you lose it. It's a great, great thing. The privacy of being just another face in the crowd.'

He concentrates on his cigarette for a moment. I wait.

'When you shot me,' he goes on, 'I realised I can't ever go back. I mean, it's not your fault but the circumstances, that whole train of events made me see what was true – is true. Do you understand?'

He finishes the cigarette.

'I agreed to *Science Fiction II* because that's what I'm good at.' He pauses. 'I agreed to marry Grace because she and I are in the same boat. We understand each other. I have to make my life with another celebrity – there's no other way.'

'So it's just another piece of business, is that it?' I'm not sure how to go on.

'Does it matter?' he says. 'In your view romantic love

is what you call a "red herring", right? Relationships are basically a matter of convenience – that's your theory. Am I correct?'

'Um,' I say.

Um.

After dinner, he wants to go for a drive. As well as his pick-up, he has a big old car. An old seventies Chevrolet, open-topped. And the night is warm.

We drive down the big wide roads in the big wide car and through some woods where there are houses set back from the road. Houses the shape of shoeboxes mostly, on little legs – this is a poorer part of town. Some of them are decorated with icicle lights dripping from the eaves. We park and walk through more woods. He takes me to where there's a spit of sand reaching out into the bay. No road, no cars, no houses, nothing. Just a spit of sand coming to the point where it meets itself from the other side. I can hear a boat tapping at its moorings nearby. I can hear the lap of one-inch waves on the beach.

'I don't think love is divisible, you know,' he says. 'I don't think loving one person means you love someone else any the less.'

I don't really know what to make of this so I stare at the trees across the water and pray for revelation.

Louis goes on, 'I agree with you about romance. You can't make it stick. There's love and there's needs that have to be met. Like I said,' he says, 'you taught me a lot.'

'Damn,' I say.

We're sitting in the sand side by side, and he turns to me. 'You wouldn't want to sell your soul, would you, just because I sold mine?'

I ask him if that's a proposal. He makes an attempt at a smile. It doesn't really work.

'I mean,' he says, 'I don't draw any conclusions from the fact of you being here.'

'I'm hanging out,' I say. 'Remember?'

'Maybe you're a *mole*,' he says suddenly. 'Maybe you're going to go away and write about all this—'

He's joking, but I jump up because suddenly I can't sit there a moment longer. This mortal coil is coiled too tight for me. I kick my shoes off and go into the water. I can see it's very shallow for a long way. I stay at the edge, a grating of tiny shells, crunchy, but not painful, under my feet.

'You know they think we *did* fall in love,' I call back to Louis on the sand.

'Who's they?'

'The media, Dick, Esther – everyone. They even think we had a night together.'

He gets up, comes and stands at the water's edge. 'But we didn't,' he says.

'They think we did, though, even though we didn't.' I can feel the air between us closing in, the magnetic field – inexorable. I dig my toes down into the sand to gain some purchase, some resistance. I feel the soft delectable squelch of it oozing up between each toe.

'Do you think that means,' he says, stepping into the water and encircling me, 'that we've got one . . . how shall I put it? Owing?'

After we've kissed, he says, 'Are you all right with this? I don't want to let you down.'

'It's okay,' I say. 'I've got my feet firmly on the ground.'

When we get back to the house there's a limo in the driveway blocking our path to the underground garage.

Louis says, 'What the—?'

He pulls up and puts the car into 'park' – the gear lever is up by the steering wheel and I see his hand trembling slightly. We get out into the still night and I have a sense of foreboding.

The chauffeur is leaning against his limo, hat off, looking up at the impenetrable house. Perhaps he's just taking the night air.

'Dan?' Louis says lightly, but there's a question in it.

The chauffeur is about to speak when there comes a series of crashing noises from the house, like plates being smashed. We all stand very still in the silence that follows.

After a moment Dan says, 'She's a little stir-crazy, I reckon. We just drove all the way from DC.'

'DC?' Louis says. There's a level of alarm in his voice that makes the hairs on the back of my neck stand on end. Dan's, too, I wouldn't doubt.

'I'm sorry,' Dan says. 'I was confused. New York. I meant New York.'

'She didn't let me know she was coming,' Louis says.

Dan shrugs, as in 'I just do what I'm told'.

Louis heads for the house. As he does a small back door opens above us and Grace steps out on to the wooden stairway. She strikes a pose, hands in pockets, before lowering her gaze to where we stand. I don't remember hearing her, I only know that I looked up instinctively the way I sometimes do when someone is watching me. But Grace isn't looking at me.

She's wearing very short white dungaree shorts, her pregnancy showing as a neat little bump. Her long greyhound legs end in a pair of wedged white sneakers. The *pièce de résistance* – the thing that shows she has *dressed* as opposed to put on some clothes like the rest of us – is a little white movie-star scarf tied around her neck.

So she stands up there on the steps and she looks down on us and, I don't know, I suppose in that moment she knows she is not wanted. Which is not about anything anybody says or does or doesn't say or doesn't do – in fact, Louis moves towards her and I smile and salute – but it is the undercurrent of information that flows between us, the data that is transmitted below the line. Above the line, Grace is being greeted and hugged and smiled at and welcomed; below the line, *she is not wanted* and there is nothing, not one thing, that any of us can do about it. Which isn't to say that Louis doesn't love her and which isn't to say that I wish to take Louis from her – neither of those things is true. But we've got a routine going here and Grace won't know the steps – she hasn't learnt the dance. It's not her fault. But we blame her anyway.

Louis and Grace go into the house and I just stand there, out in the drive with Dan, feeling like a fool. After a moment, Louis re-emerges and waves me in. I go up the steps reluctantly, my feet like stone. The three of us walk together out on to the seaward deck. Grace picks her way elegantly through the smashed dinner plates that litter the floor. No one says a word about them. Not a word.

'Stevie's been helping me build the pergola,' Louis says. 'Consuela wants to grow roses.'

'Great,' Grace says, in a way that makes it clear she doesn't want or require explanations. We give her them anyway: how I came out to the States to apologise for the shooting, how I like swimming every morning, how Louis was craving doing something physical, practical – hence the pergola – how the weather has been great. Grace just sits down in an Adirondack chair, sweeping one perfect leg up and throwing it down to dangle over the other while she listens patiently to our smokescreen.

When Louis goes inside to get iced tea, she fixes me with those delicately bloodshot crystalline green eyes and says, 'I am so happy that Louis has *finally* found a friend.'

25

That night our routine is broken, of course. I go home shortly after the iced tea. Nothing for it but to carry on, to cycle away, to move forward, turn the page. As I ride I find my consciousness is punctured by moments of realisation. The moments surface like air bubbles in oil, making their way slowly, to the upper skin of my awareness. Inside each air bubble is a *soupçon* of captured memory from the beach. A moment of sensuous recall, small, but quite powerful as it passes through my body and releases.

'Home' is the motel, and it's not until I get there and shut myself into my gloomy little room that I realise I can't be in there. I can't. I peer out of the window. The moon is up.

I think about calling London but I absolutely do not want to. I want to hear nothing of Esther, nothing of Jay and Phil – to reach over, lift the phone and dial feels like an effort beyond imagining. To exchange words across the Atlantic – surely the strain would be too much. And, anyway, how would I describe what's happening? They wouldn't understand.

I jump up, grab a sweater and head out to the bicycle. I cycle like the wind.

Cycling heaven is here – compared to London. Long

wide flat roads. Empty. The occasional sports utility vehicle making a polite arc around me as it overtakes. I pass white clapboard churches and houses straight out of the American dream – cosy porches, rocking chairs, aquamarine hydrangeas, a Stars and Stripes dangling from a door. Dogs bark and rush me uselessly, then are left behind. The lights in the houses across the marsh reflect in the salt water of the ocean ponds. I suddenly realise there is a flock of geese nearby, hundreds of them, in the long grass.

When I get to the beach I drop the bicycle into a dune and scramble out on to the sand. The moonlight seems impossible – as if it's bouncing back around the edge of the earth.

I walk along the beach, in the opposite direction to Louis's house, and soon I come across a clambake. I've heard about clambakes. What alerts me first is the smell of marijuana. I walk past at a respectful distance. The people are younger than me. On my way back, though, one of the boys is down at the edge of the surf washing something in the ocean. He smiles as I approach.

'Hi,' he says. There are two types of 'hi' – the open-ended and the finite. This is the open-ended kind.

I say, 'Hi,' back. Also the open-ended kind.

'Would you settle a bet for me?' he says. 'Are you American?'

'I'm English.' Now I have to know what the bet was. I tell him as much.

'I bet with my friend that you weren't American.'

'How come?'

'Just something about you.'

'Bad teeth?' I suggest.

He laughs and asks me if I want a beer so I go over and join the group. They all stop talking when I arrive and introduce themselves to me – each and every one (would never happen at home). They all seem to be called things like River and Meadow. I like them, though. They offer me sweetcorn, baked in foil but burnt anyway.

Soon everyone becomes very stoned and stares into the fire or up at the sky where the stars have come out. I'm not stoned, but I'm happy to stare. I decide I'd make a good hippie. I feel tired of fighting battles. I feel tired of trying to get things right. Wouldn't it be nice just to . . . *exist*. I wonder how long I would last, how long it would take for my demons to catch up with me.

When I finally cycle home it's two in the morning. Even on the warmest night the temperature drops eventually and my cotton sweater hadn't been enough – my teeth had started to chatter so I'd said my goodbyes, was invited to come again, and made my way back to my bike. Once there, I realised I didn't have a light, which was a little scary. The moon had gone. But I set off anyway, hoping for the best.

There are no cars about and the roar of the cicadas is like a high electrical hum out there in the atmosphere, the noise of friction, particles in motion. Shapes loom in the darkness, receiving light – I don't know where from. They seem distorted, threatening, impossible, and then at the last minute they resolve into familiar objects – a road sign, a tractor, a barrow. I stop and take my bearings outside the schoolhouse. There's a light here. I'm trying not to think of all those American horror

movies I saw in my teens – *Nightmare On Elm Street*,
etc. There's a sign where I've stopped and I start to read
it automatically. 'Here Captain John Stormont of the
English army was whipped with the cat o' nine tails—'

Nice. I read no further. I cycle on, turn into a side
road where there is a white shape ahead. It takes time
to work out that this shape is a person walking in the
same direction as I am cycling. I'm not sure whether to
ring my bell and warn of my presence. I am about to do
so when the whiteness resolves into dungaree shorts and
I understand, with a jolt, that this person is Grace.

I ring my bell, but hesitantly. It makes a curious
rasping noise. Grace turns – unalarmed.

'Hi,' I say, coming to a halt, 'I've been at a clambake
on the beach' – I add in case she thinks I'm following
her in some sinister way.

'Hi,' she says, as if nothing was odd at all.

'Well,' I say, and I pull a pedal into place with my
foot. I wonder where she's off to. The Senator crosses
my mind. 'Can I give you a lift somewhere?' I smile to
indicate *joke*.

She doesn't smile back. 'I can't sleep at night,' she
says, 'so I walk.'

'Oh,' I say. 'Never?'

She looks blank.

'I mean, can you never sleep?' I say ungracefully.

'Sometimes it's worse than other times. It depends.'

'On?'

'Things.'

'Oh.' I nod. 'I sleep like a log here,' I say.

'You do?' she says.

'Like a log.'

'Well, I guess that's the difference between us,' she observes, making me wonder why I was quite so insistent on being a log. I look down and fool with my bike pedal some more. 'You just keep turning up,' she says, 'don't you?'

A bad penny.

'What exactly are you doing here?'

'I'm not sure,' I say. 'But I don't think I have to explain myself to you.' The words come out with more edge than I'd intended. They give me a shot of adrenaline, my blood rushes a little. I look up defiantly.

There's a silence while she considers the situation. A silence much more unnerving than any fast retort. Eventually she says, 'Louis has decided to trust you. I think he might be making a mistake – and I've told him so.'

'What do you mean?'

'You're a journalist.'

'I'm not here as a journalist.'

She looks away, as if slightly bored with the conversation. 'I just hope I'm not proved right, that's all.'

'I care about Louis.'

'And I don't?'

I just look at her.

'Louis and I are two peas in a pod,' she says. 'Good night.'

My motel is a long, low, shabby blue building in what they call the town commons – a vast concrete car park set back off the highway boasting a WalMart, a Gap, a supermarket called King Kullen, and all the usual chains. My room is on the first floor – the second, they call it here – so I park my bike and turn into the dark outside staircase where I'm startled to see the bright red glow of a cigarette in action and then astounded to find that the owner of the cigarette is Rico.

'Jesus,' I say.

'That's right,' he says. 'It's the Second Coming.'

'Third or fourth, more like. What the hell are you doing here?'

'I'd follow you to the ends of the earth, *bella ragazza*.'

I just carry on up the stairs. Rico gets up and follows me. I put my key in my door, but pause before turning it.

'Rico, what *are* you doing here?'

'Following Grace, of course,' he says. 'How's it going with Louis?'

'It's a long story,' I say.

'I've got all night.'

'You're not coming in.'

'Then we'll talk here.' He gestures towards where a couple of plastic sun-loungers are angled to look out over the low balustrade. Quite what they are doing there I don't know. They afford a charming view of the car park.

'No,' I say, 'we can talk tomorrow.'

Rico puts a hand on my forearm, the one holding the key. 'We'll talk tonight,' he says, in a low voice, 'or I might just go away with the wrong idea. They say the camera doesn't lie, but I happen to know that sometimes it does.' He releases my forearm, pulls his camera off his shoulder, twirls it a few times on its straps then puts it ceremoniously on to one of the sun-loungers. It sits there, menacing somehow.

'Oh, shit,' I say, 'Rico, can't you just fucking fuck off?'

'I'd love a beer,' he says.

I get beers from my mini-bar, come back out and perch anxiously on the other sun-lounger. Rico fires up one of his horrible Italian cigarettes.

'Tell me what you've seen,' I say.

'First, you tell me—'

'Rico,' I interrupt, 'tell me what you've seen or this conversation is going no further.'

'I was following Grace. I saw you and Louis arrive in the convertible. I saw Grace come out.'

'Is that it?'

'I've been with Grace in DC. I got my shot—'

'Hard evidence?'

'It's a good photo.'

'And I suppose it's now your public duty to reveal this scandal to an unastounded world?'

'*Certo.*'

'And why are you telling me all this? Why are you here?'

'Because I want you out of the picture.'

'Oh,' and I laugh at that, with a glance at the camera.

Rico squints and rubs his forehead a little, his intensity is dropping, he seems tired now. 'It's not such a good story if you're in it, confusing things. If Louis has you, then it's not so clean, Grace's betrayal is not so great. And, anyway, who are you? A nobody.'

'No worries,' I say. 'I'm out of the picture. It's a done deal.' I move to get up. 'And if that's all you want, I'm going to bed.'

'*Bene*. I'll join you.'

'You will not.'

'Okay,' he says. 'But can I sleep in your room?'

'No. Get your own room.' I go over and put my key in the door again. Rico joins me.

'The motel office is shut,' he says.

'It's twenty-four-hour.'

'The office is shut. I've been to look.'

'Go to another motel.'

'There are no other motels. Come on,' he says, 'it's only one night.'

I think for a moment. 'When's the story going to break?'

'The photos will be on the news-stands Friday morning, but the story will break tomorrow evening when the paper goes to bed.'

'I want to tell Louis first. I don't want him to find out from a newspaper.'

'You can't tell him.'

'Rico!' I say, and I take my key out of the door.

'Okay,' Rico says, 'you can tell him. But not until tomorrow evening. You can tell him then.'

'Okay,' I say. But still I hesitate to open the door.

I wake up late. My body clock is set that way from lazy days. Rico is asleep, snoring lightly on the floor. I consider escape. I could go straight over to Louis's house right now. Tell him everything. But I'm only wearing a

T-shirt and knickers and I doubt I could get the rest of my clothes on without waking Rico. So I lie there ruing the fact that I ever took them off at all and then there's a knock at the door.

I freeze. Rico jumps up as if shot, wearing nothing but his sheet. When he realises where he is he falls on to the bed with a groan. I climb over him to the door.

'Who is it?' I say.

'Open up, ma'am,' comes an officious bark from the other side.

'Who is it?' I say again.

'Stevie Dunlop?' says the officious man.

'Yes?' I say and my voice squeaks.

'I am a federal officer, ma'am. And, at this time, I am requiring you to open this door.'

I turn and look at Rico who is watching wide-eyed from the bed. All sorts of scenarios are running through my head: the Senator is on to us, Grace has been murdered and they think I did it . . . I turn and check the window, in case it's an option.

'What do you want?' I squeak, buying time.

'Ma'am, I am with the Federal Bureau of Investigation. Are you aware that it's a violation of state law code four hundred and sixty-three b to *consort* on the public beaches—'

'*Shit!*' I mouth at Rico, hopping up and down now in horror. The clambake! The drugs! 'It's the FBI!'

'For God's sake,' Rico says, 'open the door.' He gets up off the bed, dragging the sheet with him for modesty.

I go for the window and am half out, straddling the frame in my knickers, when Rico opens the door. Louis is standing outside holding a bunch of flowers. 'Man, you're a good actor,' Rico says.

Louis looks at Rico, looks at me. 'Fucking Rico fucking Bargello,' he says.

'I'm not,' I say immediately – from the window.

Louis says, 'You're setting me up. The two of you! What a surprise.'

'No,' I say, 'no – no – no – no,' and I slide back into the room.

'Shit,' Louis says, and he shakes his head a couple of times as if to get rid of a fly that has settled on the end of his nose. Then he turns and walks away, still holding the flowers, and I get the feeling he hasn't noticed he's still holding the flowers. And I also get the feeling he's not that surprised. Not *that* surprised.

It's a horrible feeling.

I pull on a pair of jeans. My intention is to run hell for leather after Louis. Rico grabs me. I try to wrestle myself out of his clutches. He tackles me to the floor. He means business. Half a ton of muscle with a bullet head.

'You can't tell him,' he says. 'It's too soon.'

'Let me go!' I scream at the top of my lungs.

'Do you want Grace to get away with it?'

'I have to tell him!' I yell.

'Do you want the Senator to get the story pulled?'

'Let me go!' I screech.

'No,' Rico says. Simple as that.

And then my saviour, a woman with a mop, appears where Louis has left the door open. She looks in anxiously. 'Come back later?' she says, seeing us entwined on the floor.

'Help me!' I yell.

The woman does absolutely nothing, but she doesn't leave and evidently Rico feels obliged, reluctantly, to dismount. I leap up and pull on my jeans, jumping around like a madwoman and tripping over a couple of times in my haste.

'It's a game,' Rico says to the maid, by way of explanation.

She doesn't look convinced.

'A sex game,' he offers. 'She likes it.'

'You fucking bastard,' I add and slap him round the face for good measure, then run for the door. But by the time I've got down to the car park, Louis is long gone.

26

When I get to Louis's house, the gate out on the road is shut. I've never seen it shut before. I ring the bell but there's no answer. There's a pain in my chest, thumping against my breastbone. All I can think about is Louis thinking that I was conning him all that time – Louis thinking that everything that happened between us was a lie.

I pick my bike up off the Tarmac and cycle down the road to the beach. There I leave the bike in the small sandy car park and run along the top of the dune. The weather has turned and the sky is a pale wash of misty grey. The wind has sprung up and is restless, gusting, changing direction, sending the clouds scudding one way and then the other. And the ocean is higher than I've ever seen it – most of the beach gone. In some places the surf is even lapping at the dunes. Everything seems different – I barely recognise the place.

I stagger along the dunes, turning my ankle every now and then in the loose sand and chased by gusts of surf until I get to Louis's house. I know where to leave the dunes – a weatherbeaten group of deck chairs marks the spot. I slide down a narrow passage, wooden fencing on one side, and then through the hole in the hedge and into Louis's backyard.

The house looks deserted. I run up on to the deck to peer in through the plate-glass windows – I can only see through when right up against them, with a hand shading my eyes. I jump back with a start. Boris Karloff flings himself at the glass in greeting and Consuela is mopping the floor behind. It takes her a moment to work the catch and I am left, embarrassed, the glass between us, my explanation bubbling on my lips while she watches me, placid and insulated on the other side.

Then she slides back the window. The wind is stronger now and my hair is whipping around my face with some ferocity. I squat down and Boris Karloff climbs all over me.

'Have they gone?' I say to Consuela, raising my voice to be heard.

'Gone. Yes. For wedding.' She gives me a beatific and triumphant smile. 'Los Angeles,' she adds, relishing the words in her own language.

My face must tell a story because then she says, 'What the matter?'

'Everything,' I say.

'Not the end of the world,' she says.

'I think it might be,' I say, and bury my head in the dog. The only place for it.

'I'll get this, Consuela,' a voice says. Louis. I glance at Consuela.

'She gone. He here,' she says proudly, and turns her back.

Louis doesn't invite me in, but he steps out on to the deck and slides the glass shut behind him. I guess he doesn't want Consuela to hear.

'This is private property,' he says to me. 'I think you should leave.'

'Louis,' I say, 'please—'

He doesn't wait for me to explain. He is instantly at boiling point and I am so used to his gentle simmer that it shocks me to the core. 'I must have been crazy to trust you. Crazy!' he yells, right in my face.

'But why?' I say stupidly. I back away from him a couple of steps. I can't help it. 'I—'

'The first time I trusted you I nearly DIED!'

Boris Karloff whimpers and goes to lie under the picnic table.

'That wasn't my fault!' I say.

'What in fuck's name do you mean, it wasn't your fault? It *was* your fault. I asked you not to get involved with the madwoman. And what did you do? You gave her your ticket to the première . . . *my* première.' He stabs his chest with one finger. 'I can't *ever* forgive you for that,' he yells ferociously, defying the wind.

I back up some more.

'And then I find you hanging out with Rico Bargello. Do you have any idea how dangerous that man is? Do you have any idea what he can do to me? Do you have any *fucking* idea what it's like being me?'

Suddenly I'm yelling back: 'Oh, being you, being you, being you, you'd think every fucking thing on this planet was about *being you*. Well, I've got *news* for you. The world does not revolve around Louis fucking Plantagenet!'

'What does it revolve around? Stevie fucking Dunlop and all her fucking theories about putting it to rights? I don't think so! And you know what – the world *does* revolve around me. I don't want it to but the fact is – *to some extent* – it does! And you don't want to admit it! You don't want to acknowledge the weight I'm carrying because it doesn't fucking fit your version of how the world should be.'

'Oh, please! It's not so fucking terrible being a celebrity. I mean, what's so terrible about that? There are people starving out there you know. Working their fingers to the bone. In sweat shops.'

'Oh you love a sweat shop worker, don't you? You'd do anything for a downtrodden stranger. But what about your own fucking friends? What do you do for them? Fucking shoot them, that's what!'

'Oh, get over it.'

'Get over it?'

'You've got your consolations, haven't you? You've got this!' I fling a hand at his million dollar beach pad.

'You think I can't suffer? You think just because I've got a beach house I can't have any pain? You! You who's so sure the world is a terrible, terrible place. You who's so hung up on human rights. What about my fucking human rights? Do you think I'm not a human? Do you think there's one rule for the poor and another for the rich?'

'What is it you want? You want fame and fortune, a fucking beach house and my *pity* too! Is that what you want?'

'You crack me up. You really crack me up, you know that. You think you know it fucking ALL!'

'You know what?' I yell back. 'I do.'

This brings him up short. He's lost for a moment, takes a couple of steps towards me. 'You do – what?'

'Know it all. *To some extent*,' I add, mimicking him. 'I do know it all. I certainly know a hell of a lot more than you do.' I'm no longer shouting and my body goes from blazing intensity to icy cold which means I'm definitely out of control. 'For example,' I say, 'I know that Grace Farlow is using you like Consuela uses her mop. She's been fucking Senator Donald Bragg since time began. And she still is.'

'Get off my property!' he says.

I'm glad to comply. I turn and run back the way I came, across the garden, up on to the dunes, my hair whipping across my face in the wind, slipping and falling in my haste and in the sand, sliding – every now and again – into the shallow swirling waters, soaking my trainers in the surf.

I'm aware of a presence behind me. I turn: Boris Karloff is lolloping at my heels, mistaking this flight for fun. Then Louis comes over the dune.

'Wait!' he shouts.

I set off running again. It's no good. He catches up easily and pulls me around by one shoulder. 'Where did you get this information?'

'Louis,' I say, 'I can't tell you. I can only tell you it's true.'

I will him to believe me, but he only says, 'I'm not letting you go unless you tell me where you got this information.'

'I saw the evidence with my own eyes,' I say.

'I don't believe you,' he says.

'It's true.'

'I'll never believe anything you say again.'

'Look at Boris Karloff!' The dog has misjudged the sea on this strange unsettled day and is in too deep, too far out for comfort. He tries swimming back towards us but makes no progress. He turns sideways and gets buffeted by a wave. He is spun, goes under, paws up in the surf. For a horrible moment we lose him among the white caps, but then he resurfaces further out with his nose up. He's travelled so far so quickly, there must be a strong current.

Louis lets go of me and we both yell the dog's name. It's useless in the wind. Louis looks at the water, looks at the dog, looks at me. He kicks off his shoes.

'I'm coming too,' I say, because I can't see how he's going to get the dog back on his own. We wade out. It's shallow enough, waist deep, for quite a way and then we're forced to swim. We dive through the bottom of the waves and although it seems as if we could easily get beyond them we never do. There's no sign of Boris Karloff now. We stay out there as long as we can. Eventually Louis signals that we should go back. We swim towards the beach at a diagonal, which is what Louis knows to do when there's a current. At first it seems a long way off, the beach, but the diagonal thing works and suddenly we are there.

Louis simply sits down in the sand and puts his head in his hands.

I stand over him. 'I'm sorry,' I say. They're the only two words I can think of. Such deplorable, spineless, paltry words. But all others have deserted me.

Louis doesn't look up. I'd dearly like to join Boris Karloff in his turbulent grave, but don't have the guts, of course, for such a gesture, so I pick up my trainers and head towards the car park and the bicycle, my sodden clothes as heavy as my leaden heart.

The bike, as it turns out, is redundant. There's a car waiting for me. A warm, humming, fast car. I plonk myself down in the passenger seat like a balloon full of water that bursts.

'I think I've killed his dog,' I say.

'*Madonna!*' Rico wails. But he stamps on the accelerator and we screech away.

Of course, I don't know for sure if Louis is blaming me. I asked him, before I left, but he made no sign, his head down.

I haven't had my phone on all week – avoiding Dick's inevitable manipulative calls. But on my way to the Dunkin' Donuts concession I turn it on again. Rico, who is stunned by his own heroism – finding out where I was from Consuela and coming to rescue (his word) me – is having his breakfast there. I've been up in the motel room, changing my wet clothes and packing my things.

'By the way,' I say spitefully, mounting my Dunkin' Donuts bar stool, 'I told Louis about Grace.'

'*Va bene. Va bene,*' he says, waving away my attempt at aggression with a horrible-looking iced ring doughnut. 'It's not going to make a difference now.'

'That's not what you said this morning.'

'I just spoke to the bossman. The story's in the can.'

He looks mighty pleased with himself. 'Doughnuts are on me,' he says expansively.

'It's all right for you, you heartless bastard,' I say, 'but you've just ruined my life, you know.'

'What do you mean?' he says straightening his spine and throwing up his chin with Latinate passion. 'What do you mean I've ruined your life? I've *made* your life. He's not going to marry Grace now. He's going to fall into *your* arms!' He pauses a moment, then adds, 'I mean, afterwards, later – not too soon. Like I said, I don't want you to muddy the waters. But maybe in six weeks or so – yes – the great Louis P finds consolation in the arms of an ordinary girl, the girl next door . . .' Here Rico makes a gesture with a hand as if visualising the four-page *Hello!* magazine spread '. . . yes, it's good, and you can give me an exclusive on the pictures.'

'He's not going to fall into my arms.'

'Why not?'

'He thinks I'm a traitor. Because of you. Remember?'

'Really?' he says, with genuine surprise, and I'm just wondering whether or not to smack him in the face when my phone rings.

It's Dad.

'Dad!' Now, much as I love Dad, he's the last person on earth I want to speak to at this moment in time. The man, quite frankly, is out of the loop. 'Dad! How great to hear you!'

We make a tiny bit of small-talk. I'm well, he's well, Irena's well. 'Stevie,' he says, 'your gran's in hospital.'

It's funny: he doesn't have to say another word because in that moment I know.

I just know.

Something deep inside me lifts its weary head, something primeval, something very knowing indeed. In some way, I realise, I've been waiting for this phone call all of my adult life. When I get off the phone I tell Rico I'm going back to London because of my gran.

'Your gran?' he says.

'Yes,' I say. 'She's going to die.'

27

So I'm back at Heathrow. Back trilling down those endless grey corridors but this time with a wheelie suitcase – just as I should be. And it seems like a long, long time since I walked through this airport and bumped into Louis and got tangled up with Mike . . . and all the rest of it.

And, funnily enough, I have a little surge of nostalgia for the day that I walked through this airport, not knowing that I was about to bump into Louis Plantagenet. Odd to feel nostalgia for even the worst of times. But then I feel odd about a lot of things right now, a numb, sleep-deprived oddness.

It's true, I didn't sleep on the flight, but not because I was thinking about Gran. I was thinking about everything but Gran. My mind kept going to the Gran drawer, so to speak, but when it opened there was nothing there. So it opened other drawers instead, drawers full of old anxieties that hadn't been taken out and worried at for years, drawers full of junk. Exhausting. And when my mind wasn't doing that it just read the legend on the back of the seat in front of me – 'Life jacket under seat' – over and over again.

And as I walk through the airport I find the words are still in my head, beating a rhythmic accompaniment to the movement of my feet: *life jacket under seat life jacket under seat life jacket under seat*. Other thoughts may come in only as harmony. *Passport control life jacket under seat baggage reclaim life jacket under seat nothing to declare life jacket under seat*. Suddenly I wonder if there is a hidden message. With a small jolt of conviction I think, *It's a sign!*

My mind races off, trying for an interpretation. My *life jacket* – hope, renewal, salvation – is *under my seat*, hidden, below, beneath, the unconscious. What am I being told? That my salvation is here? That I am in fact sitting on it *and have been all the time*?

'Stevie!'

'Esther! You came to meet me!'

'Your dad told me to. You look terrible.'

'And you look pregnant!' I say admiring her much increased bump.

'How was the flight? Did you sleep?'

'No, is Gran – is Gran okay?'

Esther gives me a fearful look. 'She's not okay, Stevie,' she says, 'but she's still with us, if that's what you meant.'

Yes, that's what I meant.

At the hospital, Gran is in a room with three beds. She is in the one by the window. There are white plastic curtains that divide the beds if you want privacy. Luckily, there is nobody next to Gran. Someone was there yesterday, Dad says, but she died in the night. The woman in the bed on the corridor side of the room is full of tubes and has the kind of cough that makes you realise the difference between people who are really ill and people we call ill in the outside world, but who in fact just have colds.

Gran looks rather beautiful. Her soft halo hair is doing its halo thing, spreading out in Afro fashion on the pillow behind her head. She is as pale as rice paper and as translucent. Her veins, always a feature, are the colour of violet cream.

I say hello and take her cool, passive hand into mine – and there it lies, like a dead mouse. When she registers this gesture, her eyes move very slowly to mine. She is not at all surprised to see me. As far as she's concerned, there's no question of me having come from anywhere, I am simply *there* and that's all there is to it.

'Oh,' she whispers, dropping her gaze, 'look at that beautiful cat. A beautiful black cat.' She makes a gesture with her free hand that describes perfectly a cat leaping lightly on to her lap, arching its back, and receiving a well-timed caress.

I look at Dad. Gran always *hated* cats.

'It's the morphine,' he says.

Gran has a large cancerous tumour under her left arm. The cancer is also in her liver and brain. Apparently, she was out the day before yesterday having a picnic with Rupert on the upper reaches of the Thames. They'd had strawberries and cream. Gran's favourite. Rupert had dropped her off that night and she'd seemed fine. The next day he'd called round and, getting no answer at the door, had looked through the letter-box. He saw Gran lying on the hall floor still in her picnic outfit. He called an ambulance.

The doctors said it wasn't all that remarkable that Gran had been living such a normal life in such an advanced stage of cancer. It happens sometimes with the old. There was nothing to be done now except to give her morphine.

Thank God. No radiotherapy, no chemo, no throwing-up, no pointless operations. Thank you, God.

Rupert calls and says can he come. I say of course, and when he turns up we hug each other for ages. It's one of those hugs that takes you by surprise – once you're in it you realise you never want to come out you need it so badly. And we hardly know each other. Later Esther shows up. And Irena. We all sit around the bed. It's quite a party.

We read some poems – Rupert's idea – but Gran doesn't seem much interested. A horrible silence falls. Gran hums something to herself, a few notes that trail off, she looks over our heads and out of the window with filmy unseeing eyes.

'Right,' I hear myself saying. 'I begin with M. Who am I?' Everyone looks at me in horror, except Rupert who just looks confused. 'Twenty questions!' I say, and remind him that games were something Gran always played in her *salon* when there was any fear of conversation flagging.

Gran suddenly cries, 'Mussolini!' with great animation. We all laugh. She looks pleased.

'You have to *win* a direct question,' I say strictly. 'And it's not Mussolini.'

We start to play. Everyone gets rather absorbed. Gran shouts out enthusiastic and off-the-wall entries every now and then. I don't think she really knows what's going on but I'm sure she can feel the spirit of it. She looks from one to another of us.

At one point I'm having a sparring match with Dad over an unbelievably obscure jazz musician he's trying to catch me out on – one of his favourite tricks. I've quite forgotten where I am, gripped with the competitive spirit as we are in our family. In the midst of outraged laughter, I turn to Gran and suddenly find her looking at me. No, not at me – into me. And in that moment I see that she is not seeing me, not seeing my laughing mouth, or the colour of my eyes, or even this skin that I am in. She is looking at her daughter's daughter, the child I was, the child who meant so much to her just by virtue of existing, nothing more.

I think she's looking at my soul.

I hope my soul looked back.

And then she turns her head and the moment is over. The game goes on. No one has noticed my moment but I feel stripped bare. I think I was more loved by her in that dying moment than in all our living ones.

Nothing more needs to be said. I know I'll have what she gave me for ever.

It gets to be dark. Esther must go, she's very pregnant and tired. The doctors think Gran will last the night so Dad, Irena and Rupert decide to go and get some sleep and come back in the morning. I am staying.

Gran sleeps a little. I'm not exactly sure it is sleep, more like a light coma, a withdrawal. Then I watch TV a while. There's one angled into the ceiling in the corner of the room. Then I think I can't be watching TV when my grandmother is dying, but the dying is quite *slow*, let's face it, so I watch TV some more. Then I turn the sound to mute and just sit there. The woman in the other bed continues to cough.

I wake up to a rasping sound. It's coming from Gran – very constricted breathing. I run to get the nurse. I'm afraid to touch Gran somehow. The nurse isn't. She sits Gran up and rubs her back in a businesslike manner.

'There you go,' she says.

There you go – from this life to the next. It's all very simple. Gran suddenly opens her eyes very wide.

'Hello!' I say, startled. She's not looking at me, though. She's not looking at anything.

'There you go,' says the nurse. She leans Gran back and closes her eyes. The breathing stops. The nurse looks at her watch and then at me.

Right on cue, I start to cry. I'm quite relieved. I'd had a horrible feeling I wasn't going to do the right thing. But again, it's very simple. Someone dies, you cry. No need to worry. All taken care of.

'I'll leave you for a while,' the nurse says gently.

I take her place holding Gran, sorry that the nurse had to do it in the crucial moment, not me. I go on crying for a while. Then it comes to me that I should open the window to let her soul out. I've seen this in a film, read it in a book – I can't remember. You're meant to open the window to let the soul out.

I leap up and go to the window but it's sealed and modern, one big pane. There is a lever of a sort, but I have no faith that it will work. I have a go – nothing. I try again. Nothing. I gulp back tears and snot and head for the corridor – I am going to *complain*! Souls must go free!

The desk where the nurse sits is empty. There's a copy of the *Gazette* discarded on her seat. The whopper headline screams: DIS-GRACE! I grab it. The picture is of Grace nose to nose with a dark-haired, powerful-looking man. For a fleeting moment he reminds me of my dad.

Dad! I must call Dad. When I've done that I run back to Gran's room. She's still there. Still dead. I throw myself at the window with a howl. I put all my weight on to that handle – and, suddenly, it happens. The large pane swings open with considerable momentum taking my upper half with it. For a moment I am hanging over a seven-storey drop, but then the fulcrum turns and the pane swings back again and I am safe.

I stand back, shaking a little and then I start to laugh. A big hilarious laugh. The nurse comes in and I explain about the window and she laughs with me and we wedge it open with a pillow so that I am comforted on behalf of Gran's soul. And then we sit one on either side of Gran on the bed, quite companionable, really. And I cry some more but laugh too. For some reason everything the nurse says seems slightly hilarious. We are quite bonded so I tell her about the newspaper headline and my adventures with Louis and they seem funny beyond belief. So I sit there like that, laughing and crying, the two being quite interchangeable and really, it occurs to me, in this instance, the same emotion, until my father comes.

*   *   *

Three days later, we are standing in Gran's sitting room clasping lukewarm Hukwa tea in cup and saucer. We've just come back from the chapel of rest, so it is a wake, I suppose, although for me that word conjures Guinness and wild dancing, neither of which is on offer here. At least I've told everyone to wear colours. It seems very important that people wear colours. Loud ones. Gran's cronies have done well. The fading heiress is in a large fuchsia pink hat, the defrocked priest in deep blue velvet and even the foxy gent has stretched to a lively tweed.

But it's still there, the gloomy apologetic air that people wear at funerals, apologising, I suppose, for being alive. Rupert is doing the honours, circling the room, with shaky hands and a teapot. 'I only hope your grandmother didn't change her will in favour of that Rupert character,' Irena says to me.

'What – and leave him her collection of precious bath hats?'

'I'm only thinking of your inheritance.'

'I don't care if she did. She adored Rupert.'

Irena drops her mouth to my ear and murmurs, 'I'm thinking of leaving your father.'

I retreat with haste to the kitchen where Esther is brewing, her pregnant bulge looking quite cumbersome these days.

'This came for you,' she says, and hands me a letter.

I haven't been at home because I've been staying at Gran's, sorting through her stuff. I open the letter up.

'It's from the Crown Prosecution Service,' I say, when I've read it. 'They want me to be a witness at the mad fan's trial. I've got to go and give another statement.' My despondency settles and increases. 'I don't particularly want to be instrumental in sending that poor woman to prison, even if she is a nut.'

'Throw away the key,' Esther says. 'That's what I say.'

I don't laugh, which gets her attention. She looks me over. 'You seem doomy,' she says.

'You're meant to be doomy at funerals.'

'Quite the opposite.' She chuckles. 'Anyway, we've got a surprise for you later that will cheer you up.'

'And I've got one now.'

I turn. Dick is in the doorway groaning under the weight of a case of champagne. He delivers it gratefully on to the table.

'It's ice cold,' he says. 'It's been in the fridge.'

Esther looks at me. I look at Esther.

'Esther,' I say, 'meet Dick.'

'The Dick?' Esther says.

I glance at Dick. 'That's me,' he says proudly, throwing off his jacket and loosening his kipper tie. And then to Esther, 'I feel I know you quite well.'

'A couple of weeks ago,' Esther says, speaking to me but holding Dick's eye, 'this man was on the phone to me all hours when he couldn't get hold of you. He was practically issuing writs at one point. But now look, he's bringing champagne!'

'That's because I tipped Dick off about Grace's disgrace,' I say. 'Before I left the States. It gave him a head start of . . .' I turn to Dick '. . . oh, at least eight hours.'

'Eight very important hours.'

'So we're all friends again,' Esther says. 'That's nice.'

'By the way,' Dick says, 'we've had this.' He pulls a piece of paper out of his pocket and starts to read from it. ' "I am making this short statement in the interests of clarity and in order to bring speculation in this matter to a close. Donald Bragg is the father of my child. I loved him very much, but the relationship is now over. I am very sorry for any pain I may have caused him or his family. Louis Plantagenet has always been a very good friend to me. Due to the pressures of his schedule, however, our wedding will not be taking place at the end of the month as planned. Rumours concerning the manner of the cessation of my contract with Revlon and my withdrawal from the upcoming picture *Everlasting* are unfounded. I am simply taking a break from public life for a time in order to concentrate on the most important job in the world: motherhood." '

There's a small silence while we digest this. Then I say to Esther, 'Did you hear that? It's the most important job in the world.'

Esther puts a hand on her belly. 'My most important job right now is to get this champagne down everybody's throats.'

Now, things get slightly blurred. At one point I definitely register 'Relight My Fire' playing at full volume. Definitely. And Esther says something about Rupert and Dick snogging in the bathroom, but this may be apocryphal. At another point I'm dancing with Phil, but then I lose him again and find myself in a long, emotional conversation with a dark-haired girl I've never met before. She has a strange accent I cannot place.

'You know what he called the marriage to Grace?' I

say. 'He called it "the merger"!' It's always struck me as a very salient fact, Louis calling it 'the merger'. And today, in my heightened champagne state, it seems more meaningful than words can say.

'Louis didn't love her,' the dark-haired girl says intently. 'That boy has always been looking for a mother.'

'How do you know?'

'Oh, you can tell the motherless boys,' she says sternly. 'They look young. You can see it in their bodies. You can see it in their faces.'

'But Grace was hardly motherly,' I say.

'Ah, but she offered security, she offered certainty. She ran the show. No?'

'Yes.'

'And then she betrayed him. All children are betrayed by their mothers in the end.'

'How do you mean?'

'Just because the mother never belongs to the child. She belongs only to herself.'

'Oh, cool,' Phil says, reappearing suddenly. 'I'm glad you two met.'

'Who is this?' I say to Phil.

'Lux!'

'The i-girlfriend,' I say. 'This is the Danish i-girl-friend?'

'Yeah,' he says, laughing, and puts his arm around her.

Next I'm introducing Esther to Irena who eyes Esther's huge belly and says sternly, 'And where is the father of your child?' Irena like Lux, has no qualms about broaching these sorts of subjects – possibly something to do with them both being Scandanavian.

'Oh, he's not here,' Esther says gaily. 'He's a drunk, you see.'

'But he's in recovery,' I add.

While I was away, Jay spent six weeks in a treatment centre (they said he was a bad case) and was then sent to what's called a 'half-way house' in north London, where he lives a strict life with other recovering alcoholics. The powers-that-be said it would be dangerous for him to come back and live in his old drinking environment too soon. Esther claims she is glad not to have him hanging around at home putting his oar in, so to speak.

'It must be hard for you without him,' Irena says.

'No, no, it's marvellous. Jay and I – I tell you – two weeks with him and I'd be running for the phone, dialling oh-eight-hundred-DIVORCE.'

'You're married?'

'No, but I'd dial it anyway.'

'What is this telephone number?' Irena says getting a neat little leather-covered notebook out of her bag with pen attached.

'Oh, but it's so easy to remember – that's the point—'

I quickly make apologies and drag Esther away. 'Esther!' I say.

'Okay, but don't even think about it. Me and Jay. We are not going to be a happy co— You see? I can't even say it: the C-word. No way.'

And after that, there's Dad cornering me in the corridor to say, 'Has Irena told you she's leaving?'

'Dad,' I say, 'what have you done?'

'Nothing! Absolutely nothing.'

'I don't believe you.'

He makes a frustrated noise in the back of his throat. 'One of my horn students, she—'

'Dad!' I wail.

'Irena's got this idea in her head—'

'Look,' I say, interrupting, 'I think you two should split up.'

'No, no,' he says.

I notice that we have changed positions and I now have Dad in the corner. 'Do you – in inverted commas – love Irena?' I say.

'Yes – in inverted commas – I do.'

'Okay. What does that mean?'

'It means . . .' He casts around, sighs, even pulls out a handkerchief and wipes his forehead.

'Oh, Dad,' I say, 'you can do it!'

'It means I'd prefer to be with her than not to be with her.'

'Is that it?'

'Yes.'

'Is that what it boils down to?'

'I suppose so.'

'So you're not splitting up with Irena,' I say. 'You never will. This is how you have your relationship. This *is* your relationship. This *is* love – in inverted commas.'

I take a step back, as it were, releasing him.

'Someone said that talking about love is like dancing about architecture,' he mumbles.

I think he thinks he's let me down. 'Have another drink, Dad,' I say.

At which point the front door opens and a handsome young man walks in. He has glossy dark hair and lively green eyes. He has a healthy glow and a clear skin. He has a vulnerability about him, but a dignity too. He looks both contained and defined. He looks like someone I'd like to get to know. He looks kind, he looks intelligent . . . he looks familiar.

'Jay?' I say.

28

When it's time for Jay to go, he and I sit on the front steps waiting for his cab. The half-way house has a strict curfew.

'How'd it go with Louis?' he says.

'Not great. I blew up his relationship and drowned his dog.'

'Drowned his dog?'

'It was an accident, of course. But it was an accident attributable to me.'

I tell him the story. When I've finished, he says, 'Do you want to be with him?'

'With Louis?' The simplicity of the question taking me by surprise. '*Be* with him?'

'Well, I'm not going to ask if you love him, am I? I know what you're like on the subject of love.'

'It's not going to happen,' I say. 'Me and Louis.'

'Oh,' he says. I give him a look. He laughs. 'I was kind of hoping it was, actually.'

'Really?'

'I've been told I need to let you go.'

'Oh,' I say.

'And you need to let me go.'

'Yes,' I say.

'Because we use each other as a kind of a fall-back. It's not healthy.'

'It's true,' I say. 'And then there's Esther.'

'And then there's Esther,' he agrees. 'But she's not the reason I have to let you go.'

'No?'

'No. It's like you and Louis, it's not going to happen. Me and Esther.'

'You don't think so?'

'I don't think so.' He pauses. 'You know, I don't really have to be at the half-way house any more. They said I was ready to come home a week ago, but . . .'

'Do you want it to happen? You and Esther?'

'Sort of. But I'm not going to push for it.'

'Why not?'

'I can't.'

'Yes, you can.'

'No, really. I can't.'

'Jay,' I say, 'you'll surprise yourself. Just push.'

'What about Esther?'

'Push for the two of you.'

The solicitor at the CPS is elderly, quite personable, quite reasonable. I am taken aback. I was expecting a brute. He's pasty-faced though, and he has the air of never being surprised by anything ever. He's wearing a pale grey suit that goes with his face and a knitted mustard yellow tie.

He takes me through my statement regarding the events at the première, asks if I have anything to add, and that seems to be it. It all seems far too uncomplicated – and factual. What about the hidden motivations of the protagonists, I wonder, what about the swirling undercurrents, the dangerous passions, the damaged childhoods? What about the states of mind?

'I'm not sure I want to be for the prosecution,' I say to the man.

'You don't have to be for anybody,' he says evenly. 'You can just tell the truth. It's usually the best policy.'

'What's going to happen to the mad fan?'

'I'm sorry?'

'The defendant?'

'A long stretch. Possibly in a nuthouse. Possibly not.'

'Do you know what her defence is?'

'Insanity.'

'You know I had a cup of coffee with her a few days before the première and she told me she was "in contact" with Louis's dead mother?'

'Yes. E-mails from beyond the grave.'

'Are you serious?'

'Absolutely. She received e-mails she believed were from Louis Plantagenet's dead mother.'

'They actually exist, these e-mails?'

'Yes. I've seen them. The defence will claim the e-mails led the defendant to believe that by killing Louis she would be reuniting him with his dead mother.'

'Where did the e-mails come from?'

'Apparently they came from a prison in the United States. A women's prison, Browneville State Penitentiary, it's called. Eileen Gost struck up correspondences with women prisoners all over the world by letter and e-mail.'

'Eileen Gost being the mad fan?'

'Exactly. Miss Gost saw herself as a medium or a

psychic or some such. She provided comfort by predicting the future, that sort of thing, sent messages of apology to the prisoners' dead victims, I wouldn't wonder.'

'So most of her actual correspondents were alive – but she thought this particular correspondent was dead.'

'Precisely. And Louis's mother is dead, of course, it's a well-known fact. That wasn't Miss Gost's error. Her error was putting two and two together and getting four hundred and sixty-eight.'

He doesn't elaborate. I look confused.

'Dead mother plus e-mails from someone claiming to be Louis's mother doesn't equal a ghost, it equals a lie.'

'So who *was* sending the e-mails?'

'Some prisoner who used the screen-name Rose. The prison say they can't trace her – and, in a way, it doesn't really matter.'

'But what did the e-mails say?'

'Oh, attention-seeking, looking for comfort, delusional, claiming to be the long-lost mother of this famous movie star, caught up in his fame, wanting to be reunited with him, but feeling she wouldn't be wanted.'

'All very understandable,' I say. 'All completely absurd.'

'However,' he says, with a grimace, 'in this job it *is* important to entertain *all* possibilities.'

'What do you mean?'

'What I say, *all* possibilities. So I checked. I had a little burrow around. Louis's mother was called Nancy Porter and she grew up in an orphanage: Our Sisters of Mercy,

Portland, Maine. Apparently, she left at seventeen and married a man called John Howard. They moved out of Portland and turned up some time later in San Diego with a baby – Louis Howard. The birth certificate is all above board. Nancy's death certificate, dated eighteen months later, likewise.'

'That doesn't seem to leave any room for doubt.'

'No, but as I said,' he sighs, 'when you've done this job as long as I have, you learn to entertain all possibilities.'

I walk through Reception on my way out and decide to make the call there and then. I do it because I know, with absolute certainty, that if I don't make it now, I never will. I go and sit in the waiting area and pull out my phone. I call the International Directory first, and then the number they give me. Our sisters of Mercy, Portland, Maine.

'I want to enquire about an ex-pupil of yours called Porter,' I say, when it picks up at the other end.

'Who's calling?'

'I'm calling from a solicitor's office in London,' I say, which happens to be true. 'I think some money may have been left to her descendants. We're trying to trace them.'

'Yes, well, you won't want to talk to me. You'll want to talk to Mrs Pitt, the school secretary. And she's not here. It's six o'clock in the morning, you know.'

Shit.

'I'm sorry,' I say. I forgot the time difference. 'I'm calling from London.'

'Yes, well, you haven't woken me. I am an extoller of the virtues of early rising. But you'd better call back later.'

'Wait a minute,' I say, on impulse, 'did you know her?'

'I know all the girls. I've been here thirty years.' She doesn't go on, but I let the silence lie, hoping that she'll be tempted to fill it. 'You'll have trouble finding out about that one,' she says eventually and I wonder if this is her drier than dry way of broaching the subject of death.

'How do you mean?' I say.

'Went to hell in a hand-basket.'

'Really?' And this from a nun.

'A wild child. Impossible to pin her down.'

'Are you sure? I understood got she married quite young—'

'*Oh, Nancy*,' she says. 'I thought you meant the other one. Nancy's dead.'

'The other one?'

'There were two. Two sisters. Nancy was a decent girl. Her son became very famous, you know. A movie star. The convent was plagued with calls from the press about him, at one time. You're not from the press, are you?'

'No,' I say, 'I'm not from the press.' There's a small silence. 'And why does no one else know about the sister?' I say.

'No one else asked.'

'PU-U-U-U-U-USH!'

I'm standing on our front-door step and this is what I

hear: 'PU-U-U-U-U-USH!' I erupt in goosebumps all over my body and put my key gingerly in the door.

In the kitchen, Esther is on the floor and Jay has her in his arms and he is the one screaming: 'PU-U-U-U-U-USH!'

Phil is on the phone and Lux is between Esther's legs with a basin of hot water and clean towels. When Esther has finished with the contraction she sees me and says, 'Men should have to do this, you know. It would change everything if men had to do this. I wonder—'

'Esther!' I say. 'Concentrate on giving birth!' At which point, she's consumed by another contraction and her face crumples down, like a crushed aluminium can. I look away, frightened suddenly, and notice Jay's suitcase by the door.

'PU-U-U-U-U-USH!' he yells.

'Okay, babe,' Esther says, and she grabs his hand.

'The ambulance is seven minutes away,' says Phil, from the phone.

'Too late,' says Lux.

'How did this happen?' I say.

'Half an hour ago she was eating a curry,' Jay says.

'Ah, curry,' I say. 'For breakfast. That'll do it every time.' But I notice my legs are shaking.

'Stevie,' Esther says, when she's contraction-free again, 'talk to me! Tell me stuff!'

I look at Lux for permission. She shrugs. 'She's very intellectual,' she says.

'She likes the distraction,' Jay adds, and wipes Esther's forehead with a cool flannel.

'Men are good with flannels,' Esther says.

'Okay,' I say. I go and squat down by Esther. I'm a little scared of what's going on between her legs. I'm quite careful not to look.

'The ambulance is five minutes away,' calls Phil, from the phone.

'Too late,' says Lux again.

'Talk to me,' Esther says.

'I think Louis's mother might be alive,' I say. I tell her and Jay briefly about what happened at the CPS and about the phone call. Then it's time for another contraction.

'PU-U-U-U-U-USH!'

'Talk to me!' Esther says when she has recovered.

'Do you think I should go to the States and investigate?' I say. 'I know it'll cost money. But I could dip into the Instant Saver.'

'By the way,' Jay says, 'some guy phoned up. He's ordered forty coffins.'

'How gruesome – I mean, how great,' I say. 'He wasn't called Slobodan, by any chance?'

Jay snorts. 'An undertaker guy.'

'So,' I say, 'should I go?'

'Even if Louis's mother *is* alive,' Esther says, 'then what?'

'I don't know.'

'You get to see Louis again,' Jay points out.

'Yeah.' Esther's voice is getting constricted now and she speaks fast, trying to fit in what she wants to say before the contraction takes over. 'You get to say, "Hey, babe! Guess what? Your mother's not dead!"'

I giggle. 'It's quite a good line, you have to admit.'

'Here we go,' Lux says.

'Oh, my God,' Esther says, rising on the wave. And with one enormous screaming push, out baby comes.

29

My cheap flight into Boston is hours late, which means I miss the bus to Portland. All the downtown hotels are full so I take a long, long cab ride to the edge of town, to a tiny hotel that feels very English – fake mahogany, floral wallpaper, and a twisty-turny staircase, well carpeted, that takes me up to a room in the eaves of the house.

The young woman at the reception desk insists on carrying my bag for me, all the while giving me a lecture on how folks have to learn to fend for themselves if they want to make it 'over here'. In her eyes, I am clearly of weak decadent stock from the mother country, whereas she is a pioneer in the brave new world.

I fall on to the bed exhausted and give Jay an early-morning call. Mother and baby are doing fine, and they've decided to call her Alice. 'You don't know what you're missing,' he says. So I go to sleep with my clothes on, wondering if Pioneer Woman is right to doubt me, wondering if I should go home.

In the morning I get up as early as I can and head back into town, to the bus station. Of course, I've just missed a bus to Portland and there isn't another for two hours. I leave my bag at the left-luggage office where there's a medical type cardboard box on the desk labelled 'Handle With Care: Human Eyes In Transit'.

Once back outside I don't know what to do, but I do know I'd like some breakfast. Especially an all-American breakfast – waffles, bacon, maple syrup, ersatz coffee. There's a line of cabs at the kerb, the drivers with their windows down, elbows out, smoking, chatting. I stop at the first and ask him if he knows a good place to have breakfast.

'I know the best diner in town,' he says. 'It's run by my brother.'

So we go to his brother's diner and we have breakfast together. He's a Jamaican called Ken and a lot more welcoming than Pioneer Woman at the hotel. In fact, by the time we've had our second refill of coffee, he's saying if I didn't have a boyfriend he'd ask me to marry him.

I smile. 'I don't have a boyfriend.'

'I think you have,' he says.

'I don't.'

'Someone special?'

'No.'

'Yes, you do.'

'What makes you so sure?'

He raises two fingers and points to my eyes.

Back at the bus depot, I pick up my bag from Left Luggage. The woman behind the counter is eating a sandwich. A thought strikes me.

'What happened to the eyes?' I say.

'They're over there,' the woman says, making the statement a question, and pointing to a pile of boxes stacked by the door. The white medical box is at the bottom of the pile.

'Are they going to be okay?' I say.

'I don't know,' she says, sceptical, 'I think they're defrosting,' and goes back to her brunch.

The convent in Portland is a gloomy red-brick building, dour-looking, Catholic, of course, but redolent of Protestant work ethic. It's in a nondescript part of town, set back from the road and surrounded by dark evergreens.

I saw a lot of the sea on the way in to town on the bus, a wide, pale sea, calm and dotted with small white sails, the sky flat above – a picture-book scene. It would make a comforting watercolour called 'A Family Day Out' with tiny dabs of red in the foreground for couples, holding hands.

Of course, there's no sign of the sea at the convent, only a taste of it in the air.

In the gravel driveway a nun is taking a delivery of toilet paper and cleaning fluids. She's wearing a sensible wool dress and a short grey veil to her shoulders, very businesslike. I'm half expecting to be branded an interfering heretic and chased from the premises, so I'm reassured when her greeting is calm and incurious.

'I was speaking to one of the nuns the other day,' I say, 'on the telephone. I didn't get her name. But she was an extoller of the virtues of early rising.'

'Oh, yes,' the nun says, 'that'll be Sister Luella. A little brisk.'

'That's the one,' I say.

'She'll be in the garden,' and she waves me towards the left-hand side of the building.

Sister Luella is at the compost heap with a shovel.

She's in her sixties, wearing the same outfit as the sister out front, except in this instance the ensemble ends in a clumpy pair of wellington boots. I tell her that we spoke on the phone, that I'm not a solicitor, but that I'm not a journalist either – not on this occasion. I tell her that I'm checking some facts about the Porter girls and that she, Sister Luella, seemed like a good place to start.

Sister Luella is entirely unfazed. She stops her shovelling a moment and says, 'Well, none of it's a secret.'

I take this as a green light. 'Can you tell me a bit about the sister, Nancy Porter's sister? I'm afraid I don't know her name.'

'Lorna Porter. She was a traitorous girl.'

'How do you mean?'

'One of those girls that always has headaches. Couldn't sleep at night. Forever smoking in the bushes and thinking about boys.' She pauses to dispose of a few more shovelfuls of compost then relents a little. 'I always thought she could be quite brilliant, though, if she put her mind to it, if she wasn't so highly strung. There was something about her that was very attractive. Aside from her looks. She had Barbie-doll looks.' Sister Luella pulls her mouth down at the corners to show what she thinks of Barbie-doll looks. 'Fell pregnant, of course.'

'Do you know what happened to her?'

'I know John Howard was always in love with her. But it was no good. Lorna ran off, was never heard of again. John married her sister instead. A much better choice. John was our janitor's boy, you know.' She goes back to her shovelling.

'He and Nancy moved to San Diego quite soon after. Why did they go? Do you know?'

'Wanted a fresh start, I should think. It was tragic, though – Nancy died. An automobile accident. She would have been so proud of her son, the way he's made something of himself.'

'Yes,' I say.

'What's all this about, anyway?'

I tell her that someone might have a mother who doesn't know he has a mother.

'Well,' she says, 'it's important that he finds out.'

And so I leave the land of sturdy wellies and lobster-pots to board a plane at Logan International airport. The air steward is wearing full makeup, and X-ray Woman in the seat next to me must have bourbon before take-off.

Where are we going? La La Land, of course.

When we get there I check into a scary-looking motel right down at the unfashionable end of Sunset Boulevard. It's not at all like my English guidebook suggests. The entry for the Movie Magic Motel makes no mention of drug-dealers doing business in the next room, or of more comings and goings than a drive-thru McDonald's, to say nothing of drum and bass music vibrating through the wall.

I get out of there as quick as I can. At Reception I ask the guy where I can buy shampoo. He says there's a Duane Reade Drugs two miles up.

'I meant somewhere I could walk to,' I say.

He looks perplexed. 'We can send out,' he says.

I decide to forget the shampoo and I go and sit by

the scruffy, deserted pool and call a cellphone number Louis gave me at Anasett Point.

I get Mike.

'Hey!' he says.

'Hey!' I say. 'How goes it?'

'We live in interesting times,' he says.

I tell him I need to speak to Louis. Louis is at rehearsals for *Science Fiction II*, on the Warner Brothers lot. Louis is very busy, but Mike says he'll see what he can do.

A few hours later I'm standing outside the gates of the Warner Brother's lot. I wait there for twenty minutes, feeling like a fool. It's one of those dusty, sunny Los Angeles days when the sky stays white and it's bright on the eyes, but the buildings don't cast a shadow. The guy in the security booth looks at me so suspiciously that eventually I have to go over and explain I'm waiting for somebody.

While I'm doing this a red MG sports car screeches up to the gate. Mike drives out in it, picks me up, and drives me right back in again.

'Good to see you, girl,' he says.

We grin at each other.

'Now, is there anything I should know? Got anything up your sleeve? Any eggs? Any madwomen from Planet Fan?'

'No, Mike,' I say.

I meet Louis on an outdoor set that looks like it was used to make *The Godfather*, a slummy New-York-type street. The place is deserted, though, and Louis is sitting at the far end, on a bench, under an incongruous, but picturesque, lemon tree. When I get to him, I see that he looks different again. Somehow he's different every time I see him. His hair is even longer and he looks tired. There's a hint of age in his face, but the faint lines just give his good looks more definition.

We exchange courteous but not effusive greetings and I tell him what I have to tell him. Everything I know. His jaw goes very tight but that's all. He's not going to give me an inch.

When he gets up, Mike takes this as his cue and rolls slowly up in the sports car, ready to take me back to the gate. I go for the car then turn back to say, 'You know Rico was only in my motel room because he was following Grace. I was off the story. I'd resigned – you could check that with Dick if you wanted.'

He doesn't respond. I'm just about to get into the car when Louis, who's not giving me an inch, gives me a centimetre instead. 'Boris Karloff,' he says, and then he pauses.

'Rest in peace,' I say, glancing at The Godfather set.

'No,' he says. 'He came back. I found him half a mile up the beach. It happens sometimes with the tides.' He smiles. It's good to see that smile. 'He was kind of waterlogged. But he was alive.'

'Alive!' I say.

'Yeah,' he says. 'Alive.'

My bucket-shop plane ticket is unchangeable so I have to wait two days before I can go home. In the Movie Magic Motel. No fun. On the second day, I'm considering buying drugs from my neighbours when the phone goes.

It's Mike saying, is Louis with me?

With *me*?

'Er, no,' I say.

'Louis disappeared at lunch. His cell phone is off. No one knows where the hell he is. He's now precisely three hours late back to rehearsal – and I am officially-the-fuck worried.'

'Oh dear,' I say.

'Is this you again?'

'What?'

'Your influence.'

I don't know what to say.

'Gotta go,' Mike says.

'Wait,' I say. 'Where are you going?'

'To double-check at his hotel. In person.'

'He won't be there,' I say.

'Well, where the fuck is he?'

He hangs up and I sit there digesting this new turn of events and then it comes to me, somewhat belatedly, that once again I know exactly where Louis is.

The Browneville State Penitentiary is off one of those low-level streets in the poorest outskirt of the city. The American equivalent of a shantytown. Concrete and neon and more concrete. Most of the shops are closed, the one-storey buildings completely shuttered from tattered store sign down to littered sidewalk, giving the impression that the street is asleep, its eyes firmly shut. And everyone seems to have gone home. There's only very intermittent traffic, the odd car parked here and there. My overriding impression is of the litter – the garbage – as it blows about, skidding and spinning, in the wide gully of the road. Hamburger cartons, soda cans, old newspapers – there's even a doll doing a headstand in a drain.

I see him coming from a long way off. I can tell it's him by the walk, the way he holds himself, cautiously, apologetic almost, but unable to stifle his own presence, even with his hat tilted nearly down to his chin. I stop and let him walk up to me – I want to watch him coming. It takes a while. When he sees me he falters for a second, tips his hat back, but then he just keeps coming.

'Hello there,' he says when he gets to me.

It's like he wasn't really there at our last meeting. And now we've really met. We eye each other a while, we smile a little, we practically circle each other like lions, swishing our tails.

'I thought I'd find you here,' I say. We smile some more. The low evening sun is in his eyes and it makes him narrow them and lean away from me like he's trying to get me into focus. 'Have you been prison visiting?' I say.

'Uh-huh,' he says.

'How was it?'

'It was cool.' I give him a look, waiting for more. He just smiles. 'You'll meet her,' he says. 'She's out soon. She's done seven years. Fraud. She stole some shit, you know. She had a drug problem but they've got a good rehabilitation programme going on in there.'

'And why was she e-mailing the mad fan?'

We turn at the same time and walk up the street together.

'For one thing,' Louis says, 'she didn't know the

343

woman was crazy. She needed an outlet, I guess. She never got to talk to anyone about me. When she gave me to Nancy, her sister, just after I was born, she promised, whatever happened, she'd never claim me. My Dad never wanted to see her again you see. When he died she was desperate to contact me – but by then I was famous and she didn't want the world to think that Louis Plantagenet had a bad mother.' He says the words 'Louis Plantagenet' and 'bad' as if they had inverted commas around them. He says them as if they make him sad. 'How did you know?' he says.

'I told you. I went to the convent she grew up in. Our Sisters of Mercy.'

He stops in the street and looks at me. 'I meant, how did you know about my demons?'

'Well,' I say, 'I've got a few of my own.'

We stand there some more, just looking at each other. 'I'm sorry about when you came to the studio the other day,' he says. 'I couldn't get past the Rico thing.' And then he says, 'So, are we gonna stand here all night?' and he takes my arm in the way he does, playing with it, swinging it gently backwards and forwards like a barn door.

'I don't know,' I say. 'What about your rehearsals? You can't just walk out.'

'Hey – worse things have happened than some actor pulling out of a picture, you know. The world doesn't revolve around me. Isn't that what you told me? People are dying in the sweat shops, right?'

'And you were dying in yours,' I say, wanting to give him that suddenly.

'In a way,' he says, 'I was.'

'And it's just a job.'

'I'm not sure it was just a job,' he says. 'I'm not sure it wasn't something else. It should be just a job, though. That's what it should be.' He looks at me. 'Let's go to Wyoming,' he says. 'That's what you talked about, wasn't it? A ranch in Wyoming? How about it?'

I open my mouth. 'Okay,' I say.

He turns me round again and starts to walk me gently along the street, his arm around my shoulders, in the direction of the sun. We wander along like that, like we've got our whole lives ahead of us. Which we have I suppose.

'So we'll go to Wyoming,' Louis says lightly and he sounds like he's talking to himself, like he's rolling the words out for nobody's amusement other than his own, rolling them out over a rising bubble of laughter. 'But we're not in love, right? Because that would be a *bad thing*. That would be playing into *their* hands – the big "they". That would lead to disillusionment, right? The kingdom of coupledom being a police state and all.'

'Oh no,' I say, agreeing eagerly and starting to talk fast. 'We don't want our body chemistry to lead us astray. We don't want to fall for the myth of the happy ending. You know, historically speaking, marriage only worked well when people *died*. I mean, in the Middle Ages you were lucky to make it to forty. Current life expectancy levels are definitely a disaster in terms of—'

'Definitely a disaster?' he says swinging me round and interrupting me. 'Or just maybe?'

I look over his shoulder to where there's a twirling red

and white barber shop beacon and I watch it twirling for ever into itself and I realise I really don't care to know it all. I don't care about anything except being with Louis and watching that barber shop beacon twirling in the sunset.

'*Maybe* a disaster,' I say, capitulating. 'And after Wyoming? Will you come back to LA?'

'Yes,' he says, 'maybe.' He pauses. 'Or maybe I won't. But maybe you'll go back to London,' he says.

'Maybe,' I say.

'Or maybe you won't. Maybe I'll *buy* that ranch in Wyoming.'

'Or maybe you won't.'

'But maybe I will. And maybe you'll stay.'

'And do what?'

'Grow flowers. Healthy ones.'

'In Wyoming?'

'We could give it a try.'

'Maybe.'